The F

Rachel Lynch is an author of crime fiction whose books have sold more than one million copies. She grew up in Cumbria and the lakes and fells are never far away from her. London pulled her away to teach History and marry an Army Officer, whom she followed around the globe for thirteen years. A change of career after children led to personal training and sports therapy, but writing was always the overwhelming force driving the future. The human capacity for compassion as well as its descent into the brutal and murky world of crime are fundamental to her work.

Also by Rachel Lynch

The Rich
The Famous

Helen Scott Royal Military Police Thrillers

The Rift
The Line

Detective Kelly Porter

Dark Game
Deep Fear
Dead End
Bitter Edge
Bold Lies
Blood Rites
Little Doubt
Lost Cause
Lying Ways
Sudden Death
Silent Bones
Shared Remains

THE FAMOUS

RACHEL LYNCH

CANELO

First published in the United Kingdom in 2025 by

Canelo, an imprint of
Canelo Digital Publishing Limited,
20 Vauxhall Bridge Road,
London SW1V 2SA
United Kingdom

A Penguin Random House Company

The authorised representative in the EEA is Dorling Kindersley Verlag GmbH.
Arnulfstr. 124, 80636 Munich, Germany

Copyright © Rachel Lynch 2025

The moral right of Rachel Lynch to be identified as the creator of this work has been asserted in accordance with the Copyright, Designs and Patents Act, 1988.

All rights reserved. No part of this publication may be reproduced or transmitted in any form or by any means, electronic or mechanical, including photocopy, recording, or any information storage and retrieval system, without permission in writing from the publisher.

No part of this book may be used or reproduced in any manner for the purpose of training artificial intelligence technologies or systems. In accordance with Article 4(3) of the DSM Directive 2019/790, Canelo expressly reserves this work from the text and data mining exception.

A CIP catalogue record for this book is available from the British Library.

Print ISBN 978 1 80436 772 8
Ebook ISBN 978 1 80436 773 5

This book is a work of fiction. Names, characters, businesses, organizations, places and events are either the product of the author's imagination or are used fictitiously. Any resemblance to actual persons, living or dead, events or locales is entirely coincidental.

Cover design by Andrew Smith

Cover images © Shutterstock

Printed and bound in Great Britain by Clays Ltd, Elcograf S.p.A.

Look for more great books at
www.canelo.co
www.dk.com

Chapter 1

Dear Gloria,

You are my first celebrity pen pal.

I imagine you want to know who I am, but you'll find out soon enough. I insist our relationship is one way at first, I'm in no rush for you to remember. Take your time. You need to think things over. I understand it's been a while. I appreciate your time is precious. I used to have a job that paid well, but I still couldn't quite find enough time to get everything done.

It was a position of watching and waiting.

You might remember me.

When I watched you, I would sit quite still.

Outside the Bare Bunny on Docker Street.

I waited anywhere you needed me to, and I found trivial things to occupy myself.

Like watching the small artery in my wrist – the one which strokes my styloid process – pulsating so strongly that sometimes I thought it might rip through my skin. I traced it with my finger, because I had time to waste. Time that I couldn't afford. My life was a series of punctuations like that, stuttering to a halt, then surging forward into the unknown. Orders and expectations. Bam, bam, bam!

Not like yours.

Your success has been like a meteor in the sky, up, up and away. On your own. Always on your own, but smiling nonetheless, like Little Miss Sunshine, cohost of Good Morning Dillydale.

Stars that shine the brightest always fade first. I read they explode.

Imagine that?

I used to watch the beat, beat of life inside my wrist in awe. But now I know we're just the same, you and me. We have the same heartbeat pushing the blood straight through us. It's just biology. Imagine if I sliced it a little open. We'd bleed the same.

Stillness in a busy world.

Wouldn't it be a relief?

Sincerely yours,

Your friend.

Chapter 2

'Roger Wade, media colossus and global entrepreneur, will be laid to rest today in a private ceremony at the family's Buckinghamshire estate. Our cameras are there, and we'll get you as close as we possibly can to the guests, following all the reactions from today's events, as well as what the stars are wearing. I'm hearing that Gloria White herself will be arriving shortly...'

The presenter held on to her ear, as the producer barked new information into her earpiece. She looked dead ahead at the camera and concentrated on the words just inside her mouth, all queuing – in the wrong order – to jump out and deliver gossip to the nation. Gloria White, the ex-daughter-in-law of the deceased, worked for a rival channel, and the focus of the funeral wasn't on the bloke in the box, but on the woman who had dared to divorce his son and what she might be wearing. Gloria White had refused to be cowed by one of the most powerful men in the world and the shock split had given salacious copy to producers from London to Paris to New York.

Roger Wade's funeral was the event of the year.

'We'll bring you all the latest pictures of those arriving for the funeral and try to get some close-ups. We should see some major new designs for the autumn season, but hold on to your own hats, because the price tags might just make your eyes water.'

The anchor smiled at her own cleverness. Another prompt from her producer threw a shadow of seriousness over her face and she announced it was time to cut to another story. There was only so much visual you could squeeze out of a pair of gates in Buckinghamshire – the piece was running as dry as the low-calorie, no-gluten, no-dairy, no-dressing sandwich she had stored in the baking car for her lunch – and until some big names arrived, they had to find other material to keep their viewers from switching channels.

A pre-recorded piece gave the anchor a moment to let her shoulders sag and throw the finger to one of the cameramen who'd been eating a chocolate bar behind the camera because he knew it drove her mad. Her face felt sweaty and she needed a make-up retouch. One day, she hoped to be a titan of the media world, just like Gloria White, but she didn't intend on sleeping with a grease-ball like Oliver Wade to get there, and so she knew it'd take her a little longer.

Oliver Wade's status as an eligible divorcee had just gone stratospheric thanks to his inheritance as the only child of Roger Wade. Oliver stood to be bequeathed the kind of money that made people dizzy, but none of that could rub out the stories circulating in the press about his father.

Roger Wade had bought mostly everything in his life, except immunity from press hearsay. Bets were now on to see how long his son could keep the empire afloat. Oliver Wade was a braggart, and nobody from either side of the pond expected him to preserve the kingdom built by his father over his sixty years in the business. It was well known that Oliver Wade preferred hookers and expensive champagne over boardrooms, and Gloria White walking out on him only added credence to the gossip that he was impossible to live with.

The woman they were all waiting for was a legend of female empowerment who'd clawed her way up, passing countless men in suits on her way to the top, in a time when women were overlooked as either homemakers or ditzy blondes. Gloria was neither.

And now, even in her fifties, she was still known for being the baddest bitch on the circuit.

Roger Wade had famously once said that he'd learned everything he knew about winning from Gloria, who was the only woman he allowed to choose his trousers because they fitted her better.

The glitterati and celebrity tribe had turned out in full to clamour for a space in the tiny family chapel on the Wade estate, and those who'd been snubbed had been invited as guests across all TV channels. Wars, famine, corruption and the next killer virus took back seats on today's news segments, because all eyes were on the final resting place of a man whose personal wealth could solve perhaps 20 per cent of all humanity's problems.

But the question on everybody's lips, as the news section went back to the live feed from the helicopter circling over the M1 motorway, wasn't what time the hearse might arrive, nor was it which flowers had been sent by the President of the United States, it was if Gloria White would be wearing black.

Chapter 3

Gloria closed the door. It was a moment of quiet. Unfamiliar and uncertain, but welcome. Snapshots of hushed muteness were so rare in her world that she almost missed it. She stood with her hand on the knob and absorbed the flavour of the privacy.

'Mum?' Jilly broke the silence, and Gloria set her face once more from merely a free woman to mother, journalist, and presenter.

Today she'd add 'ex-daughter-in-law' and 'ex-wife' to the list as she prepared to say farewell to Roger and stand in the same room as Oliver for more than half an hour without killing each other. She looked at their daughter, who was a befuddlement of chaos; at once a beautiful and confident young woman on the cusp of launching her own successful career as a journalist – but 'a serious one', as she called it – as well as a tangle of emotions buzzing with the vitality of youth. Jilly was headstrong, impassioned, energetic and explosive all in one small body and was yet to find her equilibrium. She was an incendiary paradox, just like her father.

'I don't want your face all over the tabloids tomorrow,' Gloria said, trying to insist she walk under the canopy when they left for the chapel, built specifically to avoid the helicopter cameras.

Jilly eyed her mother. 'I wouldn't dare compete for your front-page splash,' she said.

Gloria was used to her daughter's sharp tongue. She only had herself to blame. She'd brought her up to be an Amazonian ball-breaker. What else was on the cards for the child of a billionaire and a TV icon?

'I don't care if they photograph me, Mum,' Jilly continued.

'That's not the point. You don't understand, once they get your photo, from all angles you could possibly imagine, that's it, you're out there, forever, Jilly. Do you understand? Forever is a long time.'

She and Oliver had sheltered Jilly from the gaze of global media as much as they could. It was one thing they agreed on.

'Can you drop the mask just for today, Mum? They'll be interested in you anyway, not me. I'm not stupid.'

Jilly's request was tinged with a mixture of frustration and boredom.

'I didn't say you were stupid, darling. I'm endowing you with my knowledge of the British press. Officially the most callous in the world. They'll be looking for your worst side, the snot as you blow your nose, a ripple of skin over your trousers, the colour of your eyes and a pattern of your fucking irises to scan.'

Gloria straightened her own dress and spotted a dot of fluff, and batted at it with her hand. She felt Jilly staring at her and knew she was being prickly.

Jilly smiled, reminding Gloria that her daughter found comfort when she allowed her camouflage to slip, even if just for a second.

They'd had the same conversation a thousand times. Gloria's only desire was that Jilly learn a few tricks to control information about her, rather than let the press command it. Gloria had made a career out of manipulating photographers, copy editors, interviewers, and more recently, bloggers, influencers and YouTube stars, but had desperately tried to shelter her daughter from fame to give her a relatively conventional upbringing. That this had been virtually impossible, given the clamour for their photograph everywhere they went, perhaps explained why Jilly had become nonchalant about the whole thing, which irritated her mother. They'd taken privacy injunctions out on several newspapers, so Jilly's face was hidden when she was a child. Now, as an adult, her parents had no control over her exposure. But to her credit, Jilly not wanting to court the attention, like some other celebrity children, was refreshing, if naive.

'All I'm saying is, if they're unsure which car you're in, and you're not with me or Dad, then it'll throw them off the scent, that's all.'

She couldn't let it go.

The voracious public appetite for celebrity copy was only fuelled by those willing to play the game. Kids like Jilly, who didn't clamour for fame at any cost, were generally left alone. Gloria saw the fact that Jilly was able to attend university and remain semi-anonymous as her greatest achievement. Her daughter's three-year degree had been completed in relative isolation and Jilly had been able to exist without being ambushed by camera-wielding nutters. The danger only arose when Jilly spent time with her parents, or her grandfather, and that had been skilfully managed by a team of experts with backgrounds in security for royalty, military dictators and A-list actors. It came with a hefty price tag, but Roger wasn't short of cash.

'And it's not a competition,' she added.

'You always have to have the last word, like Dad says,' Jilly shot back. 'I get the message, okay?'

Gloria went to speak but thought better of it. A lecture on Oliver's motives for playing the press wouldn't be well received today of all days. She forced her mouth shut.

All she'd ever wanted to do was protect her daughter from the world she lived in. The world that she'd helped to create.

Gloria felt as though time was slipping away and soon she'd have no say in how Jilly lived her life at all. She was at least thankful that her daughter wanted to remain behind the camera rather than in front of it, despite Oliver offering her a job as an anchor on one of their TV channels. Jilly had refused.

Her ex-husband loved the limelight; like his spirit flower, the narcissus, he turned to wherever the cameras were clicking, and his face was plastered over world press outlets like cheap wallpaper. Gloria couldn't go a day without seeing it staring back at her, though her physical reaction to it had been tempered with years of expensive psychotherapy. She'd learned to chant affirmations when she saw his photo and talk herself into believing she was safe out of his clutches and no longer at the mercy of his domination.

The last thing she needed was to spend a day in his company, but she was doing it for her daughter. *Their* daughter.

At Jilly's age, Gloria had been heading to London on her own to make her fortune. Now, as she cast her mind back, she wasn't sure whether it had been the most advantageous turning point of her life, or the worst mistake she'd ever made when she agreed to accompany Oliver Wade back to his apartment overlooking the Thames for a night of lust.

But if she'd turned him down, she wouldn't have Jilly, who was the single most important thing in her life. Jilly was the only thing Gloria had that hadn't been tainted by the hand of fame. It was the only corner of her world, hidden away and tucked into a secret planetary system on the edge of her universe, that was unspoiled by the hands that had shaped her.

But now, with Roger out of the way, she was unsure how long the armistice would last, and she tried to concentrate on the present moment, rather than the letter she'd folded into her desk drawer that morning.

She wouldn't go to the police.

He knew she wouldn't go to the police.

He might be watching TV now.

Of course he was. That's what he'd told her. The letter that morning was the third one she'd received, and she knew it was just the beginning.

Chapter 4

Oliver Wade peered out of the back window of his Bentley Flying Spur, and the corners of his mouth turned up at the sorry souls desperate for his photo. A flurry of chaos broke out at the estate gates, as he knew it would, and he bid the driver to slow the vehicle a little. He'd chosen not to stay over at the main house last night so he could enjoy this moment. He could have flown in by helicopter, but that would have been no fun. He gazed at the little people out of his window, which wasn't tinted, and managed a smile, which would be all over the tabloids tomorrow.

A scowl briefly crossed his face – which he tactfully hid from the invading lenses – as he realised that Gloria would more than likely upstage him, as she did everyone, but the press were fickle beasts, and he knew how crazy it would send her when images with no filter were released by paparazzi. She was beginning to look old.

Only last year he'd laughed out loud as news of her facelift had reached the front pages and some clever young spy had snapped a picture of the operation scars behind her ears, which she'd so cleverly tried to conceal. Oliver had celebrated her resulting guaranteed rage with a shot of brandy, toasting her approaching twilight years. She was only in her early fifties, but one's shelf life in front of the camera was like a footballer's: limited.

Men aged differently, and he could get more women now than in his twenties. Whereas poor Gloria's days of elegant beauty were firmly behind her. At fifty-four, things were slipping, and her favourite Harley Street doctor could only do so much.

Gloria's expiration date was looming ever nearer, and he got a kick out of watching her star beginning to tarnish. With his father out of the way, it was only a matter of time before she was moved on in the public eye and replaced by a younger model.

And with Oliver in charge, it was likely to happen sooner rather than later.

Bulbs flashed and hands holding phones hit the glass, and he bid the driver to head through the gates, up the driveway and along to the main house, where his daughter and ex-wife would be waiting.

It had been Gloria's idea for Jilly to travel separately. He acknowledged that it was for the best in terms of their daughter's privacy, but he also suspected that Gloria's motives weren't utterly altruistic. Jilly was a beauty and could easily upstage her mother.

They were to make their way to the family chapel together today, though, with the gates at the bottom of the magnificent driveway keeping the eager press grunts — who'd sell whatever they could get to the highest bidders — at bay. He would have loved to leak a few images of the inside of the chapel, and perhaps a select few shots of his guests, and blame the deed on an old colleague who'd favoured his father over him in the distant past, but there was time for all that yet. Today he was on his best behaviour.

The gates closed behind him, and he dropped the grin.

The great and good of the world's news and entertainment could wait a little longer for the stars of the show. Roger was the last of the old guard and they should show a united front in respect of what the old fucker had achieved. Tomorrow was a new day and Oliver would begin to reveal his plans for the Wade Group soon enough.

One thing he was sure of, though, was that its future didn't feature his ex-wife.

The car drew up to the main house, and the driver stopped and got out to open Oliver's door for him. He shuffled out of the seat and ignored the man who'd driven him, without even saying thank you. There was no need. Service staff were paid to serve.

He went into the house and took no notice of the army of employees fixing furniture, organising catering, and packing away outfits, hair accessories and jewels, which had presumably been paraded in front of his ex-wife and daughter to choose from. He wafted away the respectful requests for his time and marched into a large reception room, which had been turned into a dressing room.

'Daddy!' Jilly rushed to him, and he wrapped her inside his arms and held her firmly and deeply, closing his eyes and noticing what her presence did to his heart rate. His only child was gloriously attractive, and the pedigree of her genes shone around her like a halo of taste.

He released his daughter to see her eyes were red. Perhaps Gloria's decision to protect her from the press was valid. They'd eat her alive. They locked eyes.

'Gloria,' he mumbled to his ex.

'Oliver.' She sniffed.

His stomach churned momentarily as he took her in. The sight of her was enough to make his loins stir, even after all this time, and the hundred women he'd bedded since her. He spied a satisfied look on her face; she sensed his weakness. He looked away and concentrated on giving his daughter his undivided attention, but whenever Gloria was in the same room, it didn't take long for the bile to rise in his throat.

Gloria had done the unthinkable and divorced him. She'd not only left him, but she'd done it publicly, and he'd never got over the shame.

One day, he didn't know when, his fantasy would come true, and he'd watch her demise. He'd observe her wriggle in agony as her fame shrivelled and died, and she was left without the power she so craved.

He looked at her with fresh eyes and she frowned at him, acknowledging the danger of his presence, even on the day of his father's funeral.

They knew each other so well that he could read Gloria's mind by watching her body for only a second.

She still hated him.

He also saw her shiver, as if her skin crawled when he walked into the room.

Jilly was oblivious and chatted to both her parents as if their primordial hatred didn't exist.

The gloves were now off.

Their referee, the mighty Roger Wade, was dead, and almost buried, and tomorrow was the first day of the rest of their lives.

Chapter 5

Gloria felt a draught of arctic ice grab her throat as Oliver entered the room and looked over their daughter's shoulder at her. Her body fed off instinct, like it would if a serpent had just slithered from under the floorboards, and goosebumps covered her skin.

Her mother used to say that a sudden shiver was indicative of somebody walking over your future grave. Oliver did that to her whenever she saw him, and she knew he'd love the idea of jumping up and down on her final resting place. If she got there before he did.

But today wasn't the time for pitched battles and sharpened blades. That could wait.

'Traffic wasn't too bad, then?' she asked him blandly.

He smiled and acknowledged her invitation to enter a benign conversation to shield their daughter from their visceral loathing of one another.

'It's never dull in a Bentley,' he said.

She studied him and imagined him buried in his precious car.

His teeth had got whiter. His suit had got bigger. His hands were wider and his shoulders broader. His ego had grown too, since the news of his father's passing. Oliver was a predictable animal. She could tell that he was planning something.

Any revenge he might be plotting would involve his basest instincts. It would likely come in the shape of some form of sex scandal. It was the only language he spoke. He was two-dimensional when it came to women and what he thought of them. What he failed to appreciate, though, was that women were less likely to be seen as harlots and whores these days. Casting aspersions on a woman's moral character couldn't destroy reputations any more. Those days were gone. She tried to imagine how else he could harm her – falling short of murder, obviously. Not even Oliver would go that far, she thought, but a feeling of sticky doubt accompanied the flash of certainty, and it unhinged her security a little. She swallowed.

Maybe it was him behind the letters.

Prickles of sweat made her hair feel dirty, though it had been washed twice this morning. The lacquer and the heat from styling conspired to make her feel unclean, as if she'd been handed around a room full of predators.

This was no longer the eighties, she told herself, pushing the thoughts away. Maternal instinct made her check on Jilly, and she was thankful that her daughter didn't face what her generation had back then. At twenty-one, starting out in journalism in the early nineties, a woman had to have her wits about her and a lock on her knickers, as well as balls bigger than any man's. Jilly wouldn't have survived back then. Many didn't.

Even in the modern world, journalism – no matter how highbrow Jilly thought it was – hadn't been her ideal choice for her daughter's career, but Jilly was headstrong, and despite her best efforts, Gloria hadn't been able to scare her off, short of telling her exactly what she'd been through. Some things were best kept secret between a mother and her daughter, and for good reason. Besides, Jilly probably wouldn't believe her. The press was full of women raking up cases of historic abuse and if anything, it bored people. If Gloria White was to do it, she'd be accused of desperately trying to boost her ratings. Or worse, purposefully sabotaging her daughter's career.

The past must stay the past.

Gloria had hoped that Jilly might use her sociology degree from Durham to advocate for women in developing countries, as she'd shown an interest in when she was ten years old. A negotiating role in Gaza would be simpler than trying to make it on TV. But Jilly was not to be moved. Her daughter's stubborn streak was her own fault, Gloria realised; she could only blame herself.

'Don't worry, Mum, I'm not after your job!' she'd say. *'I want to report* real *stories and investigate* true *injustice.'*

'Ready?' Oliver asked.

Gloria nodded.

'Are the guests in the chapel?' she asked.

Oliver nodded.

'All set,' he said.

Their journey to the chapel was to be marshalled with military precision. The technology behind photographic detail these days was incredible, with cameras mounted on helicopters thousands of feet over a property. The march of technology that enabled people to spy on celebrities fuelled most advancements in military-grade hardware. The appetite for scandal was firmly above that for news of war, and Roger had known it. He'd launched his own technical department a decade ago and it was at the coalface of digital news. But it was a double-edged sword, and the mechanisation of gossip could be turned on them too. Like today, when they had no idea what could be lurking behind the hydrangeas that guarded the perimeter of the property. Security had been tightened for the event, and celebs had flown in their own protection teams. It had been a logistical nightmare.

But it was necessary if they wanted any kind of privacy, even for just a moment. It had proved impossible to shelter Roger's final resting place, though. He'd had an ostentatious and vulgar memorial tomb built when they'd moved to the estate some twenty years ago. It was carved from Italian marble, had space for up to ten bodies and cost a fortune. Gloria found it obscene, but it had been Roger's favourite place on the estate and where he would be immortalised.

She and Oliver took their positions either side of their daughter and Jilly held both their hands.

Oliver reeked of expensive cologne and Gloria wondered if he'd bathed in it. His scent made her gag, but she hid it well. Jilly glanced at her, and Gloria felt her breath pause as she wondered at the easy elegance of her only child. Her long blonde hair flowed effortlessly across her shoulders, and her blue eyes pierced her mind like portals to a different, softer world.

She wouldn't last two minutes in journalism, Gloria assessed uncharitably. But the thought didn't come from a place of envy or unkindness. She glanced past her daughter and saw Oliver staring at her. He wasn't showing the same signs of ageing as she was, the bastard. It was easier for men. They didn't have the pressure from the media to grow in wisdom but age their saggy arses in reverse. Nobody wanted a tight attitude, but everyone desired a tight decolletage and two pert tits. Faces were getting tighter and lips fuller in front of the camera, and hers were lagging behind. She'd had a facelift, of course, everyone had, and that had been painful enough. She stopped short of having endless tummy tucks and uplifting procedures for her butt and thighs. There was a limit. But the pressure was unbearable sometimes. She looked at Oliver's receding hairline and his jowls and thought how unfair it was that men got away with it. Men become silver foxes, geezers, ageing metrosexuals, dapper dads, rugged, seasoned, mature, and superannuated fashion followers. On the other hand, women her age were referred to as mutton dressed as lamb, hags, crones, biddies, battleaxes, old dears and witches. No wonder women queued up to spend money on reversing their biology. She reckoned half her time on the breakfast show was spent exploring the way females felt about themselves thanks to the media, and she'd been a part of the machine that created it all her career.

She'd done a piece on cheap plastic surgery only this week. The featured 'expert' in this case had a face which had long ascended behind her eyebrows, and her lips looked as though they could have saved the whole of the *Titanic*'s passenger list, not just the select few. No one had spotted the irony of the fact that the invited guests sat on her sofa and bemoaned how awful it was that women felt under such pressure to conform to constricted and male-accepted views of themselves while being lectured to by a woman who looked like Barbie, and who'd made it her life's mission to lead the field in female body armour bold enough to destroy the dreams of an army of nature-loving naturalists for generations, and adding to teenage body dysmorphic trauma. But the breakfast show wasn't the space to get into reality.

Today, right now, Gloria's focus was keeping a lid on her emotions in front of her daughter. Some people left instructions for their funeral guests to wear colours, as bright as possible, to celebrate the life of the deceased like a show in full technicolour. Not Roger. He'd wanted black, and only black. It was to be his final flourish of sombre command. She was glad the brief was so prescriptive because then she didn't have to think about how to honour the dead by expressing herself in colour. She'd respected Roger as a businessman, and even a grandfather, but she'd despised him as a man. Choosing colour would have ended in disaster.

Oliver, who was used to wearing coloured ties, bright jackets and highly polished tan shoes, looked uncomfortable in his dark suit, and Gloria reckoned he appeared almost kind in his traditional attire. Mediocre didn't suit him but satisfied her.

Gloria had managed to narrow her outfit down to a toss-up between a Dior and a Chanel. She'd gone with the Dior, who, Jilly had informed her, dressed the Nazis. Gloria had pretended to be horrified but secretly thought it strangely appropriate that she was adorned with such dark despotic vibes for one of the most difficult roles of her life. It gave her curious courage as they made their way to the chapel.

They didn't speak.

She checked her bag for her little lacquered box and patted her hand over it. She'd already taken two tablets, and she'd need another two by midday when the wake would be well under way. Networking, by then, would be in full swing, and it would be a stampede of hangers-on, swearing their loyalty to Oliver. Gloria fancied she'd also see plenty of daggers held behind their backs, just in case.

With a bit of luck, some of them would overdo it and end up in Roger's gigantic tomb with him. They already joked that the disgusting monument hid plenty of bodies.

She held her breath as she, Jilly and Oliver approached the chapel doors. Putting her game face on for the Wade family was something she was used to. Lying for them was second nature.

The printing presses would have only just begun whirring with the morning's copy by the time she'd made a start on some of the more important players in the industry attending Roger's funeral, and by the time they did, it would be front-page news, not that Roger Wade was at peace, but that Gloria White had indeed worn black.

Chapter 6

Gloria felt washed out.

The funeral had only been one part of what fatigued her, but she insisted on taking no days off. It was reported in the press that this showed her resilience, but the truth was that she had to keep busy. Her daily show, *The White Report*, was the only constant in her life that didn't add to her woes. First thing Monday morning, around 5 a.m., her chauffeur dropped her at Studio 54, and she entered hair and make-up like a conquering hero, ready to be sprayed, contoured, blow-dried and colour-charted to within inches of her life.

Her whole body was tired.

Frazzled from looking over her shoulder. Worn out from trying to work out who the hell was sending her the letters.

It was the kind of weakness that tormented her in the middle of the night when sleep should come. But when the shadows danced around her ceiling, mingling with the moon's tormented glare through the cracks in her blinds, slumber eluded her – hence why she'd gone to a private doctor for something to help. Gloria had noticed that in the last couple of years, rest was something in her past that she could only recall with fondness, having never appreciated it at the time. She hated whingeing about the menopause. Strength, to her, was still a bastion of 1980s shoulder pads and manly resilience, which had lasted well into the time she was rising through the ranks. Complaining was for people who weren't busy. She felt the weariness in her shoulders and deep inside her chest, like an anchor keeping her chained to something she couldn't explain.

The weight of it submerged her under a chasm of water, and she had trouble catching a breath when she emerged from hair and make-up. The familiar pull of fear followed, galvanised by anxiety.

Was it someone here in the studio?

Who knew about her past?

People fussed around her, like they always did, and she saw no signs of any unusual behaviour, except perhaps an assistant who kept loitering. Aides coiffed her hair and preened her by fluffing up the pieces of material laid on her body like a shroud, keeping her straightjacketed before she was paraded in front of the cameras. Her lack of repose was something she simply got used to. Peace and quiet were things she could only talk about with her guests from her orange sofa. It was where she was able to find out about the outside world, in lieu of living in it.

But more frequently of late, she'd caught herself wondering who Gloria White really was and how she'd arrived at this place. Her body was changing, and where she'd once been belligerently capable of protecting her outer skin, lately she'd begun to allow doubt to creep in. Everybody else seemed to know who she was, everyone but Gloria herself. Sometimes it was as if she woke from a disturbed rest in the middle of a fuzzy ball of wool, and her head felt full of a substance akin to jelly. Her joints ached too, and she'd toyed with having vitamin shots. Her skin sagged and her waist grew ever thicker, and there was only so much nipping and tucking she could do before it became blatantly obvious she was faking it. And when that happened, she wanted to hang up her Louboutins and catch the next plane to a tiny Pacific island she fantasised about, where she'd shag a local fisherman and swim in turquoise water and eat coconuts off the back of a dolphin for the rest of her days.

As far as she could remember, she was strong, smart, sassy and powerful. A shining beacon of hope for all women out there who wanted to succeed in a man's world. But this morning, she felt all her fifty-four years. They had crept up on her slowly, as if they had always been waiting around a cheerless corner, ready to pounce when she least expected it. But now the malaise was back: the terrible gloom, the loneliness; the despairing hole of inevitability. She couldn't shake it off simply by putting on the daily mask of TV-ready glamour. It was here inside her, following her around, eating away at her core.

And somebody, somewhere, knew she deserved it.

The Pacific idyll seemed as far away as ever.

Nobody else saw it, this crushing insecurity about getting old and becoming irrelevant, but it was always there. The young lad who was responsible for her face paint told her that she looked fabulous, as if he was oblivious to the darkness radiating out of the two black caverns in the middle of her face. She felt a wreck. The funeral had taken her energy and sapped it, wasting it away and leaving it washed up under a pile of late-summer blooms, wilting in a corner of an unused sitting room in Buckinghamshire.

The sycophancy of the make-up artist was probably written into his contract, she thought. He wasn't to know her apathy. He was an expert liar. Everybody was. Everyone was a pedlar of fraud. The make-up artist's tools were his brushes, and Gloria's was her mouth.

He'd covered the ghastliest circles under her eyes and filled in the cracks. He'd painted over the worst excesses of her past, for which she thanked him, of course.

Did he know? Is that why he'd paid particular attention to her this morning, trying to cover her sins?

He sashayed ahead of her now – along the white corridor, lit so brightly that it stung her retinas – full of the inexperience of youth and its attendant arrogance. She envied him. His hips swayed with the contentment that he'd done his job again today, but Gloria knew he'd rather be in musical theatre.

Another actor jumping through hoops like she had.

Make-up was just another ruse to convince the audience of their superiority and make them strive for such perfection, keeping them glued to their TVs, but it was giving her a headache this morning, and she wasn't in the mood. Increasingly, she felt her screen clothes and face were suffocating her.

Voices assaulted her as she made her way to the studio. People, young and old, male, female and everything in between, scurried around her like an army of ants, desperate to get to the nest first with their prize for the queen. The buzz was softened somewhat by the two little blue pills she'd thrown down her throat earlier with a shot of watered-down vodka. She kept a bottle of it in a drawer in her dressing room and it was used like a lubricant to smooth the edges and lift her spirits. It wasn't as if she were Judy Garland, boozing at the age of six; it was just a little livener.

'Yes, Gloria, no, Gloria.'

'Gloria, your belt is too tan.'

'Gloria, your first live thread is at seven.'

Staffers and runners closed in behind her as she entered the set. The lights were softer than the ones in the long corridor and her head let up its complaints, for now. Her guests for the day were a mixture of mothers with sob stories of their kids being bullied in the playground, a man with a dog that could count to ten, a woman who cheated death on a water slide in Turkey, and an ex-politician who was trying to save his marriage by apologising live on air at 11 a.m. for snorting cocaine off a prostitute's breasts in Paris.

She dealt with the disgrace-now-and-pay-later generation who were catching up to the instant nature of the internet. It wasn't so much what people *did* that caused controversy; it was the getting caught that counted. The media didn't care what morals people held, just if they were in fashion or not, and if they weren't, then it sold more copy.

She walked over to the orange sofa and questioned her interior design choices that didn't suit her current demeanour. The cushions were lime green and grey, last year's black. No one else was allowed to sit there. It was Gloria's space alone. The sofa was suddenly reminiscent of the womb, where babies were nurtured and fed while they grew into humans, ready for the world. The sight of it made her want to cover it with something drab, but it was too late, they were live in ten.

The assistant cameraman who'd caught her eye was staring at her and she held his gaze brazenly. He was young and attractive but with the look of a psycho.

Telly was the ultimate hoax, and she was in the magic business. Her guests thought her serenely secure, trussed up inside a cocoon of privilege and fortune. It was her own deception, and she took full responsibility for it. She'd cultivated it and now carried the burden of it in its perfection, though it trapped her in a prison. It was a penal colony full of conformists, though, not convicts who broke the law but upheld it.

And this morning, it suffocated her.

Anybody, from her producer Elaine to the guard on the door, could be the one who'd sent her the letters. Or it could be all of them, colluding in her downfall.

She sighed audibly, trying to get a clean breath. There must have been twenty people in the studio, busy doing their jobs, checking camera settings, angles, lighting, sound, scripts, feeds and playback. A body from Wardrobe still loitered, fiddling with a stiletto on Gloria's right foot. She read her notes and felt the drugs in her system beginning to work. Warmth began to radiate from her heart and spread to the rest of her body, and she felt connected and safe on her orange sofa, which suddenly felt familiar again. Her guests would sit opposite her on another one – a cheaper, less extravagant version – ready to answer her pre-checked questions, giving their rehearsed answers. Around eight million Britons would tune in this morning, perhaps more because of the events of the weekend. What she said, as well as the inanity of her guests, would be reported in the tabloids and broadsheets. Everybody was hungry for escape. Chatter about food, fashion and fakery had taken over information pathways and Gloria knew she was guilty of being a significant part of the process. They peddled knowledge but no understanding.

The producer was barking questions at her.

Elaine was a fellow product of the institute of illusion. She was preened and concocted to within an inch of her Stella McCartney blouse. A caricature of herself that everyone looked to for leadership. Gloria knew Elaine had slept with her ex-husband for the job. But she didn't judge – that's how most of them got started.

'How do we pronounce her name?'
'Will he have his dog with him?'
'What if it shits everywhere?'
'How long has he known about the murder of his mother?'

Gloria asked last-minute queries of her subjects and answers were fired back from all corners of the studio. She nodded; she no longer took notes, but she did read them. She'd been in the game for so long that she felt comfortable enough on her sofa, commanding answers from the vulnerable, and seeing where the morning took her, within reason.

Her manicured hands separated pieces of paper and she handed them over to an assistant, having memorised them all. She was almost ready.

She put the weekend behind her and tried to take a deep enough breath to forget about it. Oliver had excelled himself and suggested a quickie to ease their grief after the funeral. He'd been drunk. She'd responded by telling him that a screwdriver through her skull might have a more desirable outcome, and he hadn't seen the funny side. He simply couldn't see that, to her, he was about as desirable as a supermarket bra.

The only positive outcome of the weekend was that they'd successfully shielded Jilly from being photographed and steered the majority of the stories to Roger's past money-making exploits, which were as murky as they were many.

Jilly had returned home to her flat in London unnoticed, and safe, to concentrate on the piece she was keeping close to her chest. Gloria had asked to read it but Jilly had told her it wasn't ready. She was being exceedingly cagey about the whole thing.

It was an investigative article on the penal system and the statistics on re-offending. Gloria sincerely hoped that she'd get her obsession with adverse childhood experiences out of her system quickly and rejoin the real world, where people made their own luck, but Jilly was an advocate of the underdog and insisted on championing the needy.

A cup of water was placed alongside a three-shot cortado coffee, mellowed with steamed – not frothed – milk and sweetened with two sugars. She glanced up and saw the creepy assistant cameraman flash her an awkward smile.

Oh, Jesus!

The china espresso cup tipped over, spilling coffee all over the table and splashing some of it onto Gloria's chinos.

The ensuing silence was deafening as everybody waited to see how she'd react. Then there was an explosion of fuss as she watched the unfolding drama. It was as if everybody else in the studio was moving except her. She held her hands in the air as the mess was wiped up and Wardrobe runners sprinted about shouting instructions for where to find a spare pair of trousers in under four minutes.

The assistant cameramen fiddled desperately with the mic attached to her white silk blouse when he knocked the drink again. He stood still in horror, and she thought he might piss himself. She glanced at his crotch, expecting to see a spreading sodden stain. Suddenly, he grabbed the cup, trying to help, but made more of a mess.

'Stop! Christ! I'll do it!' she snapped, instantly regretting it. Nowadays, they were supposed to be more inclusive and sensitive to other people's feelings, it was called 'mental health awareness', but it was hard for veterans of Gloria's era to come across those sorts of skills naturally, and the bloke was terrified of her.

She found herself wondering if he was displaying stalker behaviour, but told herself to stop it.

In under a minute, Wardrobe had sourced a spare pair of chinos, tailored for Gloria White only. They were ripped out of their plastic dry-cleaning bag, and a screen was placed around her while she changed. Hands whipped the stained pair off her, over her stilettos, which didn't fit properly, and the trousers were pulled onto her in time for the final ten-second countdown to air.

She emerged, fully restored, with her blonde hair sprayed and her lipstick renewed.

Behind camera one, as they launched with the programme's jingle, was a chaotic electrical short-circuiting of nerves and terror. In front of it, she greeted the nation and introduced the show's big stories.

The robot inside her was awakened and ready for action. It was as if a switch had been flicked on and her face began moving in the ways it had been trained to do, with perfection and poise. Elaine smiled at her and gave her thumbs up.

After the segment, they cut to the news and her shoulders sank. Her smile, which had been plastered onto her face, turned to a grimace, and she stared at Elaine, who nodded enthusiastically.

The camera technician who had spilled the coffee was nowhere to be seen. Gloria asked after him.

'He's packing his locker – he's been told to fuck off and never come back. Don't worry, we'll give him a glowing reference so it doesn't blow back as a bullying story, I'll get him a job on another channel.' Elaine beamed at her and Gloria imagined if the assistant had been her own daughter.

She peered into a mirror thrust into her face and nodded with satisfaction. The shaky start hadn't ruined her visage, though she did notice a tiny speck of lipstick on her front teeth. It was wiped away for her and she faced camera two as the news segment ended.

It was time to welcome her first guest, who looked about twenty years old, close in age to Jilly. But the young female guest could have been from a different planet. She'd been held against her will in a dungeon under a house in Amsterdam, by her father, for fourteen years. It had been a coup getting her to appear and it was their big story of the day, apart from Roger's funeral, and the horny politician.

An image of Jilly appeared in her head, and she thought how easily a different life could have been hers.

Chapter 7

Dear Gloria,

You looked beautiful today on TV. I have to pinch myself because it's really you.

Perfect in your place on the big orange sofa on the breakfast show. The White Report is the highlight of my day. I wouldn't call it an obsession, because I have other pursuits. I'm not neurotic about one thing, but lots of things, so technically, I'm not compulsive, but measured and organised. Compared to most, I'm ordinary, and that's how you would describe me if we met again.

I know you better than you think, but you probably don't even remember me from Docker Street, do you?

Proximity to you costs more than money, and I was so close to you once I could have touched you. I can't open a door for you any more, and I can't take your coat, or pour you a drink after a hard day, but I can caress your soul, because I know that better than anyone.

And it's hurting, I can tell.

One still, moonless night, I watched you sleeping. You murmured softly in the back of the car because you were so tired, you'd passed out. I can tell when you're close to burnout by the look on your face and the way your eyes close a millimetre more than usual; they're doing that a lot lately. It's difficult to tell sometimes because your eye lift, and all the make-up masks it, but I can see.

I touched your face that night and your skin was so soft. I felt your breath on my hand.

When I woke you, there was no evidence you'd been asleep for more than a minute and that somebody had sat beside you and put their hand inside your blouse.

The memory of your skin makes me shudder. If I could sell that memory, I'd be a millionaire, and that's the test of something valuable: lots of people want it.

To thousands, you're a two-dimensional cut-out on the TV screen, but to me, you're flesh and scent.

Real and warm, your body was next to mine for full minutes, and you allowed me to hold you as you cried in your slumber.

I know what keeps you pacing your bedroom all night long. You go downstairs for a cool drink of water, you relieve yourself, you try to read, and you listen to soft music, but none of it works, does it? And I know why.

You looked flustered this morning and I'm putting it down to your awful weekend, but I don't want you to cry, because you know as much as I do that Roger never deserved your tears. He was an evil man who forced secrets on those he controlled, like me and you.

Yours sincerely,
Your friend.

Chapter 8

Gloria tried to balance the sick feeling in her gut with a milky coffee. The voice from the letters swirled around her head whenever she had a moment to think. The solution was to keep her head noisy.

A special tribute programme to Roger Wade aired after the breakfast show and the staff stuck around to watch it, as they often did when they were curious how something would look on screen. Each department had a job to do: Gloria's was to present, Elaine's was to produce the original content, the editors slimmed it down and tightened it up, the lighting crew added atmosphere, and so on. A single piece might be the work of fifty people when it finally went out to the public. Gloria loosened her trousers and threw off her heels, curling up on a chair pulled up in front of seven screens usually manned by the production crew, led by Elaine.

They sat away from the main group of staff, inside the dark production suite, and the respite from the studio lights gave Gloria some relief from a recurring headache, which wouldn't go away with pills and vodka.

She'd given her 'friend' from the letters a voice, but even though it was her own invention, she couldn't give him a face. She'd racked her brains to see if she could recall a driver they'd used back in their Manchester days, but had come up with nothing memorable. They'd used plenty of cabs, but trying to pin one down almost thirty years later was impossible. She pushed the reference to him touching her deep down into a place even she couldn't reach. She didn't want to reach.

The credits rolled, and she and Elaine pointed out visuals that worked well and critiqued those that didn't. The piece on Roger had been a few years in the making. Like senior royals, the media was always ready for them to expire and homages to high-profile personalities were put together years in advance.

Gloria smiled when Roger's young face came on screen. The visual was tagged with the year 1967.

'Jesus, he was a looker, wasn't he?' Elaine said. 'All those Wade boys are,' she added, winking at Gloria, who forced a smile. Any reference to her husband made her slightly wary, as if he might be in the next room, testing her responses. Most people in showbiz had trust issues and if they didn't, they stood to lose a lot of money.

But she had to admit that Roger Wade had been a handsome bastard. His shock of auburn, almost ginger hair, flopping over his eyes, framed by a wide jaw and an open smile, with good teeth, smacked of strength and surety. He had the chiselled jaw of a movie star, and a coloured and privileged past, which nowadays would be called 'troubled'. But the piece wasn't about that; it was about his triumphs.

Film reel from the 1960s was tricky to work with, and the editors had done a sterling job finding it and piecing it together for a digital production. There were interviews with colleagues, politicians, actors and media giants, all of whom only had positive things to say about the man.

Gloria shifted in her chair. She wondered what it must have been like coming from a family where your future was certain. Roger had been the product of generations of success, and he wore it like a medal pinned to his tailored shirt.

Gloria was beginning to regret agreeing to watch the short film, as she couldn't help but see Oliver in his father's face. They were cut from the same cloth and Roger's mannerisms, regardless of whether he was in his twenties or his seventies, mirrored his son's exactly. It was like watching Oliver on screen, and the visual assault made her feel uncomfortable.

The programme celebrated Roger as a husband and a father as well as a media tour de force, having created the Wade Media Group from nothing in Manchester in the late 1990s. It included footage from when Oliver was a baby and clips of family holidays. Oliver's mother made a brief appearance and could have been a maid for all anyone knew, judging by her skulking around in the background, wearing an apron and standing behind her husband. Then there were snippets of Roger sailing with his son, hiking in the Himalayas – oh yes, entrepreneurs *love* life – and then, finally, there it was, in all its glory.

Gloria closed her eyes, sinking down in her seat, as everybody cheered.

The wedding of the decade.

Gloria had worn a diamond tiara borrowed from DeBeers by Roger. Since the death of his beloved wife, prematurely to cancer – before Gloria met Oliver – Roger had been desperate to spend his money on another woman. Gloria stepped into those shoes and Oliver revelled in his father's generosity. Her dress was handmade by Miuccia Prada herself, and the cake was flown in from New York, on Concorde, so the cream wouldn't spoil.

'Wow,' she heard Elaine breathe, as if thoroughly pissed off that she looked so damned gorgeous.

Gloria felt daft for a second or two and suddenly bashful that all eyes were on her. It was a strange sensation because she was used to living under the microscope, but it was more for Jilly, because she wished she was watching it with her daughter. She was happy to be examined in the make-believe world of TV, but not like this. This was real.

The vulnerability made her feel queasy.

Gloria found herself laughing along with the production team as archive clips of her holidays, appearances on chat shows and photos of her and Oliver at exclusive parties flashed across the screen. She hardly recognised the stranger up there.

A traitorous voice told her she'd made a mistake and that she should never have divorced the man who gave her everything. But nostalgia was the enemy of truth, and she was under no illusion; the shots she was watching were merely polished baubles of trickery designed to sell a brand.

She stopped laughing.

'Is this about Roger or me?' she asked Elaine.

A few murmurs around the small studio indicated agreement that the focus was off, but that was telly. Roger's death only sold copy because of who he left behind. People didn't tune in to watch an old bloke age and die; they followed his story because of the glamour he attracted and those who surrounded him, like Gloria.

She was the story.

Thankfully, the segment ended, and Gloria got up to go back to her dressing room to take off her make-up and put on her own clothes. She'd be photographed as she went to her car, but there was an appetite for that too, because it showed how normal she was outside of her showbiz skin, and women related to it.

Gloria had created her own brand outside of the Wade Group, and she no longer relied on them to survive, but hadn't found the courage to go it alone – yet. For now, she still needed them.

In her dressing room, as she wiped away her make-up, she reflected on Roger's life and the parts people were choosing to honour.

She would have written a very different story.

A knock on her door made her jump, and a runner poked his head around her door, holding a large mail-bag.

'Your mail, it's all been through the scanner,' he told her, dropping the huge bag of post on the floor beside her. 'Do you want me to sort it?' he asked.

She shook her head. The young lad backed out and closed the door, and she stared at the bag, which was bursting at the seams.

The others had got through the scanner.

The line between love and obsession was a fine one and Gloria was always wary about fan mail that went beyond a thank you or display of ordinary appreciation.

The letters were no fan mail.

She finished wiping away the layers of thick make-up and washed her face, then applied a soothing cream. She'd give her skin an hour or so to calm down before applying her own light cover, then she'd leave to go home. But first, she emptied the bag, looking for something in particular.

It didn't take long to find it.

A letter, like the others, in the same handwriting.

She picked it up and tore it open, speed-reading it until the familiar sense of nausea overwhelmed her and she had to sit down.

It was from him.

Chapter 9

Jilly smelled pasta sauce, though she knew from the effect the smell was having on her senses that she wouldn't eat it. She'd likely push it around her plate and watch her flatmate eat. Max's appetite wasn't about to be curbed by the fact she'd spent her weekend in front of the world's press, at her grandfather's funeral, or any other news, for that matter. His five-a-day was interpreted as the number of times he required meat to be paired with a full plate of accompaniments, usually rice, pasta or pitta. She stood on her balcony, watching the sun dip to the west over London, peeking through the gaps in the metal skyline, and contemplated the sky as it turned orange.

'It's ready,' he shouted.

They'd lived together all summer, since finishing university, where they'd also shared a house near the centre of Durham for three years. They'd decided that London was the next best city to explore, after existing in the charming and cobbled haven of the North-East, which was like living in a pocket-sized snippet of academia. It hadn't resembled real life at all, and they thought it was about time they grew up.

Jilly was wary of new friendships. She'd met Max during freshers' week. He was a technical engineering student, a computer wizard, and socially awkward. He'd spilled rum and Coke on her. He was a misfit too, but not in the sense that his parents were so famous he couldn't move around freely; with him it was more that he'd always been painfully shy. He'd lost his sister when she was only nine years old and had been unable to fathom the world after that. Jilly had recognised in him a kindred spirit yearning for real connection. They understood one another.

They found their way together and had been inseparable ever since.

He'd cooked to welcome her home again after the funeral and he'd bought extra tissues to get through her telling him the story of the whole weekend. She'd wanted him at the funeral, at her side, but couldn't have dealt with her mother's questions about whether he was her boyfriend or not. Frankly, it was none of her business, and it was out of a sense of protective fierceness that Jilly had told Max not to come, and kept the nature of their friendship from her mother too. And Jilly was glad he hadn't been there. All she'd done all weekend was blub. She'd been introduced to enough faces to cover a thousand magazines and she'd forgotten most of them. Her life had always been littered with moments of weirdness when pop stars, actors and politicians accompanied them on family holidays, in private theatre boxes or as guests in their home. She'd never found it strange, because that was her life. Her family had visitors that happened to be on the TV, others didn't. It wasn't worth talking about.

In Jilly's world, she didn't make friends, she discarded them. They swarmed around her when they found out who she was, and it was her job to filter through them and jettison the hangers-on. Sadly, that included most of them. But not Max.

He didn't care who her mother or father was, and even less, her grandfather.

She went inside and saw that Max had set the table with pretty napkins and crystal glasses and was opening what looked like an expensive bottle of Malbec. She sat down and allowed him to pamper her. He'd make a great husband one day, she thought, and wondered who the lucky lady might be. She knew that when the time came, she'd be like a protective big sister who vetted every candidate, looking for the one who'd treat him how he deserved.

'Your mother called you eight times today,' he said as they sat down and she took her first sip of wine. It was delicious and she fancied just drinking tonight, without having to be sensible and line her stomach with food. But people – including Max – thought that grief was a little like convalescence, and that the patient needed comfort food to survive it.

They sat down and Max began eating in earnest. She watched him hoover his spaghetti while she pushed hers around.

'It's funny how you think famous people will live forever,' she said.

Max slowed down his sucking and rested his elbows on the table.

'Tell me your favourite memories of him,' he said.

She smiled and put down her fork, giving up on her food.

'When I slept over at his estate on my own – usually because my parents had an event or something – my room had a doll's house in it, which was the size of our place in Durham.'

Max laughed and shook his head. She knew he was fascinated by her tales of excess, but not in a judgemental way, more because it was like describing a different world.

'I don't know the man on TV they're all talking about,' she said, a cloud crossing her face again.

'So, don't watch it. Keep hold of the memories you have just for yourself,' Max said.

'I know he wasn't loved by everybody,' she said.

A breeze wafted through from the balcony, and they heard horns punctuating the London night.

'It doesn't matter. This always happens. Fame is a double-edged sword. You're either loved or hated, there's nothing in between. I wouldn't last a day!'

They laughed. It felt good.

Her phone buzzed: a message from her old university tutor, whom she kept in touch with.

'It's Professor Love,' she announced to Max, who stopped eating and grinned.

'Open it, then!'

She'd been waiting for some news.

She did so and scanned the message quickly, covering her mouth with her hand.

'He's agreed to see me!'

'Shut up!' Max said, exaggerating his words slowly for effect. He put his fork down and went to her side, peering over her shoulder, reading the message for himself.

'My hands are shaking,' Jilly said.

Max turned to her and stared into her eyes. 'This is amazing, and just what you need. We have to celebrate. Fuck the food, let's go out. Where shall we go?'

Jilly couldn't answer, so Max clicked his fingers and said he knew the perfect place. He'd read about a small tapas bar that had opened along Southbank, close to Borough Market. It was their favourite area to wander in London because it was the most anonymous. Full of city people during the day, and tourists at the weekend, it was neither pretentious nor gimmicky.

'Get your bag,' he said to her.

She stood still and didn't move.

'What?' he asked.

She burst into tears.

He went to her and gently put his arms around her and held her until the shaking stopped.

'I didn't think I had any more tears,' she whispered.

'It's okay,' he replied.

'Should I call my mum?' she asked him.

He thought about the question for a moment and then shook his head. 'She didn't like the other piece you did on prisons, did she?'

Jilly shook her head.

'I thought you wanted to do this alone,' he added.

'You're right.' She nodded. 'I need to do this alone and break away from her, and if she doesn't approve, then that's her problem. Do I need make-up?' she added.

He smiled and wiped her cheeks softly with his fingers. 'No. You don't need to cover up. Besides, no one will care. In this city, people just think about themselves.'

Chapter 10

The drive from London to Surrey seemed particularly long. Gloria had been commuting by chauffeur for years, but she'd only just recently begun to notice the details, like how uncomfortable it was to sit for sometimes four hours with a tight waistband digging into your fat, or how quickly she got drunk nowadays on the wine provided in the mini fridge. The Mercedes limousine was supposed to be the ultimate in executive luxury, but tonight she felt out of place. Her skin felt hot, and she couldn't wait to have a shower. It wasn't simply the sweltering London heat this time of year that she felt choking her. The air conditioning was working just fine, but her skin felt wet with awkwardness, as if her body didn't fit her any more.

She wanted to throw the windows open and hang her head out, but the network had strict protocols when it came to exposure. Image marketing for celebrities was difficult to control in the era of the mobile phone, but still, the network tried to limit it. Even on her way home, she was for sale.

By the time they reached the outlying suburbs of London, she'd kicked off her shoes, undone her trousers and settled into the back seat, trying to get some sleep, but slumber eluded her, and her brain filled with noise instead. She'd tried to count or think of pleasant things to get her mind to switch off, but it never worked.

She'd texted Jilly and tried to call, but her daughter was blatantly ignoring her. It seemed that all she needed was her flatmate, Max, who seemed nice enough but was still a hanger-on. He came from nowhere, suddenly emerging to make friends with her daughter on her first day of university. The relationship had lasted, to Gloria's surprise, and Jilly had denied any romantic involvement, but why would a young man hang around if not for sex? In Gloria's world, men always wanted *something*.

She sipped from a cool glass of white wine. The car-fridge was her idea. A job in telly and the ability to sink copious amounts of wine used to be a classic pairing, like Batman and Robin, Thelma and Louise, or Ken and Barbie. But nowadays, in the health-conscious new millennium, getting smashed was frowned upon, especially on the job, so old sweats like her saved it for when they were alone. Crystal glasses were also provided in the back of the car, but their luxury failed to make her feel any better. She couldn't decide if it was her fear or the liquor burning her throat. She scrolled through her phone for something to do; anything to distract her from her reality. But boredom with the news forced her to peer at the outside world through the tinted windows: a world she couldn't touch.

It was normal out there.

People went about their business. They fed kids, took them to swimming lessons, had conversations with friends, made love to partners and paid bills.

It was a life she'd wanted but could never have. Not now. Not ever.

There had been a time she'd been free, but she could hardly recall it. Now she lived in a gilded cage, and people paid to watch her perform.

Warmth travelled up her chest, and she imagined herself diving into her pool, away from the animalistic heatwave that was gripping the nation. It was big news and had killed three pensioners already, as well as countless domestic pets.

She stared out of the window and watched as lights whizzed by and she wished herself somewhere else for a while. Somewhere anonymous so she could wander along a street, stopping to have coffee with a friend – a genuine pal, not somebody who wanted something from her.

The person sending her letters wanted something from her, but she didn't know what. The notes were the truest thing that had happened to her in a long time, and in a weird way she trusted the voice behind them. It was clear, direct and intentional. It gave her a sense of belonging. She knew it was perverse, but she couldn't deny the desire to work out the message he was trying to give her.

She assumed it was a man; she'd never known a female driver and the thought suddenly depressed her.

If he was merely a pervert, she'd have had no problem reporting him to the police. But he knew things about her. Things she never shared.

Each time she received a new one, her breath caught in her chest, as if she was about to be held under water, but then curiosity aroused within her, and she hadn't felt that since before *The White Report*. Success had dulled her edge.

The letters awoke a new hunger in her.

An appetite to find the fucker and confront him.

On her own, to prove she could still do it.

A lusher treeline informed her that they were nearly home. Another wave of fear washed over her. In the car, at least she was going somewhere. At home, she'd face a sterile domain that stood still. At home, she was supposed to be herself, but she didn't know who that was any more. She'd taken calls in the back of the car, from her agent, her accountant, her milk-delivery person, and a courier service that had screwed up the arrival of a parcel, but none of them spoke to *her*; they only had words for Gloria White.

Sometimes she flicked through old diaries, searching for contacts she'd lost touch with, trying to drum up the courage to call one of them and ask if they'd like a coffee, or a glass of wine, or even a meal. But then she recoiled, realising that it would only lead to disappointment. She'd done it once and arranged a drink with an old university pal, but it became clear when they sat down that the woman – who was nice enough – had only come to see if some of Gloria's influence might rub off and propel her into stardom. She'd even organised for a friend to sit at the bar and take photos of them, which she later sold to a tabloid. The incident put her off doing it again.

Looking back was like stumbling into oncoming traffic blind. Best avoided. But to refrain from looking backwards, she needed to look forward, at least with her eyes open, and she couldn't do that either, because she didn't believe there was anything there for her. A great fear had begun to take hold when she turned fifty and Jilly moved out. Like there wasn't much left to look forward to. The end was inevitable and looming ever closer, and she couldn't help feeling despair.

That's when she'd gone to the doctor for something to take the edge off. But instead of HRT, she'd been given Adderall.

Her home in Surrey was burrowed away underneath a canopy of trees, the same ones that surrounded nearby Virginia Water. She chose it for privacy, to escape the constant threat of people wanting to meet her. Strangers had a habit of wanting to consume their celebrity idols, and they thought nothing of touching her uninvited. There was a fine line between interest and harm.

She approached the house with a heavy feeling in her stomach. It was an empty reminder of what used to live there. Her daughter had gone, and she was too scared to invite another man into her life after Oliver.

Divorce was messy, but a public break-up was eviscerating.

Finally, the car pulled up to the electric gates at the front of the house, and the driver punched in the entry code on a keypad inside the car. The large gates yawned open and, after they'd driven in, they slid shut behind them, as if confirming that her life was a series of pockets of isolation, each protected from reality by an army of sycophants and assistants. She simply moved from one zone to the other, and back again.

The driver opened her door, and she paid attention to him when she got out of the car. She didn't recognise him, and she searched his face for evidence that he knew what was happening to her.

Could it be him? Lots of people had access to her during the day. He smiled and the moment passed. She thanked him and went to her front door, unlocking it and going in, closing the door behind her without making eye contact with him for a second time.

She'd made the mistake of shagging a driver once, and he'd sold his story to a prominent newspaper. Thankfully, the Wade Group had spun it to her favour and she'd emerged a triumphant cougar.

Trust no one.

She peeked behind the curtain to make sure the driver had gone, then checked her front door was secured with its treble-locking system.

Inside was just as she'd left it this morning at 4 a.m. The sickly perfume from the flowers in the hallway made her slightly nauseous. Lilies reminded her of death, but they were the most aesthetic and dramatic of all flowers, especially when paired with a white vase and a glass table. Peonies and other exhibitionists were pretentious and should be kept for celebrity dinner parties, which she no longer had.

She threw her things down in a pile on the floor and kicked off her shoes. The housekeeper came in every day and tidied them away, like she stripped everything from the fabric of the house that didn't belong. Perhaps if she laid down on the cold tiles and fell asleep, the housekeeper would tidy her away too.

She searched for evidence that somebody – anybody – had been there, but there was none.

But *he* knew where she lived.

Or at least that's what he'd suggested in one of his letters: he'd watched her pace up and down in the middle of the night, unable to sleep. Or was he guessing? It had been a good guess. When the effects of her tablets and the booze wore off, she paced all night long sometimes. How could he know? She'd checked outside her house; on the long leafy lane, from across the road, you could see her bedroom, just.

But surely no one could get inside? Her domestic cocoon was spotless, so much so that any evidence of her living in it had been brushed and hoovered away. Even the housekeeper herself was invisible; Gloria didn't recall her name. She chided herself for assuming it was a woman who cleaned her house, but it was probably true, like the drivers being male. The cushions in the lounge were still as plump as they had been this morning and she idly wondered when she'd want to sit on them again. She didn't want to spoil them. The week's post waited on the table for her, but she'd already been through it, looking for his handwriting. The letters always came to her work address.

Her bare feet slapped satisfyingly on the polished floor as she crossed the hallway, and the noise relaxed her. It was reassuringly human. She needed another drink. She entered the grand kitchen, half expecting it to be turned over, with smashed glass threatening to tear her feet apart, but it was pristine. The blinds were still half drawn to protect the space from the intense heat of the day. She flicked a switch and they whirred upwards into their housing until the mechanism stopped and the beauty of the south-facing garden was revealed by clever lighting on timers.

Her desire to jump into the pool had disappeared, along with any interest in eating dinner. She opened the bifold doors by remote control and felt the warm air fight with the cold. She undid her blouse and slipped off the loose trousers she'd worn home. She stood in her underwear, and it made her chuckle to herself because there was nobody to seduce there, not that her body was up to it these days anyhow. She was no longer young and sexy, though she did receive fan mail from those who fantasised about dominant middle-aged women like her. Maybe that's what it was? Fan mail.

No, it wasn't. She was certain.

She took a large glass from the overhead rack and got a bottle of ice-cold Chablis from the wine fridge. She filled her glass to the very top and took a slug.

Her landline phone ringing made her jump. The sound pierced her ears and begged the question: who used landlines any more? Her breathing quickened. She listed in her head all the people who knew where she lived. It wasn't that many, but journalists and weirdos always had a way.

Always.

The noise stopped, but as soon as it did, her mobile buzzed and she retrieved it from her handbag.

Her body relaxed. It was Jilly.

'Darling,' she said, trying not to slur her words, but she needn't have bothered because Jilly was clearly drunk too and didn't notice. She was with Max and they'd gone out to dinner to celebrate something, but Gloria couldn't work out what it was. It didn't matter, the important thing was that Jilly was happy, almost like a normal young woman.

It was unusual for Jilly to let her hair down and Gloria relished the moment.

'I'm so glad you're having a good time, darling,' she said. 'What are you celebrating?'

'My professor, she set me up...' Jilly's voice trailed off.

'Set you up?'

Jilly hiccupped. Then Max came on the phone and they chatted politely for a few minutes. Gloria found him awkward but accepted that he made Jilly happy. At least there was no evidence he'd sold them out yet. Gloria still didn't grasp what they were celebrating, but it didn't matter, she didn't care, as long as her daughter wasn't crying over her grandfather. This was just what she needed: something to distract her. Max passed the phone back to Jilly, whose voice had changed. Gloria sensed seriousness in it and braced herself. Alcohol could be like truth serum to her daughter, and Gloria guessed that she'd called to get something off her chest. Her joy over her daughter's seemingly spontaneous call evaporated.

'Dad said you think I'm "swanning around trying to save the world". What exactly does that mean, Mum?'

Gloria braced herself and cursed her idiot ex-husband, who loved to drive wedges between them just for kicks.

'I didn't say that.'

Gloria felt caught out. She *had* said that, but it had been a private conversation. She saw her daughter throwing her life away on the altar of righteousness just so she could say she hadn't succumbed to glamour media, like her mother. And this was the rub; Jilly had chosen a branch of journalism to spite her, not because she was serious about it. But talking to her drunk really wouldn't progress the debate further.

'I don't believe you. Why would Daddy lie to me? What is it about my work that you can't bring yourself to support? You used to write serious journalism,' she said, slurring the long words. 'I've read some of it. You were good. Why can't I do it too?'

Jilly wasn't letting go.

'Let's talk tomorrow, shall we? Now isn't the time,' Gloria told her daughter. 'All I said was that it's tough to be taken seriously in this industry. Your dad knows how hard it is.'

'Daddy says I have a bright future and I can work at the network any time I want to.'

Gloria closed her eyes. In that one sentence, Jilly had crushed any good intentions Gloria ever had about not raising a nepo baby. She and Oliver had promised each other that they wouldn't use their trade to further their child's fortunes. But when divorce ripped apart marriages, it destroyed promises too.

'Sweetheart, you're getting the wrong impression. Let's talk tomorrow—'

'Of course it's tough! You think I can't do it?' Jilly asked.

Gloria heard Max in the background trying to take the phone off her daughter.

'I'm sorry, darling, I fully support your work, and I loved your last article, despite what your father told you. We need more journalism like yours to replace the facile shit I churn out every day,' she said sarcastically.

Jilly laughed, and Gloria knew she'd smoothed things over with her. If she denigrated her own career and promised Jilly that she'd be winning awards for investigative journalism before she could say 'Elvis shot Kennedy', she'd keep her onside, but it was a devilish trade-off, and it wasn't true. Gloria was devastated that Jilly wanted to join the game. And she was angry with Oliver for encouraging her.

At least Jilly was unlikely to have to do what she'd done to get ahead.

She'd endured eleven long years of marriage before ending what the media called 'a marriage made in heaven'. The Wades provided the money, and she delivered the mouth.

Gloria managed to steer the conversation onto safer topics, and she forgot to ask her daughter what it was she had called about. Her news – the kind that made her want to get drunk – must have been important, but it disappeared underneath the resentment that always reared its head when Jilly mourned the loss of her parents' marriage and lashed out.

Jilly had a yearning to make things right. She'd been born with fire in her belly, and Gloria admired her sense of justice. Hers was a world where the right thing got done, but Gloria's wasn't like that at all, and she wanted to protect her daughter from inevitable disappointment and pain. Jilly had always wanted to save the world and those in it.

She hadn't yet learned cynicism, while Gloria was riddled with it.

For a tiny moment, she wanted to believe her daughter's passion and understand her need to improve the human condition.

She had no idea how she and Oliver raised such a behemoth of good.

Jilly ended the call as drunk people often do: abruptly, and Gloria was left alone again.

She watched the sky turn orange from the back of her house – the colour of her studio sofa – and the late-summer heat began to turn down a dial or two, bringing some relief of sorts. There was a scant breeze coming through the open doors and she stood in the opening, expecting something. She didn't know what she desired. Some sort of peace, she supposed.

Going back to the hall to retrieve her bag, she promptly tripped over it and tutted. Her foot had turned it over, exposing all the folded letters in there and adrenalin rushed through her body. She hadn't taken any Adderall since the morning and her right hand shook gently.

She stared at the latest one, in its envelope still. She wanted to burn it but she daren't touch it lest it scorch her skin.

'*Your job is controversial, you have enemies…*' Elaine told her all the time. It was true, Gloria got sent crazy stuff in the post and online all the time. It was her normal. Celebrities in the spotlight attracted weirdos. It was part of the job spec, and the Met Police's files were full of TV personalities reporting perverts and stalkers.

But this one was different.

He knew her.

She leaned over to pick up the envelope, taking the letter out and reading it again. It was grubby and she shivered. She'd read it over and over again since receiving it at work.

Whoever owned this particular piece of paper before it made its way to her was unclean and unfortunate. The handwriting was immature and reminded her of an essay written hastily by a teenager with no interest in the topic, yet it was articulate and considered. A long-ago memory stirred inside her: sitting at the back of English class listening to Mrs Thompson drone on about Romeo and Juliet. She and her buddies distracted by a piece of paper doing the rounds. *Sharon is a slag.*

The author was educated but downtrodden; that much was certain.

A driver? Perhaps.

She put it back into her bag, not wanting to sully any of the surfaces of her home, and then she went back to the kitchen to wash her hands, throwing the bag on the table.

She took the wine bottle from the fridge, as well as her glass, out to the garden, where the night had begun to caress the surface of the pool. It glimmered with orange, purple and blue, and looked like a postcard from paradise. The water was still, and she stared into its depths, wanting to jump in and forget everything for a while. It was quiet and the perfect surroundings engulfed her. A little wine spilled on the patio and the disorder pleased her curiously, as if reminding her that she was just another citizen.

But try as she might to rid her brain of the letter, she couldn't, and the thought of it followed her everywhere she went.

Chapter 11

The words were emblazoned in neon across the night sky.

Bare Bunny.

The club of promises.

It had been exclusively for stars back in the day. Footballers, pop stars, soap actors and journalists. By invitation only.

The celestial bodies Gloria stared at tonight were more dependable and less needy. Above her pool, deep into the night sky, constellations hung like a canopy of crystals.

She knew Cassiopeia, because of its 'W' shape, but it wasn't quite straight and reminded her instead of the wonky smile kids stick on snowmen, with rocks or bits of coal. She knew that stars twinkled, and planets didn't, so she reckoned she could see Jupiter, which shone yellow, and Venus, which was the brightest. Her life seemed so little alongside the universe, and it brought her strange comfort to understand that she was only one tiny speck of dust in the planetary system. She caught herself leaning into metaphysical contemplation and it made her chuckle, because she'd had too much wine and had reached the stage where she was being silly.

Even the letters seemed humorous now. Who would want to bother with her at her age? The tiredness and the effects of the pills didn't help. But the seriousness of the vast possibilities above her was not lost, and she stopped smiling and stared at her phone. She couldn't help it. She was puzzled by the mechanics of the thing, how it got its life from something up there, a satellite – or fake star – that beamed messages all over the globe.

Sometimes, it was vital not to be important.

Her phone rang and she saw it was Oliver. She was cross with him for breaking her trust, but then again, it was no shock. They spoke when they had to, but Roger's death had seemed to give Oliver a renewed sense of need to contact her.

He was lonely.

Panic gripped her.

What if he'd set this whole letter thing up? He knew her every move back in their Manchester days. It would be easy for him to pull off. Just to mess with her head and confuse her at a time when Jilly needed her.

She stared at his number flashing.

She could never find peace.

Oliver liked to think he had power over people, including her, and it drove him crazy when she was unavailable to talk. She was tempted to ignore him, but she was lonely too and fancied a chat, even if it was with him. Besides, she had something to ask him.

After all this time, they still occasionally used each other as crutches.

'Oliver?'

'Gloria. I saw the piece on Dad. Congratulations, it was stunning.'

There was genuine emotion in his voice, but he'd had years to perfect the illusion and Gloria knew better.

'Thank you. It was mostly Elaine.'

'Modesty doesn't suit you.'

Her guard flew up. She suddenly felt sober. Her thoughts of flying away on a star were forgotten and she listened to his every word, expecting a trap. It wouldn't surprise her if he recorded his calls in an attempt to discredit her at a time of his choosing, which was more likely with Roger now gone. Her ratings were excellent; too good for him to sack her, but she knew he wouldn't be able to tolerate having her around forever.

'How can I help? It's late,' she asked in a functional voice.

'We've created a genius,' he said. The praise came out of the blue, but she knew he was prepping for something else. He was softening her up.

Her skin broke out in goosebumps all over and she got up from the lounger. The black night was cool, which was a relief, and she didn't want to go inside, but Oliver had suddenly made her feel as though she must. She felt watched without warning. She couldn't see all the way to the bottom of her garden, beyond the pool, to the summer house or behind it, and her imagination ran riot as she imagined seeing shapes down there.

'We have,' she agreed with him. 'She's amazing. Her brain is full to bursting with ideas.' She walked towards the house.

'She's just like you, I can't take the credit.'

Her stomach flipped over. He was like a cat offering to share his bowl of milk with a mouse.

'Well, I'm flattered, but I reckon it's in the Wade blood,' she said.

The mere mention of his parentage was sure to send him into a pit of nostalgia that would hopefully suck up the rest of the conversation. Oliver loved talking about his family's rise to power. She'd heard it a thousand times, but tonight she wanted to distract him. She knew he wanted something and the thought of what he had in mind unnerved her.

'I still can't believe he's gone. I went into Dad's study today and went through some papers.'

She sensed he was building up to something. She allowed him to wax lyrical. She'd heard it all before, how his parents built their network from nothing in the sixties, when land in Manchester was cheap and aspiring journalists worked for basically nothing but the story. Oliver had been born with a typewriter in his cot, or so the family joke was told. But then he mentioned Jilly again.

'She was born with a typewriter in her cot.'

Right on cue.

'Or a Mac, at least.'

He laughed and agreed with her assessment.

'She was upset that you gave her the impression I thought her work a waste of time,' Gloria said, not able to bite her tongue any more.

'Ah, that's what I was ringing to apologise for.'

'So you did tell her that?'

'Well, it wasn't quite in those words.'

'Never mind. I've patched it up with her.'

Really, Gloria seethed inside. She imagined him manipulating her words, repackaging them for Jilly to make her think that her mother had no respect for her starting out in journalism.

'How was she? I didn't want her to leave here until she was ready,' he said.

She imagined him rattling around his father's mansion, needing somebody to listen to him. She really wasn't interested in what Roger had left behind.

'It's good for her to get back to her own space. She was exhausted,' she said.

'Tired at her age! We had so much more get-up-and-go, didn't we?'

Gloria was unsure if his words were a veiled reference to their historic sexual activities, or simply an off-the-cuff reminiscence. Nothing was accidental with Oliver. Either way, she wasn't comfortable with where the conversation was going.

'She seemed a bit overwhelmed,' she told him, changing the subject.

'She wants to be like you,' he said.

'Really? I thought she wanted to be *nothing* like me,' she replied.

The words were out before she could help herself. She'd invited his criticism and now he wouldn't stop.

'I didn't mean daytime TV, I meant how you started,' he said.

'Of course. Well, if she wants it enough, she'll get it. She's determined and very talented. I did like her article, by the way.'

'I know you did, I tried to explain that, tried to smooth things over, but she was upset. She took it the wrong way and didn't give me a chance to explain.'

Liar.

'So, I hear you had a little spat at work this morning?' He plopped into the conversation.

Here we go, she thought.

This was really why he'd called. She rinsed her wine glass in the kitchen and glanced over her shoulder at the shadows, glad she'd come inside. She pressed the buttons to close the doors and the blinds, and they glided together.

'Spat?'

'Coffee-gate.'

She'd forgotten about the young man who'd spilled coffee over her trousers, and it was typical of Oliver to call out something trivial to make her question herself. It put her on edge. As the blinds clicked shut, she considered employing a bodyguard.

'Remember the Bare Bunny nightclub?' she asked him. It was her turn to change the subject.

'The what?'

'Exactly, I know, it seems a million years ago. It's just I saw something on TV about it being bulldozed.'

It was only a small lie. But she'd looked it up after receiving the last letter because she couldn't stop thinking about it. The warehouse on Docker Street, where the club had stood, had been converted years ago into flats, and now, due to recession and rising unemployment in the area, they were being razed to the ground to make way for a new shopping centre. The old making way for the new. The area had reinvented itself more times than she could keep up with. Back in their Manchester days, it had been the place to be. Not just a club, but *the* club, which is why she and Oliver used to go there, when their stars were rising as cut-throat journalists. They used to frequent it, not only to chase stories, mainly of gangs and famous people getting into trouble by evading taxes and meddling with call girls, but because it was a damn good night out.

Everybody who was anybody partied at the Bare Bunny, leeching off the gold dust which floated off the halcyon days of the Hacienda scene. Rich and famous people flocked there to shed their skins and relax. There was a no-camera policy. Not like now, when anybody could hide a phone in their knickers and snap a celeb with their pants down. Literally.

Life was much simpler then. Neither of them was famous yet and nobody knew their faces, which is why she questioned the identity of the author of the letters, because he *did* know her face. Back then, she'd moved freely around the city. The move to London by the Wade Group had been the beginning of something else and signalled the end of that life.

A new start.

An opportunity to move on from mistakes. Bad memories, but also good ones.

'The Bare Bunny,' she repeated to him. Maybe he hadn't heard her correctly.

'I heard you.'

His voice had changed, and her gut dropped to her toes.

She'd done it again; she'd forgotten why he called her late at night. He did it when he needed to bolster his ego, when he felt like he required the exercise of some power. How stupid of her to forget.

'Let's forget it,' she said. But it was too late.

'But you brought it up,' he said.

'I'm sorry, I shouldn't have—'

'No, you shouldn't have, but you did. Is this because of Dad? Your timing sucks.'

'No. I simply mentioned it because it was in something I read.'

'You were always a good liar. But not good enough for me to not see through it.'

'Oliver, let's not do this.' She knew he was right, but she wouldn't tell him why. *Couldn't* tell him why.

'I can't believe you'd do this to me now, after everything,' he said. He was the victim again.

She was trapped on a tightrope of doom. On the one side was the pit of monotonous hell, where she had to listen to Oliver's self-pity for hours, and on the other was the cavern of guilt, where she slammed the phone down and instantly regretted it.

This time, she decided to listen, not just to ease his whirring mind but also to quieten her own.

It was over an hour before she got off the phone and by then it was gone midnight. Her car would pick her up at 4 a.m. for the journey into London. She rubbed her shoulders where they'd been taking the barrage of everybody else's trauma. Sometimes she felt as though that was all she was: a sponge for the demanding. She must have had a sign slapped on her head at some point, inviting everybody who saw her to offload and transfer their shit onto her.

She had a headache.

She drained her glass – which she'd retrieved from the sink to fill up again for the long conversation with Oliver – then placed it back into the basin and took some paracetamol out of a drawer. She swallowed four propranolol as well, to calm her down and give her a decent chance of sleep.

As she turned off the lights and set the alarm, she heard a crack outside and froze.

The letters were delivered to work. Everybody knew where she worked. They didn't know where she lived. But he did. He'd told her as much.

If he'd waited this long to find her, then how hard would it be to trace her home address? It was from somebody who knew the Bare Bunny. It was from somebody who saw her and Oliver there back then, dancing, laughing, drinking, having fun, like a pair of normal twenty-something-year-olds; before kids, free and easy.

If only it had been that simple.

Chapter 12

The club pulsated as if it were alive, and bodies gyrated up against one another to the beat. The noise rattled through the mass of flesh as Gloria's eyes searched for somebody. It was a young woman she sought. A small girl, almost a woman, but not quite. Pretty but not beautiful. Simple and steady, with a whiff of innocence. She looked out of place, Gloria remembered. As if she'd snuck into the place uninvited, but Gloria spotted her, because she knew who she was and what she wanted. Curiosity made Gloria sit and watch her, but lack of entertainment caused her to follow the young woman through the club and take note of who she spoke to.

The girl was as keen as a puppy, desperate to impress, and had no idea that her darting eyes and sober steadiness marked her out as unusual to the big men on the door.

Gloria watched as the girl grew frustrated because no one was interested in talking to her, and she fidgeted with the dress that she'd clearly worn specially for tonight, thinking this would be her big scoop. Gloria bumped into bodies as they twisted and twirled in front of her. The people in the club would call it a good night out. To Gloria, it was a work night. She recalled the difference, even though she was fast asleep and imagining the whole thing. She could feel the urgency of needing to follow the girl and watch out for her. But Gloria was only there for one thing. To get the story. But so was the other woman – or girl – who had no idea the danger she was in. In her dream, Gloria watched her pause at the bar, trying to squeeze herself between two large men holding bottles of beer, but she couldn't get past them. They blocked her way, and she tensed. She was so tiny and the bodies of the two men closed her exit. She was trapped between them, and they were so close that Gloria thought she must have been able to smell their bodies. The club was hot and sticky, and Gloria imagined the stench of the two men enveloping the girl. The men grinned at the girl's predicament, and she was powerless.

In the place between sleep and waking, Gloria's chest thudded, and it matched the booming of the music, though the beat soon turned to the sound of fear.

Fear for the girl.

Fear for herself.

One of the men moved a little bit to the left and Gloria saw her head still trapped in between them. The girl's face had changed from brazen courage to evident terror. Gloria felt her body twitch, but there was nothing she could do for the girl now. She wondered desperately if Tommy, the club manager, was watching on his endless TV screens. Why wasn't he doing something?

The men sensed their opportunity, and one took hold of one of the girl's breasts. She flinched, but there was nowhere to go. Gloria's skin felt clammy and, in her daze, she felt perspiration cling to her top lip. She wiped it away absentmindedly, but it stayed, stubborn and determined, and began leaking down her face. The silliness of her standing in a club with water running down her whole face made her realise that it was a dream, and she tried to tell herself to wake up.

But she couldn't.

Now it was the girl's face that streamed with liquid, and make-up and tears.

Gloria wanted to tell the men that the make-up wasn't an invitation to touch the girl, but it was too late.

Rage engulfed Gloria and she tried to charge between the men, but they didn't see her. She was invisible. But she could see everything that was happening to the girl.

The men's hands in her crotch, rough like a rock. *It hurts*. Gloria wasn't the one being violated but she could still feel it. The girl wriggled, but instead of breaking free, her face collided with the man's chest, and he was encouraged by the supposed invitation. Gloria watched him suck on his bottle like a newborn calf, and it was repulsive. She was so close to him that she could hear the liquid forcing its way into his gullet and he burped in her face.

She smelled beer, but at the same time Gloria knew that she wasn't close enough to the men to be able to do so. In her dream, she'd become the girl and she felt her fear.

The other man was sandwiched behind the girl now, and he'd managed to raise her skirt, forcing his hand between her buttocks. Gloria held her breath, as if that would make him stop, but it just made her lightheaded.

Then she knew he was inside her.

In the dream, Gloria couldn't feel it, but she knew it. The girl was in grave danger.

Hot prickles charged around Gloria's skin, and she felt as though her body might explode. She tried to scream, but the only sound that emerged from her mouth was silence, and she was forced to endure witnessing the assault while passers-by danced, got high and smiled at the girl, unaware that she was pinned between two monsters.

'I've got a message for you.'

One of the men whispered into Gloria's ear and, for a second, she wondered where the girl had gone. She looked at the floor and saw no sign of her. Nobody else seemed to hear them, despite the fact that she was shouting at the top of her lungs, so hard that they screamed with agony. Even though her mouth didn't move and she was still asleep. But the fear of losing the girl was stronger than what the men had done to her.

Suddenly, Gloria found herself outside the club, flying above it in the cool Manchester air. It was familiar to her inside her dream, and she also knew it in daylight, as an ugly, cheap monstrosity.

Why had Oliver taken her there?

She could still hear the music, even though she was flying in the sky above the club; she felt the bass thump through her body and then a voice calling to her to look down. There, beneath her, smiling up at her, was a man. A driver, waiting at the door of a car. His face was black and his eyes empty and he was calling her.

Gloria jerked her body as she roused from her place of inertia and found herself awake and staring at the dark lamp next to her bed. Her body was covered in sweat.

It took a few seconds to believe that she wasn't flying over the nightclub, or inside it with the men she'd dreamed about, or looking into the face of the man next to the car. Her heart rate recovered, but the vision remained vivid and taunting, and sadness overwhelmed her.

There was no mistaking the cavernous warehouse in the centre of Manchester, a Mecca for hedonists by night, but in the day just another unattractive building hiding secrets. The neon lights and heat from a thousand bodies disguised its true purpose: to trick people into thinking they were living their best lives. Fun, fun, fun.

But she'd seen it during the day too.

She'd watched the cleaners scrape off the evidence of the night before with their mops and fill hundreds of sacks with the detritus of young (and old) people, throwing their lives away inside a needle or a condom. The reality of the place was nothing but grubby.

Her head throbbed with despair as her body recovered from the flying visit to a place she'd left decades ago. She was startled at the terror a simple dream could evoke. But it was not surprising given the contents of the letters. Her mind was processing the shock of the intrusion into her life from somewhere she'd hidden long ago.

Maybe this was the beginning of it, and it wouldn't stop until she faced the ghosts from the past. But how could somebody else know? Unless…

She knew then that the only way the visions would go away was if she found out who was sending her the letters. There were endless possibilities, all terrifying.

She thought of Roger's past associates from their Manchester days: gangland chiefs, underworld leaders, crime gods...

She threw off her covers and walked to the bathroom, where she pulled her pants down and sat on the toilet. A strange sensation caught her attention and in her half-awake state, she was puzzled as to why her pants were wet.

Then she remembered the man's hands on the girl in her dream and shivered, feeling as though she might be sick.

Suddenly, she felt alone. More alone than she had when she'd witnessed what those men did to the girl. It felt as though their hands had been down her knickers. But she remembered that it wasn't her in the dream, it had been somebody else; another woman suffering the same fate. A woman no older than a girl, and she was tiny and innocent, and didn't belong in the club. But her desperation for a story had sent her there and made her take risks she never would under ordinary circumstances. If women had access to the top stories without taking unnecessary gambles, then she would never have been in the club.

If Oliver had given her the job she desired, she would never have been in the club.

Gloria remembered the night it happened.

Her dream hadn't been fantasy, but a very real memory of something she'd seen.

Gloria flushed the toilet and padded back to bed, knowing she'd get no more sleep because she'd be wondering what happened to the girl in the club after she'd lost sight of her.

Chapter 13

Max held his arm steady for Jilly to hold on to as he guided her along the river outside the tapas bar.

She was drunk. They'd been discussing him paying rent. The apartment overlooking the Thames was hers and she wouldn't accept payment from him. Her feet were unsteady, but he managed to coach her into putting one in front of the other, all the while listening to her mismatched odds and ends of stories cobbled together by a brain saturated with grief and booze.

He'd been advising her on what to ask a convicted killer.

He was patient, like a good friend should be, and he listened to her sentences that didn't make sense or connect to any of the others she delivered. She needed to get to bed, but it was still a long walk home.

Her body was heavy against his because she hadn't the coordination to hold it up herself, but Max didn't mind as he half carried her. As they staggered together, he felt lucky to have met her, not because of living rent-free in the grand apartment overlooking the London skyline or the clear connection her family had all over the world, or indeed, how beautiful she was, but simply because she was his best friend. His only friend.

And after three years, he knew she needed him more than ever.

He propped her up while he adjusted his position, and she almost fell over as he took one hand away. Worry gripped him as he became annoyed with himself that he hadn't realised how drunk she'd got. He knew she wasn't able to take much booze. She never had been. It was one of the things he found endearing about her at university; while other students downed bottles of wine for bets and lined up chasers on social nights, Jilly would always hold back and watch.

'I'm going to be as good as she was,' Jilly slurred.

'Who?'

'Gloria White! She wrote an article about him, you know – he was famous.'

'Who?'

'Declan Lewis. My mother wrote an article about him when she was a journalist in Manchester.'

'No way?' Max followed the conversation with half his brain, as the other half tried to keep her from falling over.

Jilly nodded unsteadily, unbalancing her footing. Max caught her.

Their university lecturer had confirmed that Jilly had been given permission by the governor of HMP Frankland to interview one of their category A prisoners. The murderer Declan Lewis. That's what they were celebrating.

Max questioned if she'd actually pulled it off without her famous family pulling strings, but Jilly had insisted they had nothing to do with it and it was their secret.

'Why didn't you tell her? She could have told you what he was like back then, before he did it,' he said.

'I don't need her help. I'm not interested,' she said with the gusto of somebody who'd sunk too many cocktails.

It was confirmation that Jilly hadn't had nepotistic help from the Wade family to nail the interview. But he wasn't so sure about Professor Love's motives. Just because she lectured on social corruption and moral bankruptcy didn't mean she was immune to the effects of it herself. Max wasn't that naive. Lecturers' wages weren't impressive, and he could understand any of them being seduced by an extra buck. Max was inundated with offers of work, based on his very specialised degree. He took part-time projects on that paid handsomely. The rest of the time he spent with Jilly. The same couldn't be said for arts and social degrees, and he was suspicious of the professor.

A man stepped out in front of them, and Max was forced to yank on Jilly's summer dress, to stop her from crashing into him, but he held on too tight, and her dress ripped. Before he could work out what was going on, the man was filming them. Max held his hand up to cover their faces, but he accidentally swiped Jilly across her face. She tripped and fell, and Max was torn between getting the man to fuck off and seeing to Jilly, who'd crumpled in a heap to the ground.

He used his body to shield her from the bloke, who seemed determined to film her, then he realised what was going on and belted the phone out of the man's hand, sending it flying across the pavement towards the river. The man scurried after it, throwing insults over his shoulder. Max wanted to chase him but knew he should stay with Jilly.

'Are you okay?' he asked her as he breathed deeply and knelt over her, making sure she could stand up. She began to giggle, and Max couldn't help but smile.

'What was he doing?' she asked.

'Filming us,' he replied.

'Why?'

She looked puzzled, but then he saw realisation dawn across her face as it became clear the man with the phone knew who she was. In fact, he was probably a member of the paparazzi.

'How did he know where to find you?' Max asked.

Jilly went quiet, her face screwed up with anxiety, as he helped her up.

'Oh my God, he's still filming,' she said, pointing at the figure who had retrieved his phone and was now stood about twenty feet from them.

'That's not an ordinary phone,' he said.

Jilly looked at him quizzically, and he could tell she was trying to process the concept of journos carrying tiny phones that looked like personal handsets but were actually sophisticated cameras; it blew her drunken mind. But she'd told him what paps were paid for exclusives and it was more than a whole year's rent.

Max left her and marched over to the guy, Jilly calling after him.

'What the fuck are you doing? Just stop. Leave her alone,' Max shouted at the man, who backed off.

Jilly swayed and steadied herself, and she seemed to discover some sobriety as she walked in a straight line over to Max and tried to persuade him to drop it.

'Are the stories about your grandfather true?' the man asked.

'What?' Jilly replied.

She had no time to probe further because Max had dragged her away and they were walking back to their apartment. The man had got the message and held back, deciding not to follow them any further, but he stood still on the spot and watched them disappear around a corner.

Max and Jilly didn't speak until they got inside.

'What do you think he meant?' she asked him. 'What stories?'

'Nothing. I wouldn't take any notice,' he told her. 'He was trying to get a rise out of you, and they'll do anything. Everybody knows your grandfather just died, so it doesn't take a rocket scientist to work out what'll get you going, and then all they need to do is film you losing your temper, and they've got a story,' he said.

She smiled at him, and he unlocked their door. He noticed she was walking in a straight line now, the shock of having her privacy invaded in such a disgusting manner turning her mood serious.

'I should ask my mum,' she said.

He looked at his watch. 'It's really late. She'll be in bed, and didn't you say she gets up ridiculously early to go to her morning show?'

Jilly nodded.

Max could see that she longed to call her mother, not because she wanted information on what the man might have meant by asking about her grandfather and stories about him, but because she was scared and needed reassurance. Max threw his keys on the side and they sat down and he held his arms out to her. He'd been doing it a lot lately, and Jilly moved into him and settled there. He noticed the rise and fall of her chest and how her breathing began to slow after ten minutes. The lights were out and the blinds open, so the room was illuminated by the glow of the city beneath them. It was quiet up here and Max stared at the orange and pink neon glow from the buildings outside, wondering what was happening inside some of them and who was out there. His world was such a small one, though he preferred it that way, and Jilly was one of the few people he wanted inside of it. She was the same and the feeling was reciprocated.

They only needed each other.

He held her tighter and then felt her sobs rather than heard them.

And so began another night of cradling her, wrapped together on the sofa, getting up only to pass her tissues and fix another pot of tea, until the morning came and her worries subsided a little.

But as she drifted off into another world – infinitely better than the one she was in – he couldn't help but think what the man had meant about the stories of Jilly's grandfather.

He reached for his phone in his pocket, careful not to wake Jilly, and googled Roger Wade and a torrid torrent of accusations popped up on his feed.

Jilly began to snore gently, and he made sure she was comfortable before gently sliding away from her to sit at the kitchen table with a cup of strong coffee to finish reading the articles.

Chapter 14

Gloria woke to silence. Morning was usually her favourite part of the day, if she'd slept. But even after feeling as though she'd waged war in the night, the dawn brought with it a sliver of hope and the chance to start afresh. However, the positivity soon faded when she saw the bottles next to her bed and an open pill box. Her face burned with shame. She was too old to feel dread in the morning, to fear whether she'd make it through the day without vomiting. But it wasn't a hangover that caused her anxiety. It was the slippery feeling she was losing control.

Her eyelids felt heavy, and she shook off the crust of the night before – evidence of her restlessness – by wiping her face with a flannel, then stepped into the shower. She felt grimy, having been too tired to bathe last night, and she stood under the water, hoping it would invigorate her. She was vaguely aware of her phone pinging when she was in the shower but ignored it. Every day, when she awoke at dawn, she was always staggered to learn that somewhere inside Wade Media Group, somebody else was already up and at their desk, bothering her with questions.

She felt dead.

She lathered soap across her body. The warm water performed magic tricks and she felt lighter as she stepped out of the shower to dry herself. She spent time creaming her body, and by the time she'd pulled on loose clothes for the journey into London, she felt more awake, despite the events of last night preventing her from appreciating more than a few hours' sleep. She skipped breakfast and just made coffee, so she had something pleasant with which to wash down a couple of pills to calm her nerves. Even for her, it was too early for vodka.

Hair and make-up would need to perform miracles this morning, she thought.

She told herself that she was going through a rough patch and the anxiety would dissipate with time. She had a lot on her plate: Roger's death and funeral, Oliver's control of Wade Media, her daughter moving out and embarking on the unknown journey of life, and the savage loneliness she came home to every night. These things alone were enough to send anyone mad. Gloria thought she was holding up quite well, compared to some of the basket cases she interviewed for daytime TV.

She smiled to herself and her mood lifted. Now she was ready for work.

Downstairs, she busied herself with the coffee machine and noticed her phone buzz a few more times, but she stuck to her policy of not checking it until she got into the car. If it was Jilly, she'd call.

She heard the intercom buzz and saw on the monitor that her car had arrived outside the gates, so she took her handbag and briefcase, checking that her phone was inside, and went to leave the house. Her hand touched the envelope with the letter in it and she recoiled. It brought back vivid images of her dream – or had it been a waking storyboard? A daydream? A nightmare. She didn't know which. She tucked the envelope underneath her purse, out of sight, but not out of mind.

She had four letters in total now, and she still hadn't decided what to do with them. The police wouldn't be interested. Stalkers were notoriously vague until the point at which they decided to confront their victim in the flesh. She'd had enough 'experts' on her show saying as much, talking about how stalkers are the most sophisticated of criminals: perverted and intelligent at the same time. And observant. They know their chosen quarries intimately, as a general rule, and before they strike, they do a huge amount of work preparing their finale.

She wondered how long her pursuer had planned before sending her the letters? Had he been thinking about it for a long time, years, perhaps?

The thought made her nauseous and she wished she'd had more than black coffee with her pills. But the feeling would abate as soon as she got in the car and began thinking about the day's schedule. Her diary should be uploaded onto the car's computer, which was set up for her in the back seat, and she'd spend her journey reading notes on her guests for today.

She closed the front door and watched the driver manoeuvre the Mercedes into the driveway, then get out and open the car door for her. He was different to the one who'd dropped her off last night. She made a note to notice their faces more, and she realised that this one had been here before; she recognised him. She watched him for signs that he could possibly be an axe murderer, or any other such nutter with intent to kill and maim, but she had no idea what she was looking for and felt foolish. His hands were clean and manicured, so she discounted him from her list of potential tormentors.

She settled into the back seat and opened her phone, ready to face whatever it was that was causing it to light up rudely at such an unsociable hour.

As soon as she did, she couldn't read the messages fast enough, and she scanned the information they had so far. Elaine had been up since three, picking apart the two main stories that were breaking with the day's news. Then there was the piece online which was splashed across all formats: the video of her daughter and Max, with him allegedly hitting her and dragging her to the ground in the centre of London.

She felt sick.

Then her phone began to ring.

Chapter 15

Gloria's head hurt with the sound of Oliver's voice. He was shouting and had been for the last ten minutes. He hadn't drawn breath. He, too, had read the articles and he'd sworn to draw blood. She was sitting in the back of the car, pulling her head away from the phone every time he shouted into it at his end. There was something about the pitch of his voice that, she knew, led to the kind of overload that resulted in a migraine, and that was the last thing she needed before work.

She didn't know who he was angrier with: the authors of the articles about his father, or the one about his daughter. He was calling Max names and threatening to do things to him that, if overheard by a single journalist, would land him in a cell for the night, despite his money and influence.

'Calm down,' she ordered him. Fatigue gripped her shoulders, and she resented having to be the one to control Oliver's outbursts. He should have a PA to put up with this crap, she thought. Or a lover, but she knew they never lasted long.

'I don't believe for one second that it is what it looks like,' she said, though she was unsure. After all, the video must have been shot after she talked to them last night, so she had no way of knowing. And Jilly wasn't answering her phone.

'Have you spoken to her?' he demanded.

'Stop shouting at me. We're not married any more, remember?'

'Sorry,' he said.

Her shock at hearing the word pass his lips stopped her momentarily and she thought she might faint, but remembering what they were arguing about in the first place, she bounced back by asking him if *he'd* spoken to their daughter.

'No, she's not answering her phone.'

'Me neither,' she said. 'Look, all we can do is wait until she calls us back. She's twenty-one, Oliver. She's an adult.'

'What if he's got her tied up somewhere and is beating the shit out of her?'

'Have you met Max?'

'Yes, you know I have.'

'Well, stop being so gullible. It's a random photographer trying their luck, and it's staged. You can tell by how it's edited. Let me talk to her. Just don't go firing off at the hip and pinning this on Max until we've heard from her. She looks slaughtered in the video,' she added. 'She's staggering because she's drunk, not because Max hit her. She had some news last night but I didn't get it out of her because she was drunk even then, early on. She was celebrating something. That was when she called me out for not supporting her.'

But despite her words of encouragement to her ex-husband, Gloria wasn't sure exactly what Max was capable of. It wasn't the manipulation of the footage that bothered her, the way Jilly had been made to look like she'd been hit by her friend. It was more about how a journalist had known where she'd be when Jilly had told her specifically that they'd gone out to celebrate something out of the blue.

She'd played the game for long enough to know that journos and photographers paid handsomely for such tip-offs.

Oliver didn't reply.

'I suggest you put your energy into thinking about how we're going to deal with the other stories today. About your father.'

Silence.

Two stories had broken in the broadsheets, which cast doubt over Roger Wade's past. On the one hand, it was a sign of the times. Any male over fifty who'd risen to fame before girl power gripped the nation was in danger of having their personal lives investigated. Gloria reflected at times that sometimes at night she could hear the creaking of old men's panic across the city, if she listened carefully enough. They weren't all Jimmy Saviles, but they weren't all blameless either. Death often provided the catalyst needed to open a book on someone; maybe Roger's time had come. But so soon after his funeral was callous, and even Gloria was taken by surprise.

Five women had gone on record accusing Roger Wade of rape and false imprisonment. The historic charges related to a period before Gloria knew him. It couldn't be any worse.

The Wade Media Group hadn't been pre-warned, which was unusual. It indicated that the stories had legs, and the fact that broadsheets had gone to press meant their lawyers were involved and they had witnesses.

Roger Wade was no saint. Everybody knew that, but there was a fine line between saint and sinner. The goalposts had moved, and Gloria couldn't help but feel a little excited that a man like Roger might be facing a stain on his otherwise impeccable reputation. Her one concern was his granddaughter, who thought he was flawless.

'I've scanned both articles. Neither mentions names. Have you got legal onto it?' she asked.

'Done, and Elaine is on it.'

'So, all you can do is remain fierce and vigilant. We might be looking at a legal fight, or a payout of some kind.'

'Hmm,' he agreed. But there was something else. He hadn't simply called to share their shock at Roger Wade being called out as a pervert and a possible predator. This wasn't news. Roger had climbed into the news scene when office girls were still felt-up as they bent over to empty the bins. Unmarried women were called harlots, and men were providers for and gods over their wives. He was an anachronism, one of the extinct beasts that had died out in another era. Only their bones remained, and it wouldn't be too long before their kind would be studied in books.

But their legacies still endured, and there were women who were out there, now willing to come forward and tell the truth.

'I've instructed our side to find the women and bring them over to us,' Oliver said.

Gloria's skin crawled and she wanted to shout at him to stop, but her throat had constricted, and the words wouldn't come out. He was going to fight them, and he was expecting her to support him. She felt sick.

'Oliver, I… Remember what he did.'

The words had escaped before she could think how he might react. She'd managed to squeeze them out of her windpipe, but now she wished she hadn't.

'What?' he said quietly. 'What did he do?' His voice was tinged with disgust, and she had a flashback of his temper, when he'd used the same voice to try to make her feel ashamed. It had usually been after a successful awards ceremony when Oliver had been overlooked and she'd won something; after they'd got home, and the lights were dimmed, his body saturated with booze, and he'd start to attack her. Verbally at first, emotionally savaging her, and in the end, physically. But of all the torture methods he used, the mental punishment was the worst.

She thought the line was dead and she went to end the call. But he was still there.

'I'm curious,' he said. 'You mentioned the Bare Bunny the very night before those stories broke.'

His voice was like syrup and his words slithered around her mind like slippery fish. Her mind conjured a vision of the pond surrounding Roger's tomb and she suddenly felt as though she was being held underneath the murky water. She wasn't quite sure what he meant but she knew it wasn't good for her.

'Oliver, I…'

But the line had gone dead.

Her phone rang straight away, and she almost dropped it, as if it was a hot rock from a lava flow.

It was her daughter.

'Jilly!' she gushed. 'How are you?'

'I'm fine, what's with the ten thousand calls?'

Her voice was groggy, and it was clear she'd just woken up.

It was also obvious that her daughter hadn't seen the news this morning.

Chapter 16

Dear Gloria,

I'm squeezing my knuckles together from pure joy. They're turning white at the peaks where the cartilage joins the bone and I'm grinding them against one another and staring at the flesh stretching over them.

I've spent many years gazing at my knuckles, Gloria.

I should have had them separately insured, like musicians do with their instruments.

I wasn't well educated as a child, but I read books and I'm a fast learner. I was a naughty student at school, a working-class boy, easily distracted and liable to go off at a tangent towards something more interesting. My reports all said the same thing, I could try harder. My mother used to pull in her breath with disappointment when she read them.

It's taken me all this time to work out what they meant, because I was trying my hardest when they slapped my knuckles with a ruler and told me to do the work again. It was like a sum in maths that I kept missing a part of the equation for. But I was applying my absolute best, it was just I couldn't work out what I was doing wrong because of the pain across my hands.

Now I understand that what they really meant to say was that it doesn't matter how hard you try, if your effort is pursuing the wrong thing, you'll fail anyway. 'Must try harder' is actually a euphemism for 'must try harder to please'. The equation had nothing to do with it.

Everything changed when I found a boss who understood that.

Before that, the aspiration was to do the work, and that's what I thought they wanted, but it wasn't. What they desired all along was for me to comply. To try to please them. To fit in. To be a part of the system. That's what 'try hard' meant.

But it took me until I was much older to find salvation in education.

I still don't like mistakes. They make me feel as though my body is falling asleep. I'm always alert to the potential to fail, because only then will I find out what I must try harder at.

Today, I must try harder to discover what's really behind those headlines that have been released by your rival channels. It must sting to hear about Roger that way.

I wouldn't know, I was nothing to him. I just sat with him occasionally and listened to his mumblings later on in life. After he'd made all his mistakes.

But that isn't what's important. It's not about truth, it's whether people believe it about Roger, and if they do, then you really have a problem, don't you? Me and you already know the stories are true. But I won't tell.

It was never my job to judge, just to drive.

You're the one who's going to tell.

The stories circulating around about him are gifts for you and your daughter. They'll make you wary and put you on your guard. That makes my job a little harder, but not impossible. It's far too easy to penetrate your world, and I was thinking you should up your security.

Now you will listen, because I can feel your whole family and the Wade Media empire sweating over whether the stories might drag you all down.

And I know the truth just as surely as you do. But it's your job to tell them.

For the sake of all the women he hurt. Girls like Jilly.

Are you a good mother, Gloria?

Will you choose her when you have to?

Sincerely yours,

Your friend.

Chapter 17

When Gloria arrived at work, there were more photographers than usual waiting for her. She checked her hair before she allowed the driver to open the car door and covered her sunken eyes with sunglasses, then plastered her best smile across her face and stepped out to the clicking of lenses, which sounded like bullets to her.

'Gloria, are the stories about your father-in-law true?'
'Gloria, can we see a smile?'
'Gloria, how are you feeling today?'
'Gloria, show us your best side!'
'Gloria, are those mules Gucci?'

But this morning, she was in no mood to play games and she walked past them silently. Ordinarily, she'd stop to sign a few autographs, even at this time of the morning; it was amazing to see the number of people who turned out to see their favourite telly presenter. But that was the point. It was what made the Wade Group stand out. They weren't just TV stars and news giants, they were part of a household brand. Roger had courted business leaders and politicians along his long path to glory and counselled them on how to get rich and stay rich. He had been a self-styled business guru who people trusted because of his own success. Roger put his money where his mouth was and walked the talk. He did what he said he was going to do and gathered many allies along the way. He accumulated enemies too, but they could never gain enough traction against him to dent his golden armour.

But now, with his dead body turned to ash, Roger was more vulnerable than ever, and with Oliver in charge in his stead, Gloria felt a shift in the old guard.

Roger's name, along with that of his whole family, was no longer safe.

Some of Roger's old stalwarts had been approached for interview, and where they'd once have been belligerent and short with the garrulous attempts at sound bites, batting them off with formidable grounds, now they only provided yawning silence and whispers of 'no comment' for public consumption. The stories were growing arms and legs.

The Wade Group couldn't afford to sit on the fence, because that's when it was liable to break.

Gloria walked into Roger's office and saw Oliver sat in his chair. It had been years since she'd seen Roger in there, but it was still his office. Oliver looked out of place and out of his depth. He'd been seen on occasion visiting the office more in recent years, but nobody expected him to take a serious role when Roger was gone. Elaine had taken the reins for much of the period of Roger's illness, and Gloria had fulfilled an executive consulting role; in other words, Elaine had come to her to finalise any decisions and Gloria had signed them off.

She saw Elaine across the room and an understanding passed between them. The presence of three men in suits stopped her in her tracks. This was not good. Oliver at the helm wasn't healthy for the company and it wasn't fortuitous for them, but bringing in outsiders was even worse. Oliver tended to create mess wherever he went, like a seagull that flies in, shits everywhere, then leaves.

Oliver stood up and Gloria recognised his tie. She'd bought it for him in Paris. The knowledge unsettled her.

He began by introducing the three men who were standing behind him. They came forward when their names were mentioned. They were lawyers, and it was their job, Oliver told them, to pick apart the libel potential in the stories that had gone to print this morning.

'The narrative is that a total of five women have come forward with allegations of historic sexual abuse, in the Manchester office, and at five hotels, three in Manchester and two here in London.'

Gloria had read the articles and she knew the accusations but she still closed her eyes when the more salacious commentary was read out. After the last charge had been aired, Gloria opened her eyes and caught Elaine's gaze. Was she thinking the same as she was?

Roger was guilty as hell and everybody in that room knew it, except perhaps the lawyers. They were young and ambitious, and no doubt most interested in money. The law wasn't about right and wrong, it was about who had the best case and these pups were here to prove it.

Gloria thought they should hold on to their hats, because if five women had come forward overnight, two days after Roger's body was cremated, then there'd be more.

'We've got our own investigator looking into the women,' Oliver announced. 'One of them was on the game in the nineties.'

Gloria winced. It was a good job that this wasn't a public press conference, else Oliver would be mincemeat by the evening news.

She put up her hand.

Oliver nodded to her, unused to the protocol of meetings at the Wade Group.

'What's that got to do with it if she accused Roger of sexual harassment?' she asked.

Oliver glared at her.

One of the lawyers stepped in. 'She's right, we shouldn't be investigating their characters, just challenging their version of events, by looking at timelines and suchlike.'

Oliver didn't know how to handle the objection, and Gloria felt a tinge of sympathy for him. She held her breath and hoped he did the right thing, but before she could encourage him by sending him a facial signal, he'd launched into a tirade that left no one in any doubt over what was being investigated.

'If you test me again with your insipid woke fluff, you can kiss this job goodbye. That's exactly what I want investigating. I want it reporting by tonight that at least one of those women was a prostitute in the nineties, in the centre of Manchester, working around the Blue Bird club area. I've got a team on this, and if you don't want to contribute to it and tell me what I can do, rather than what I can't do, then fuck off.'

The room went silent and Gloria almost applauded. It was a solid performance. She pitied the three lawyers who might have thought getting the Wade Group as a gig would launch their careers and bring in some big money. They'd been seriously misguided. Oliver left no ambiguity about what he wanted, and Gloria thought there was hope for the Wade Group yet.

However, her stomach churned sickeningly at the prospect of what he was about to do to the women who'd come forward. Despite him showing signs of growing into a decent leader and a boss with a clear vision, albeit from the dark ages, Gloria also knew that she wanted no part of it. Men like Oliver Wade were no longer part of the future – her future – only the past, and there was no better evidence than that in front of her. His little speech told her everything she needed to know about how Oliver chose to tackle their problem and future issues too. There'd be no public acknowledgement, no apology, no display of sympathy for the victims and no acceptance of liability.

This was war, and Gloria felt as though the ground had just opened and swallowed her up. She had an inkling of what it felt like to be in the court of a madman and Oliver had literally only been in Roger's chair for five minutes. She glanced at Elaine and saw the same shock fixed on her face.

Nobody moved.

Oliver was a neanderthal who belonged in the nineties, back when the girls his father was supposed to have abused could be dismissed because they didn't play ball and let the boss bend them over the photocopier whenever the hell he fancied. Society hadn't caught up back then. To Oliver, it didn't matter. His empire was under attack, and he wouldn't have a word said against his father.

She needed to stop him and talk him round before he made an even bigger fool of himself, and brought the Wade Group to its knees. He stood to lose everything, which wasn't a problem for her, but it could be for Jilly.

She kept quiet until Oliver had dished out jobs to everyone, then it was her turn.

'I want a live segment on women who fake sexual abuse claims,' he said.

Gloria's guts turned over.

She'd seen personal attacks before in the press. They weren't pretty, and everybody did it, but there were limits of taste and decency, and this would smack of personal gain because of the timing.

Oliver dismissed the lawyers, who were perfectly clear on their allotted tasks. Gloria caught Elaine's arm as she went to leave with them.

'Can you stay behind to calm him down with me?' she whispered.

Elaine nodded.

'I haven't got long,' Elaine replied, looking at her phone. 'Frankly, though, Gloria, I don't fancy our chances.'

'Well, that seemed to go well,' Oliver said from behind his desk.

'Can we recommend a collective deep breath here?' Gloria said to him.

'Gloria,' he began. She knew there was a condescending lecture on its way and realised that working with him in charge of the network was going to be impossible. She'd been independent for far too long.

It was time to go.

She looked at Elaine.

'Gloria,' he repeated. 'If you're going to tell me to lay off, or in any way back down in the face of these allegations, then I don't want to hear it. I'll ignore it this time, but I'd appreciate your loyalty.'

Elaine had been about to say something but changed her mind and made an excuse to leave.

Gloria found herself alone with him after all. Just like in the good old days when women who promised to stick together didn't have the courage to in the end because the odds were always stacked against them. Elaine closed the door behind her.

'Oliver, what are you doing? You know those women are telling the truth.'

He banged his hand so hard on Roger's desk that it made Gloria jump.

'What the fuck!' she said and went to leave.

'Gloria, I won't have it. You either support the Wade Group or not.'

'Is that a threat?' she asked.

'We must stick together on this.'

'And lie? You could save the company a lot of damage if you handled this cleverly. You don't have to admit liability, but don't trash the women. Think what they've been through already.'

'It was thirty years ago!' he said.

'So what? To them it was like yesterday, and we all knew what he was like. Isn't this an opportunity to make amends? It was coming anyway – we can't escape it.'

'You are seriously asking me to betray my own father? He was a jolly old pervert, yes, but these days any kind of touching or feeling leads to that ugly slur of: "Rape! Rape!"'

'Oliver, I can't support you on this. And remember that thirty years ago, those women who you're dismissing as "asking for it" were the same age as Jilly. And on that note, you haven't asked how she is, or how she's handled her name being in the news. She's not used to it like we are. She's mortified.'

'I thought you said it was fake?' he said.

'Of course it is, but it's still in the news for God's sake!'

She walked out of the office and slammed the door before he could rile her any further. As she made her way to the lifts, she felt eyes on her as the stories about Roger multiplied across the media world. But she had more important things to worry about, and her daughter was one of them.

Chapter 18

'Calm down, darling. You should take a few days off and stay indoors. Believe me, this will die down. We've got bigger stories breaking today,' Gloria said over the phone to her daughter.

'About Grandad?'

'Yes.'

Jilly sniffed, and Gloria wanted to wrap her up inside a hug and make everything better like she had when she was a child. She'd had a shock, but her reputation wasn't in tatters, like her grandfather's. An amateur photographer had simply chanced his arm and it had paid off for him, this time. Some tabloid had paid a few thousand quid for the footage of Jilly Wade, but it was an embarrassment, no more.

What she was more interested in was the behaviour of her daughter's flatmate.

'I can't even recognise you in it, and Max covered his face. He's a quick thinker – pity he didn't cover yours.'

'If it wasn't for him, it would have been a lot worse,' Jilly said.

'And how is Max?'

'We're thinking of going up to Durham for a few days.'

'That's a fantastic idea!' Gloria gushed. 'Get away from it all, go and visit some of your university friends, away from London. Does Max need to go?'

Jilly sighed. 'Mum, I don't have any university friends. I know what you're thinking. I really don't need this right now. Max had nothing to do with that photographer following us.'

'How did he know you were there?'

'Mum, leave it.'

'Of all the places in London, he just so happened to see you coming out of a bar near Borough Market?'

'Mum!'

'All right! Go to Durham. Stay away from the fuss.'

'I could do some research while I'm there. My professor works inside HMP Frankland a few days a week. I'm looking into a couple of their lifers for my next article.'

Gloria sighed, but not too loudly for it to be obvious. Her daughter still clung to her obsession with the underclass.

'Well, if it was me, I'd rest. Do a bit of sight-seeing up there. Did you ever go inside the cathedral apart from your graduation? You've had a shock. I'm not keen on that professor. I'm not sure about her research, either – it's all very one-sided.'

'I know you think she's a Marxist, Mum.'

'I didn't say that.'

'She's a very respected criminologist.'

'Well, how wonderful.'

Jilly laughed. It was the first time Gloria had genuinely heard joy in her daughter's voice since Saturday, before the funeral, that wasn't because of drunkenness. Maybe the video had been forgotten already after all. It had been a flash in the pan; a second of fame for the photographer and no more. If anybody was interested in Jilly Wade and her alleged boyfriend slapping her, then there weren't that many of them because it had dropped from the online news in two hours.

'It's nice to hear you're feeling better. Are you sure you're okay?'

'I am. Max is packing now. Please don't think badly of him, Mum. He had nothing to do with it, I swear.'

'But how do you know?'

'How do you not? Have you got something on him? Did you and Dad pay to have his background looked into because he's not one of us, like Professor Love isn't either? She's an expert on profiling,' Jilly persevered.

'Killers? You want to study men who've been sent to prison for their whole lives? Why?' Gloria was genuinely incredulous.

'Because it matters, Mum. Professor Love studies why certain groups in society commit the worst felonies.'

'You sound American. "Felony" is an American word – is she American? What sort of name is "Professor Love"? She sounds like a James Bond villain.'

'Mum!'

'Sorry. So, what does it involve? She profiles these criminals, and you study her findings?'

'Yes. And...'

'And?' Gloria asked. She waited for an answer, but Jilly heard Max in the background.

'That's it, I have to go. I think we'll plan to leave later this evening and wait for the traffic to ease up the A1.'

'You sound better already, darling,' Gloria said. 'I think you're handling it remarkably well.' She softened, relieved her daughter was in one piece. And she admitted that she had Max to thank for that. He was Jilly's voice of reason and, between them, they'd calmed her down and reassured her that these online stories were like the pappus of a dandelion: they floated around for a few seconds in a blaze of glory, then fell to the earth in a puddle of dust, to be forgotten forever. This had been Gloria's philosophy on fame since being thrust into the spotlight thirty years ago. Maybe Max had more nous about him than she realised and she shouldn't fear him at all.

And it was good news about Jilly going to Durham for a few days. For three whole years, her daughter had been able to be anonymous up there, among the cobbles and the dead saints. She'd been pleasantly surprised herself when she'd visited. She'd thought she'd need a bodyguard and a disguise to fight off the press but they left her alone. She'd stayed in a private room provided by the chancellor of University College, who was a personal friend of Roger's. They'd had immense fun coming up with a disguise for her, but in the end, she hadn't needed it because nobody was really interested, and it had been liberating. Of course, she'd been approached for autographs and photos, but nothing like in London. It was the perfect place for Jilly to be now, even if she insisted on seeing Professor Love, who sounded as though she should be walking out of the ocean in a bikini with a pistol, and not counselling cons in HMP Frankland.

Gloria had done her homework on the academic; the woman was a far-left campaigner, who could be guaranteed to turn up to anything that involved chanting or generally causing trouble. She was an enemy of privilege and tradition, and Gloria didn't trust her intentions towards her daughter. The last thing they needed was somebody like her using the accusations against Roger to make Jilly feel even worse. But there was no reason why Jilly should see her old professor if she was going there simply to relax and escape from the attention, and perhaps read a few papers.

'Be careful,' she told her.

'I will, Mum. That footage freaked me out. I won't get that drunk ever again.'

'You needed a blowout. We all do it. Don't beat yourself up. It happens, just be aware of who is around you. I do trust Max, he's a good friend, but I'm still not sure about that professor.'

They hung up, and Gloria felt as though at least one of her problems today had been taken off her shoulders.

Chapter 19

Back in her dressing room, Gloria read the latest letter.

Her hands trembled.

She felt backed against a wall. This was the moment she should enlist all the help she could get from, if not the police, at least the network's security department.

After all, it was their responsibility what got through in the mail bag. But if they didn't know what to look for, then they wouldn't know how to stop it.

She imagined a man's knuckles, dirty and swollen, but the image was short-lived because Oliver burst in, and she hid the letter under her seat.

'Can you at least listen to my plan?'

His insistence on being present in her life again suffocated her. Nowhere was sacred. She felt hunted on all sides. He eyed her suspiciously.

'Are you all right?' he asked.

'All right? Are you serious?'

The idea that she was on tap to him, and he could seek her out whenever he pleased, was repulsive to her and she was desperate to leave the building for the day. His presence in such close proximity made the room stuffy and airless. They'd finished filming for the day and she'd been in the middle of removing her make-up when the mail had arrived. She'd eyed the staffer delivering it, as she had come to do lately, but saw that he was a 'her'.

A creeping feeling of suspicion had settled in her gut when she realised where she'd seen the young man who'd spilled coffee on her before. He'd also delivered her mail bag occasionally. She was sure of it. She recalled his shy grin and the way he dropped the bag and backed out of her dressing room silently, leaving her feeling slightly violated.

But today it wasn't him, because Elaine had sacked him.

She looked back to the gigantic mirror covering the wall and carried on wiping off layers of make-up. Her skin dragged with the pad, and she examined the loss of elasticity. They'd had a skin specialist on the programme last week recommending a miracle serum, and she'd said she'd used it for seven weeks and it'd made a difference. It was a lie, but they'd paid her over half a million to say it, so she had. Was she really that cheap? She thought about knuckles again and the working-class boy...

Perhaps that's why she didn't trust Max.

She eyed Oliver in the reflection of the mirror; he stood against the wall with his arms folded, still raging, mumbling under his breath.

'You've got me cornered, I'm all ears,' she said, pulling silly faces to get her cotton pad into her crevices. Oliver watched her, transfixed.

'What?'

'I don't know how you wear all that stuff,' he said.

'It's called TV,' she said sarcastically, as if he'd suddenly forgotten.

He actually smiled and for a second, she thought they might have a civil conversation. But then she tensed again when she recalled what she was sat on.

'Dad used a private investigator for a few issues he had.' Oliver paused and looked at her in the mirror.

'Understood,' she said.

Money could make anything go away if you dug a grave deep enough. She seemed to recall a few shady characters hanging around Roger, and she wondered if his ghosts were now all laid to rest alongside him in his tomb.

'So, I think we should at least give him a shot to find out what these women want. It's usually money.'

She didn't react.

Her skin looked tired and begged her for a break from the make-up that was slapped on her every day. She reckoned she could save a thousand trees just with the face pads alone that were thrown into the waste bin at her feet.

She and Elaine had managed to talk Oliver out of filling the breakfast programme with derogatory aspersions on the women who'd accused Roger of sexual harassment and assault. Instead, they'd ploughed on with what they'd planned and only the news segments touched on the allegations, which the Wade family was vociferously denying.

Each time the camera came back to her in the studio after the news, she'd plastered on a smile and led into the next part of the show with seamless professionalism.

Now she was exhausted and wanted to go home.

She turned her chair around to face him.

'I'm surprised you need or even want my approval. I would have thought you'd have given the go-ahead already.'

'Good, so that's settled, then?'

She shrugged. 'If you think they're genuinely mistaken, then obviously we need to protect the business.'

It was a caveat that she knew would never hold up in court. Of course, Roger was guilty as hell, but that didn't mean they'd lose. And she still had time, if it got that far, to persuade Oliver to settle out of court. She knew that rather than slowing down and taking a break after Roger's death, perhaps to take Jilly away somewhere hot like she'd planned, she'd have to stay here and babysit Oliver, to prevent him from doing something stupid.

She'd promised Roger before he died that she'd look after the Wade Group. She'd visited him at his estate in Buckinghamshire two weeks before he passed away. He'd held her hand tightly, and she'd recoiled at his touch. His hands were like claws covered in thin, icy-cold silk, and he'd clasped her flesh between them and stared into her eyes hopefully. It had made her heart ache.

Roger had been kind to her, but she was under no illusion that he'd seen business potential in her from the very beginning. She wondered how much he might have loved her if she had been of no use to him. She'd revived the flagging ratings of daytime TV and sent his stock sky high, making him, and the Wade Media Group, viable again. They'd won awards, covered the biggest stories, expanded their coverage, and launched new magazines and papers, as well as their online reach.

'You *are* the Wade Group,' he'd whispered to her in his raspy, dying voice. 'Oliver needs you.' He'd held on to her hands for as long as his strength allowed, then he'd fallen back onto his pillow and closed his eyes. As she'd backed out of the room, quietly so as not to disturb him, he bellowed, 'I'm not dead yet!' with all his might and made her jump. Then they'd both laughed, hard and long, as if their lives depended on it. She'd sat with him then, more relaxed and appreciative of his brain, which showed no signs of fading in power.

His vitality pervaded the room and when the staff came in to give him medicine or change his bedsheets, she'd sensed his grip still holding on to the reins of the Wade Group, and she'd known, like he knew, that Oliver wasn't ready – nor would he ever be – to take over. He didn't possess the necessary temperament for it, and she knew that when this was all over, Wade Media Group would look very different, if it existed at all.

Her job was to manage the fallout and minimise the impact of the missiles being thrown at them. Missiles like the stories in the press today.

She knew the editors at the newspapers who'd given the go-ahead on the articles this morning, and they'd doubtless sat on the stories until Roger was dead.

'Why don't you concentrate on that and go ahead with a private investigation, and in the meantime, leave the production of the show to me?' she said to Oliver. 'Find out what you can. Compile it all and let's give it to the lawyers to pick over.

You're right, they don't stand a chance. But let's not look like this is a case of sour grapes. The content we put out needs to be first class and professional. The two issues are separate, let's not confuse them. It looks desperate.'

Her face set in a regal stare, and Oliver began to smile. It started slowly at first and then spread to the rest of his face. She'd done the right thing and got him off her back.

For now.

Her own smile sat fixed on her mouth like a trophy waiting to be presented to a child for their efforts at a school cricket match, but her stomach churned and shame bubbled within, knowing how inside this room, with a few throwaway sentences, she'd sacrificed those women who'd been abused by Roger — and God knows who else — all those years ago.

Everybody faced difficult choices and hers was this one. She could save those women, or she could save the Wade Group.

The right and good thing to do would be to champion the voices of the forgotten and make right the scourge of toxic misogyny across the industry by speaking out about its failings. But the right and good thing was rarely the thing that was the best option. The best option for her family was to allow Oliver to conduct his own investigation, with the help of a suspect PI called Pete — who'd been trusted by Roger, and was thereby automatically questionable in his methods and morals — to make the problem go away and protect what was theirs.

A creeping feeling spread under her ribcage as she remembered the author of the letter asking her what she'd choose.

'Are you a good mother, Gloria?'

He knew what she'd do before she did, and she concentrated on keeping her hand steady as she turned back to the mirror. Was this all about Roger?

'Throw everything into the investigation and I'll keep running the media wing,' she added, trying to sound breezy.

'You've surprised me, Gloria. I love it when you do that. I always have.'

She knew the tone of his voice, and the tilt of his head and the curl of his mouth as his best flirtatious moves.

'I'm not doing it for you,' she said, casting a warning look to him.

This made him smile wider, as if she'd challenged him to a naked mud wrestle. She noted with disgust that he was excited, like a new puppy at the prospect of a walk.

He threw up his hands and nodded. 'Whatever you say,' he said.

She allowed him to believe whatever he wanted, as long as it would get him to fuck off out of her dressing room.

'Haven't you got somewhere to be?' she asked him.

'I have. You know I would have done this with or without you.'

It was typical Oliver flexing. He was warning her, but she was one step ahead of him.

Whoever was sending her the letters, now she knew it wasn't Oliver behind them. It was somebody who wanted to see the destruction of the Wade Group and she had to decide if she wanted that too.

'I know,' she said. 'This was your idea. I would have done it differently, I don't rate PIs, but I agree with you: it needs to be done.'

This wasn't quite true. She respected private investigation on the whole, just not the kind paid for by Wade money.

The massaging of Oliver's ego was complete, and he left the room full of self-importance. As soon as the door closed behind him, she flopped over her desk and pushed her hands into her face, and then she retrieved the letter from under her body. She now had five. The silent scream that erupted from inside of her forced hot breath onto her palms and she dug her nails into her face and rocked backward and forward, as if she was crying real tears and sobbing with endless abandon, not caring who heard.

But she wasn't.

She didn't have the luxury of feeling. She must pretend.

She brought her head up and stared into the mirror. She had no idea who those women who'd come forward were, but she'd just given them further life sentences. Not only had Roger ruined their chances of living normal, healthy lives, but she'd just silenced them again, because whatever Oliver and his PI discovered, it would be massaged and tweaked until it destroyed the reputations of these women, and they'd drop all charges.

Because of her.

In a second, she'd demolished five human beings who were probably telling the truth, because if the real truth came out and the press got hold of the stories she was keeping hidden, then they'd be facing certain obliteration.

But what if somebody beat her to it? Somebody who knew what happened?

She stared at the letter in her hand and straightened it out. It was warm from her body heat and she recoiled at the idea that it had been in the hands of somebody who was playing a game with her.

A game of life and death.

Chapter 20

Gloria was almost ready to leave the building and sign out for the day when a message came from Oliver to meet him in his office.

She tutted. What now? Why couldn't he simply text her like normal exes who couldn't stand each other? But Oliver couldn't communicate, that was the point. She gathered her things and decided to leave them in her dressing room and collect them on her way out. She checked her phone but there were no messages from Jilly, so she assumed she was well on her way to Durham by now. At least with her daughter out of the way, Gloria could concentrate on sorting Oliver out – and the rest of their lives while she was at it.

Gloria left her dressing room and headed to the lifts, smiling at the employees she encountered. People moved out of the way for her and held open doors; occasionally, they covered their mouths and had serious fandom moments. Gloria was used to it and treated them all with the same grace.

She had a reputation for being a down-to-earth star who had time for her fans.

But today, she wasn't in the mood. The shit kept flying and she'd had enough.

She marched into Roger's office without knocking. Oliver was sat at his father's desk, overlooking the Thames and the Tower of London beyond. Roger's office was beautiful. The leather and cedar interiors, bookcases, drinks cabinet: all the trappings necessary to give off a stench of privileged charades suited the son and heir just as well, but he still looked out of place. He fitted in perfectly with the view from the huge windowpane – which had been positioned by crane, taking two weeks to fit and finish – but his demeanour looked uncomfortable. Something else had gone wrong.

'What is it?' she asked him.

'Close the door.'

This was the third time in one day they'd been in close proximity and expected to behave like adults rather than quarrelling exes, and it was just as uncomfortable as the first time. Gloria closed the door and stood in the middle of the room waiting for the bad news, whatever it was. Her nervous system couldn't cope with seeing him three times a day for the rest of her career, and she knew her time was nearly up. She'd already made the decision. If they survived this, she was gone. She didn't need the money and she could do without the fame.

There was an era, long ago, when they'd relished one another's presence in a room full of people, attending board meetings together, sharing lunches, dashing about chasing stories and sources, then pausing to stare at one another, hungry for what would come later, in their bed.

Now, her body rebelled as she was forced to wait.

'What are we waiting for?'

'Elaine.'

'Why?' she asked, but he didn't reply; instead, he looked out of the huge window.

Oliver sat on Roger's chair, pretending to be the man himself, and Gloria almost expected him to smoke one of his father's cigars or flick through the TV channels on the giant TV hinged on the wall.

She stood awkwardly, waiting, looking at her watch, deciding she'd walk out if Elaine didn't appear soon.

Roger used to have the news on loop twenty-four hours a day, getting sleep for a few hours in between when he was certain that nothing was breaking as an exclusive. When there was a war on, he'd get no rest at all, yet still function with bellicosity. Everybody at Wade Media saw him as a superhuman specimen, proud and different, and they'd all stand in awe, watching him dishing out orders to anchors managing the news of the day. He'd called the breakfast show Gloria's own mini empire and he'd let her get on with it the way she saw fit. She'd been made by Roger Wade, and the feeling, this morning, waiting for Oliver to impersonate him, sat oddly with her.

'Gloria, I trust you,' Roger had told her. *'Don't bother me with the detail.'*

He'd then, more often than not, go on to ask her about his granddaughter and what she was up to. In his later years, that's all he'd cared about, and he travelled into the office less and less. Jilly had provided for him all he'd ever needed or wanted.

He'd spoiled her.

He spent his days taking Jilly to parks and on helicopter rides over the city, or to art galleries where he'd rent the entire place for a private viewing. Years ago, they'd slept at the Natural History Museum one night, under the tyrannosaurus rex, and he'd paid a curator to tell her stories about the prehistoric world as they'd snuggled down in their pyjamas on luxury blow-up beds, set up by an army of employees and whipped down again just as quickly in the morning, before the doors opened to the throbbing crowds and the old bones became public once more.

As Roger's only grandchild, Jilly would inherit everything one day, and it was their job, for now, to keep it intact.

A knock on the door broke Gloria's nostalgic trip down memory lane and her attention was dragged away from the huge portrait of Roger on the wall, which she'd noticed Oliver staring at too, as if the old ghost was warning him not to fuck up.

Elaine came in, and a look passed between them. Gloria had been aware of their affair for years before her divorce. Apart from the obviously uncomfortable meetings they shared, she didn't much care about the liaison. Oliver had, by that time, begun to sleep with anybody who'd have him, and Gloria had felt more pity for her producer than anything resembling jealousy or anger. But the physical presence of Oliver between them now was new. They'd never faced up to it before, had never discussed it.

'What's this all about, Oliver?' Gloria asked.

Elaine sighed.

Oliver turned to them and closed his laptop with a flurry of energy, as if what he was working on was something terribly important.

Roger had known where the future was in TV, and putting Gloria in prime-time position on his shows, over his son, had been a game changer in the nineties. It had been groundbreaking then, and Roger had won awards for it. Women's daytime TV exploded, and Gloria White was born, kicking and screaming in her shoulder pads and lacquered hair, wrapped up and mummified as a woman who could have it all: baby, home, man and career.

She was a pioneer. And Oliver had hated it.

Was she here for another beating? With Elaine as his witness?

The irony wasn't lost on her that while Roger was alive, she'd been propped up by his generosity, and now he was dead, she was in danger of being buried by it.

'We've got a problem,' Oliver said finally.

'Another one?' Gloria asked.

'The technician that you scared half to death, Gloria,' Oliver said.

Gloria's brow creased; she had no idea what he was talking about. And she was in no mood to guess.

'He spilled coffee on you yesterday,' Elaine said.

'Ah, him.' The penny dropped. 'What about him?'

'He went home and hanged himself,' Oliver said.

'What?' Gloria felt as though the ground might swallow her whole and collapsed into the nearest chair. Elaine remained standing; she had known already.

'His family has hired a lawyer to sue us for negligence. Bullying. They've mentioned your behaviour on set,' Oliver said.

Gloria strained her ears, thinking she'd misheard him.

'What?'

'I know, it's terrible, Gloria, but we must take it seriously. This cancel culture is real.'

Elaine's voice echoed in Gloria's head, and she felt her mouth open wide, but no words came out. Her insides turned to stone. She looked at Elaine, who refused to glance her way. Instead, she threw her a side profile, like a side dish. A cold one of fish.

The silence was awkward. But for Gloria, she sensed, it was also lethal. This was the perfect ammunition with which Oliver could control her. Her guts turned to mush.

'Cancel culture? Bullying?' She was aware that she was panicking.

'Of course, I'm sure there's nothing for you to worry about...' Oliver said.

'He had mental health issues that he didn't tell us about,' Elaine quickly sandwiched in. 'And money worries.'

It made her feel slightly better, but a man was still dead.

'What was his name?' Gloria asked.

'Andy Knight,' Elaine said.

'It was only fucking coffee,' Gloria said.

'Elaine sacked him,' Oliver said.

Gloria glared at her. 'So he killed himself?'

'I thought it'd show him that—' Elaine began.

'That what, Elaine? Jesus, the poor fucker. Oh, God, I feel sick. You said you'd take care of him...'

'There is talk that he did it on purpose to get close to you,' Oliver said.

'Yes, that's right – he had a fixation on you,' Elaine added.

'No,' Gloria said, louder than she intended, shutting them up. 'No, that's not how it happened, it was an accident. Oh, Christ.'

'If we go down that route, we'll be crucified,' Oliver said.

Gloria felt the slippery sensation of fear grip her body.

Visions of headlines calling out a bully at the network, in today's toxic climate, wriggled restlessly around her head.

'Somebody has already approached Elaine and told her that he might have been hungover, and that he was barely holding on as it was.'

Gloria winced. Andy Knight hadn't seemed hungover at all, or in any way compromised. They were in here to slaughter the reputation of an innocent man after his tragic death, just as they were preparing to massacre five guiltless women who'd lived with devastating secrets for thirty years.

Suddenly, she saw Oliver as just a man. Not a boss, or a media force, or a manipulating son or husband, just a man. And he was as vulnerable and scared as she was. As Elaine was. The ground underneath them was shifting, but inside that room, in that moment, they had a choice to make.

Decisions like it had been made a thousand times by Roger, but Gloria had pretended it hadn't been her making them or complying with them. She'd told herself that association didn't amount to guilt.

Now, she wasn't so sure.

The three of them looked at one another and an agreement was silently reached.

Gloria rose from her chair quietly.

'Where are you going?' Oliver barked at her.

She turned to him.

'What did you mean he had a fixation on me?' she asked.

'Something about him being seen entering your dressing room,' Elaine said.

Gloria put her hand to her head.

'Gloria, are you okay?' Oliver said.

'I don't feel well,' she said.

'Of course – Elaine, help her,' he demanded.

'I'm fine,' she insisted. She shook away Elaine's offer of a supportive arm and left the office.

Chapter 21

Jilly read from her phone as Max drove her car.

The traffic was as quiet as expected for a Tuesday evening, and the biggest problem with the A1 was how dull it was. The road didn't ever seem to twist or turn in a different direction, and the scenery was all the same. Jilly knew the exits off by heart from three years of driving the same journey every couple of weeks.

Max enjoyed driving, though, and she was happy for him to take charge of her new Tesla. She suspected he'd offered to make the journey to appease her because he felt so guilty about the photographs. Whatever the reason, she was happy to be with him.

Once they'd broken free of London, they'd stopped for milkshakes at the services near Baldock, just north of Stevenage. They had around three and a half hours to go and Max was an easy companion. Jilly found that the further north she travelled, the less anxious she felt inside her body.

She'd been reading the link Professor Love had sent her on Declan Lewis. He was a fifty-nine-year-old man serving a life sentence for the murder of his pregnant girlfriend in 2005. He'd served twenty years already and Jilly found it hard to comprehend how long that was. To her, it was a lifetime. He'd been sent to prison when she was a baby.

Her memories were made up of a woven mesh of events that flashed before her like a neon road sign. They were individual snapshots of things she had lodged somewhere deep inside her brain and recalling them was like being underwater at an art fair: all the colours merged into one and she found herself surrounded by blurred images, not being able to tell which were the masterpieces and which were the daubing of amateurs.

The point was that life, especially twenty years of it, was infinite in its duration and its value. Jilly saw herself as mature, though not as old as her parents, but grown-up enough to have a full history behind her, and the thought of all that time spent incarcerated filled her with compassion for the felon.

Her father would baulk at the idea of trying to understand a killer, but for Jilly that was the whole point of Professor Love's work and why she wanted to write something on it for an amnesty charity.

'I don't know how you can read in the car,' Max said. 'It makes me feel sick.'

'You get motion sickness? You have to concentrate on the horizon. I've never suffered with it. It doesn't bother me.' She yawned and stretched. 'Where are we?'

'In Cambridgeshire, I think, or Norfolk, I'm never sure which counties the A1 goes through.'

'What the fuck?' Jilly exclaimed, staring at her phone.

'What is it?' Max panicked.

'A newspaper article I've been sent. Oh God, I can't believe it, Mum said this might happen.'

'Do you want me to stop?' Max asked. 'Is it about us?'

They were only just recovering from the shock of the piece online about their supposed fight last night, so if there was something else, Max deserved to know, but it wasn't about him this time. Jilly found the news excruciating at times, especially when journalists interviewed real people about their awful experiences and asked them inane questions about how they felt. That's why she wanted to report on issues with time and sensitivity, not like her mother did, in sound bites and snapshots, making it seem as though people's pain was momentary and disposable. The story about the two of them last night, accusing Max of beating her to the ground, was a good example.

A single frame of visual had led to the potential destruction of somebody's life. Luckily for them, they were aware of the trickery. The story was ridiculous, but Jilly wondered: for every story that was easily dismissible like that one, how many ruined somebody's life with their lies? But it wasn't about her.

'No, it's not about us. It's about my grandfather... Yes, please can we stop.'

Max changed lanes to the inside and told her there was a service station coming up in two miles. They drove in silence until he indicated to come off and Jilly held her phone face down on her lap, to prevent her reading any more.

Max pulled off and turned into the car park and stopped the car, turning to her. She passed him the phone, and he opened the page she'd been reading.

He was quiet for a long time. Jilly looked out of the window at the people coming and going with takeaway coffees and food to eat on the go. Children skipped alongside their mothers, people smoked cigarettes, thankful for their nicotine hit until the next time, and couples held hands and smiled together.

Life went on.

Jilly stared at them and wondered how many had read the news.

The video of her and Max had been grainy, and it had been dark, so her mum had assured her that no one would be able to recognise them, and a name meant nothing to the ordinary reader. By tomorrow, no one would care what had happened to Jilly Wade, or if her 'boyfriend' was a violent control freak.

Lies sold papers, but they didn't endure.

But this was different.

Everybody knew who Roger Wade was. And everybody loved a great fall. And the stories just kept coming.

It all fitted together nicely. Roger Wade was rich, powerful and dead. Of course he was guilty. Jilly saw the trial by public flogging playing out before her and she knew that this was just the beginning. She'd seen it a thousand times before and often the allegations were true; it was only occasionally that they were proven to be fabricated for personal gain. She had a sudden desire to know who the five women were and what they wanted.

'Do you want to call your mum?' he asked her.

'No, she'll just gloss over it and tell me not to worry. She still treats me like a five-year-old.'

'Your dad?'

'He'll do the opposite and tell me too much, and that he's got it all sorted, and that those women are whores and liars.'

'Fair enough.' Max waited. 'Would he really call them whores and liars?'

Jilly smiled briefly. 'Somebody has attacked his family. He once told me that if a boy at school continued to pull my hair, he'd be able to make him disappear, and his body would never be found.'

'Are you serious?' Max asked. He laughed, but then stopped when he saw that she was. 'He didn't?'

Jilly nodded. 'He did. He makes bad news go away and he probably will this time too. I feel sorry for them.'

'Where do you think he'd hide the bodies?' Max asked.

'Max!' She swiped at him playfully.

'Who do you feel sorry for?'

'Those women. What if the stories are true?'

Max shook his head. 'Of course they're not true. Your grandad would never...'

'Never what? Have sex and pay for it? Why not? Then pay for them to stay quiet? Then go a little further?'

'But he didn't need to – he could get any woman he wanted, surely.'

'You're confusing the ability to acquire with the desire to own. Why would they say those things if they weren't true? What about libel laws?'

'People lie, Jilly, all the time. Don't think that of your grandfather just because you're scared. It might be bullshit – it probably *is* bullshit.'

'But what if it isn't?'

'That's why you should call your parents and see what they say.'

'It's obvious why they haven't discussed it with me. I knew my mum was distracted but she gave me the impression that the stories would go away. Now I know why she told me not to read them. They haven't gone away and they're getting worse. Their silence means they don't know what to do. And they always know what to do. Which means he probably did it. My parents think I idolised my grandfather, and I did love him deeply, but I'm not entirely stupid. I've read other things about him.'

'No, you can't think like that. You're getting sucked into the media circus because you're angry about this morning, and what they did to you, to us. But that was all lies, so why isn't this the same?'

She thought about it for a couple of minutes and turned to him, feeling a little better. 'You're right,' she said. 'It's so easy to get sucked in.'

'Do you believe your grandad had it in him to do something like that?' he asked her.

She shook her head. 'No, I don't.' But then she screwed up her face. 'How would I know? God, I don't know.'

'I guess men like that are adept at hiding it,' he said.

She stared at him.

'I mean, that's what I read. Men who've been getting away with it for years, you know, like serial killers, and their wives and family have no idea.'

They drove away.

'Did you tell your mum about Declan Lewis?'

'No, she'd go crazy and tell me I can't see him.'

He laughed. 'So, you are going to see him?'

'Of course I am. Maybe he can tell me why people lie and get away with it.'

Chapter 22

Finally, Gloria arrived back to her home and went straight to bed. It wasn't long gone six o'clock in the evening, but her body could no longer support her weight and all she desired was to forget the day and the news it had delivered. She wanted to switch off and travel to a world beyond this one, in the safety of her own bed.

But she couldn't settle, and her heart flipped in cycles of resting and racing, like a bolting horse that appears to have been tamed, but then rears up again.

She rolled over in her huge king-sized bed and then rolled back again. Her body believed it was making pasta and she'd turned into a massive rolling pin, smoothing out the sheets underneath her, back and forth, back and forth. One side of the bed was cold, so she moved there to absorb the chill, breathing calmly and welcoming the drift that accompanied the beginning of sleep, but then it was too hot, and she swayed the other way.

Finally, she sat up and sighed loudly. Shadows danced across her darkened room, and she walked to the window to check outside. She saw nothing but the day going by gently and harmlessly and she let the curtain fall with frustration.

She'd taken two Adderall and her nervous system had calmed a little, but she'd been up hunting for white wine on top of that. Only a drug-induced coma would bring her the relief she craved.

She thought about her guest list for tomorrow's show, hoping that might send her to sleep through sheer boredom.

They'd decided to go with the breaking story of Gary Chambers, a fellow presenter on a rival channel who'd fallen on hard times in the last couple of years. Oliver was hoping it would distract viewers from the story about Roger. Vehement denials and threats of lawsuits all morning had tempered the worst effects somewhat and the story had slithered away to the shadows while the women's lawyers figured out their next move. Meanwhile, their channel would run with another predator – Gary – and they had a woman coming in who had accused him of harassment.

Gloria had had her arse felt by Gary too – most people had – but that wasn't the point. She was one of many, going back to the eighties, and it had the industry reeling again. Oliver was hoping it'd distract everybody for a while. Every couple of years another old dinosaur got cancelled because their shady past caught up with them. It was a precarious dance that made the rest of them look over their shoulders, because most of them were complicit.

Going with the story of Gary was a gamble, but they couldn't ignore it. They had to face it head-on and they hoped that by throwing mud on someone else, it'd buy them time with the stories on Roger, and now the suicide of Andy Knight.

She'd known Gary for a long time. He had loose hands and a habit of staying late at work and keeping a female typist busy in a quiet room full of paperwork.

He was a nobody nowadays, but that wasn't the point.

If she believed Gary should pay for his sins, then why not Roger too?

Are you a good mother, Gloria?

She tossed and turned, flitting between thinking they were playing with fire and doing the right thing to save the company.

Neither option was ideal, or pleasant. But Gary Chambers had it coming.

It was years ago. Suddenly her young life seemed apart from her. It was something she could see hovering in the distance, but she couldn't touch it, because she wouldn't know how to. In the dark, she questioned her own sanity and her ability to recall true events, and she resigned herself to the indisputable knowledge that memory, like success, was relative. She could smell his body, and feel his breath on her cheek, and she could even hear his tongue clicking around his mouth, grotesquely spreading tobacco-laden saliva across his orange teeth. It had been in the days before veneers became a thing. Before her big break. Before Oliver.

Presenters back then appeared as they were in real life; they had wrinkles, rashes, thinning hair, crooked teeth and sweat marks around the tops of their shirts.

She felt his wandering hands as if they were on her now, in bed, under her T-shirt, grabbing at her skin. She remembered he had a broken nail, and it grazed her flesh. But more than anything else, she recalled her sense of loss. There was no barrier between his hands and her body. No one was there to stop him and tell him what he was doing was wrong. She was trapped between him and a wall, and what she once believed was a strong and smart body ceased to operate and froze in a response she'd never experienced before, or since. It was as if her body refused to work normally. She couldn't move. She couldn't breathe. He covered her like a blanket, but this one wasn't warm or cosy like the ones she covered Jilly with when she was a baby. This one had been like a brick wall, and it stank of predator.

She remembered his smile, as if deep down, if she was really honest with herself – and him – she should admit that she was really enjoying his attention. Because girls like her 'wanted it'.

She recalled the look on his face that said to her he was doing her a favour by paying her attention and, if she was lucky, she'd even get a few more articles printed. Her terror in the face of true, unrelenting and all-consuming power was total.

This was the true reason she didn't want Jilly to go into the business. To come into *her* business.

But it was different now, she told herself.

Or was it?

This was why she'd shielded her daughter from fame itself. Maybe it was also why she pushed for so many 'ordinary' stories, as Elaine called them, to appear on the show.

She had the power now, but only because she'd enjoyed the protection of Oliver and Roger all these years. Her stomach dropped to her toes as she dared not think of what Oliver had done to maintain her immunity, just because she bore him a daughter. She was off limits. Safe.

Sleep eluded her and she got up and went downstairs, flicking on a lamp in the kitchen instead of opening the blinds, which allowed tiny specks of light in through the slats. Even in the dusky light, the haze told her that the temperature was roasting out there. The soft light soothed her and was preferable to harsh bright illumination which reminded her of studios and made her anxious.

She poured a glass of wine, knowing she wouldn't sleep, and then googled Gary's name. Countless articles popped up, all vicious and damning. The knives were out, and so they should be, but she found it curious that the claws that might kill him had been retracted for twenty years or more. Devils only become evil when it suits the mainstream establishment.

She recognised the names of the authors of the pieces and clocked their easy betrayal. They were all guilty of it. Gary made some of their careers. His success had built an entire mountain of wealth, recognition and power, until it came crashing down for financial reasons – he spent money faster than he earned it – and was blown out of existence by hungry prospectors wanting their pound of flesh. But he was still fair game, and she remembered what he did to her, and she knew he deserved it, because everything he owned was on the back of women like her who'd suffered his hands down their pants, in their bras, or worse.

She felt hot liquid behind her eyes and wiped them with the back of her hand. Her body was betraying her.

She drained her wine and realised she was hungry. The sight of an old banana made her stomach growl, but she couldn't even be bothered with that.

A cloud must have passed over her house because the speckles of light peeking through the blinds dimmed and Gloria felt as though she was living inside a fortress. Her home was a citadel, built behind high walls, designed to protect her inner world, but what good were barricades when all you wanted to do was get out?

Chapter 23

Dear Gloria,

I know we're not the same. People like me can never be like you, can they?

But once, a long time ago, you were insignificant too. You yearned for recognition and power. And now you have it, you don't want it any more, do you, Gloria? The pressure has got too much. If only being a mother was enough for you.

She dreamed of being a mother.

It was the only thing she ever wanted. To bring another life into this crazy world and love it unconditionally.

And it's your fault she can't.

You got to have your baby daughter all to yourself and give her all the love she ever needed.

Mothers and daughters are inseparable. To watch them is to learn how a human bonds with another. The trust of a child is all-consuming. Pure, true faith like no other. As soon as the newborn looks into the eyes of her mother, she knows she's safe.

You yearned to mother too, and you got given your one true desire. You have a healthy, beautiful and courageous girl who you smile and laugh with.

Mothering or smothering?

Is there ever a difference?

Jilly will never know.

I watch mothers looking at their children everywhere: in films, on the street, in playgrounds, in restaurants, at the school gates, in the swimming pool. It's how you look at your daughter. But I don't know if you're play-acting. I don't know if it's real, because I can't tell with you, Gloria.

Your duplicity is slathered all over you, and it stinks.

You've had your chance to be a mother. A woman. The softer side of hell.

You had me fooled. You have everyone fooled.

I'm not the only one to see through the netting you drape over yourself. Your second skin is coming off. The scales are falling away. Slowly but surely, bits of you are slewing away and all that will be left is a pile of old discarded dress-up clothes, ripped and overused, abandoned in a heap by a woman who disappeared.

Into Suite 724.

And people will ask where she went.

They will want to know the truth.

And that will be your choice to tell them.

I'll give you that choice.

That will be my gift to you after everything you did.

What will you choose?

Mother or child?

As ever,

Your special friend.

Chapter 24

'Darling, don't read the news. How many times have I told you? There are people who want to sully your grandfather's name now he's gone. It's what the media does, it's in their DNA.'

Jilly noticed that her mother had neither denied nor confirmed the stories about her grandfather when they spoke on the phone early Wednesday morning.

Make-believe, like TV, was in her mother's DNA.

The conversation hadn't lasted long. Jilly was growing impatient with her mother's checking up on her and her incessant skulduggery regarding Max's intentions.

Two could play at that game because she'd been conservative with her own truth. She and Max had enjoyed the city last night when they'd arrived in Durham, and they'd walked along the Wear, then stopped at a boat bar to drink cocktails.

But that wasn't the reason she was here.

Jilly's house had been bought by her father as a gift, but also as an investment, when she was a student. She didn't need to rent it out. It was a bolthole for times when she needed it, times like this. And handy for its proximity to Frankland Prison.

But her mother thought her incapable of lying. Jilly knew that in her mother's eyes, she could do no wrong. The early life of Gloria White was shrouded in mystery, apart from the fact she'd come from a working-class background – from nothing, essentially, or so the story went – and made her way to the top through her own hard work.

Jilly wasn't stupid. She suspected her mother had allied with her father to further her career in the media. It was why Jilly was so determined to make her own way. Without Gloria White's help.

Her mother also believed she was the only one who could play games with people. Just because Jilly had been sheltered from some things in life, it didn't mean she couldn't see them. Her mother couldn't keep her in an ivory tower forever, which is why she'd moved out.

She had her own life to live.

Jilly admitted that being plastered across social media yesterday, drunk and all over the place, had scared her, but it was perfect timing to toughen her up. She had to get used to it. Her mother blaming Max and hinting that perhaps he tipped off a journalist had got under her skin. She'd never move back home, not for all the money in the world.

Besides, she had business to attend to. It was a perfect opportunity to forget the articles and concentrate on something else.

The visit to meet Declan Lewis had already been arranged.

The fact that she was doing it behind her parents' back made it even more attractive.

She thought about the convict inside his concrete jail, locked up for twenty-two hours a day and unable to make basic choices about his own body.

Denied a compelling future, human beings withered, she believed. It was one of the tenets of life: to strive towards something. Inside a prison cell, one looked forward to nothing. She was eager to ask Lewis what he thought about when the lights went out and the bolt on his door clanged shut. She was more excited to meet the convicted lifer than she was about anything else in her own life. In fact, it was a welcome escape from the turmoil going on in London. But her mother's advice, though predictable, was way off the mark. The articles about her grandfather, rather than making her want to avoid the news, made her want to read it more, and discover the truth.

Perhaps Declan Lewis had something to say on powerful men and how they ruined women's lives.

She joined Max outside, in the small terrace garden, and placed a tray of cups, biscuits and a cafetière between them. The walled space was private and was a haven of summer dreams on days like this, which were rare in the North-East. The sky was bright blue and Max shaded his eyes as he poured from the cafetière. Jilly sat down and went over her notes one more time. Her hands were clammy, and her stomach had been churning all morning. She hadn't eaten. She took a biscuit and munched on it eagerly.

It wasn't anger she felt towards her mother, or disappointment in her grandfather, but nerves at the prospect of meeting Lewis.

The sun shone in her eyes and she considered the case the convict was pursuing against the UK government for vitamin D deficiency caused by the lack of natural sunlight. Jilly smiled at his boldness. The idea that a bunch of suits in Strasbourg were compelled to discuss the human rights of a category A murderer who craved a bit of sunshine on his skin amused her. The more she'd studied sociology, the more she'd come to realise that the law was an ass, and open to interpretation. Law wasn't about right and wrong, but about the way you played it.

And Declan Lewis knew how to play it.

Professor Love had already told her he was a slippery character, which was what made him interesting to her.

Jilly had asked the professor several times why he'd said yes to an interview with a novice journalist when he'd turned down scores of others more qualified than she was.

'That's the point,' Professor Love had told her. 'You're not tainted by the system, yet. He likes that.'

Of course, it had to be approved by the governor, but it wasn't unheard of. Plenty of writers and authors gained access to prisons up and down the country for research. She calmed her breathing and felt the sugar from the biscuit soothe her tummy.

'This is what you really want, isn't it?' Max asked her.

She looked at him oddly.

'Of course.'

He looked away.

'What is it, Max?' she asked.

'I don't know how to say this.'

'Just say it.'

'You are an absolute warrior of equality, it's what I've always admired about you.'

'I sense a "but" coming,' she said, smiling at him. 'You've read the articles about my grandfather. And now you're starting to think he did it,' she said.

He looked down and sipped his coffee.

'It's okay, Max. I'm thinking the same thing. My mother thinks I shy away from reading negative shit about my family. But that's wrong. I'm an expert. I know everything that's ever been said about them. It's ugly, and most of it is bullshit, but this stuff about my grandfather has something behind it.'

Max looked relieved.

'Are you nervous?' he asked her.

She nodded. 'Yes, but it's also a distraction from my family.'

She looked down at the piles of paper on her lap and suddenly there seemed no order to them.

'I'm not allowed my notes in the room, but I can take notes while there.'

'All set?'

'Professor Love will be in there with us the whole time.' She moved the notes to the table.

'Of course she will. You won't find yourself alone with him.'

'I'm not scared of him,' she said.

'I know. You're not scared of anyone. I still wish I was coming in there with you, though.'

'If only my mother knew.'

'That's her job, to protect you,' he said.

'She thinks you might have tipped off the photographer the other night.'

Max stopped sipping.

'Oh.' He looked bereft, as if the approval of Gloria White meant something to him.

'I'm sorry, I shouldn't have said anything.'

'I know she doesn't think much of me,' he said.

'She's just paranoid,' she said. But it was too late. Max looked genuinely hurt.

Jilly got up and checked her bag.

'Ready?' he asked, but his enthusiasm had dipped.

Professor Love had coached Jilly as much as she could to prepare her for what she was about to walk into. The men inside Frankland were constantly under threat, physically and mentally, she said. Drugs were endemic, and depression and mental health at breaking point. The professor had painted a desperate picture of a sinkhole where men went to be forgotten.

She'd also told her what Declan knew about her and her interest in social injustice.

Her biggest fear was that somebody would find out who her parents were. She'd toyed with the idea of changing her name for university but had decided against it. Wade wasn't an uncommon name and her parents had kept her out of the spotlight successfully so far.

Professor Love assured her that, to Lewis, she was just an ex-student of hers whom he could trust.

The professor's reassurances were tempered by a certain amount of reality. Jilly wasn't foolish enough to think that cons couldn't get their hands on anything they wanted if they had the right contacts on the outside, and Declan Lewis had links to the Manchester Cheetham Hill Gang, and his nightclubs had been just a cover. She'd studied his profile. He was as powerful on the inside as he had been on the outside. However, during his discussions with Professor Love about being interviewed by a young aspiring journalist, he'd showed no signs that he was interested in anything but telling his story. The man, still – Jilly shouldn't forget – was a brutal criminal. And that was just on the outside. In prison, Jilly knew that it was a mafia-style ghetto, where discipline was maintained through violence. She had to be alert at all times, the professor told her.

Lewis was kept on F Wing with other notorious criminals at 'Monster Mansion', the affectionate epithet for HMP Frankland. It had housed Peter Sutcliffe and Harold Shipman, and was now home to Levi Belfield and Wayne Couzens.

'I'm going to take it slow with him,' she said.

'He's got time,' Max replied.

'I'm going to ask him about growing up with the Cheetham Hill Gang on the Waterloo estate in Manchester in the 1980s, and what it was like running drugs and getting involved in petty criminality, until it turned serious around his thirteenth birthday.'

'Pull him in slowly.'

'I'll ask about his murder charge at the age of seventeen, and what he thought of the subsequent reshuffle at Manchester Metropolitan Police drugs squad.'

'Don't hold back,' Max poked fun at her.

'I want to know if he felt resentment towards those who'd investigated him. With juvenile court behind him, I want to know what happened to him after keeping his nose clean for the next twenty years.'

'Clean?'

'Nothing was proven,' Jilly said. 'He was never arrested.'

'Though you can't ignore the rumours.'

Jilly acknowledged that Max was technically correct. Throughout the nineties, Lewis had survived under the radar of law enforcement, but hearsay pinned a life of organised crime at his door.

'Will you ask about his girlfriend?'

The disappearance of his girlfriend, Linda Wilson, in 2005 had put Declan Lewis back on the radar of local police and they'd pounced, charging him with her murder five weeks after that. He'd always insisted on his innocence, but Jilly knew that in prison, cons all said the same: they were stitched up. Jilly wanted to know by whom. Lewis was found guilty by a jury that had seen no body, and given a life sentence by a judge who said he was a cold-hearted killer. Linda had never been found. Lewis was to serve a minimum of twenty-one years and that made him eligible for parole next year, but due to him denying the charge and never changing his plea, it was unlikely he'd ever get out. The crime that tripped him up in the end had been one of passion.

Everybody – including Jilly and Max – wanted to know where Linda's body was.

Max walked Jilly to her car.

'Are you sure you don't want company?' he asked.

'I'll be fine. Make yourself at home.' She laughed. 'Besides, you've got work to do.'

Max was busy developing a program for a major bank and he was very modest about the whole thing. He was a genius, but fiercely independent. She knew, deep down, that Max envied her wealth, and she'd seen it when she'd stupidly told him what her mother suspected. It would make him feel even more of an outsider.

But he was quickly becoming a substantial earner himself and had talked of owning his own place.

She waved as she pulled away and drove through the city towards the outskirts, wondering how many tourists milling about Durham knew that one of the nation's toughest prisons languished on its borders in a tiny village, five miles outside of the city. No one would guess that such a hellish place existed so close to one of England's prettiest cities of ancient and esteemed history.

She heard the professor in her head, giving her last-minute tips. *'Keep it professional. If you let your mind wander to what he did, he'll see right through you. Don't let him in. He knows all the tricks.'*

She approached the sprawling facility. It looked fairly benign, like a primary school or a medical centre, but with lots of barbed wire on the walls and a sinister darkening of the windows that gave away its true purpose.

He'd be in there right now, perhaps being led from the centre of the prison, where visitors weren't allowed, away from the cots and keys, towards the education centre, where Professor Love used an office when she wasn't lecturing at the university. Would his wing mates know where he was going? Was it big news? Would he be taken past them, handcuffed, out on his little trip to eat up an innocent young girl for breakfast?

Her mind played tricks on her and the butterflies in her stomach threatened to leap out and fly freely above her head.

She found a parking space and got out of her car, leaving her bag behind, and taking a clean notepad and pen. Her laptop was in her bag, and she planned to type up everything she remembered from the interview as soon as she returned to her car. She understood that inside the room, she might go blank, or freeze with uncertainty, or even be struck dumb by the macabre fascination of being so close to a killer. It happened.

She spotted the professor waiting for her outside the gates and waved, then joined her so they could go in together. Professor Love was in her sixties and was officious in her demeanour and wore a tweed suit, like she did for lectures. Her jet-black hair was likely dyed and she wore bright red lipstick, reminding Jilly of photos of eighties bands her mother had shown her on YouTube. They went through several sets of gates together, which clanged behind them. Then they walked through a body scanner and had to hand over their belongings to be tested for drugs. Cons were always inventing ingenious ways to smuggle contraband in, and visitors were the most favoured method. They were shown along a corridor behind another two sets of metal gates, and Jilly felt as though she was now in the bowels of the prison. It felt different from the outside; the noises were muted and big men with dozens of keys towered over them. It seemed like the further she got into the belly of the prison, the bigger the guards became. But they were pleasant and clearly knew the professor.

Finally, they were taken to a door and let in by a guard.

Inside the tiny undecorated room, the professor set out her things and put Jilly at ease by asking about her summer and they discussed Jilly's published work so far. She'd had a few pieces appear in national newspapers and journals, and the professor had already hinted at her impression that Jilly had only been considered because of who her parents were. It was no surprise and she appreciated it took most aspiring journalists years to get noticed.

The notion that she was a freeloader still stung.

Jilly noted a familiar resentment behind the professor's interest and suspected she was helping her to get her own leg up in the industry. Her lecturer had struggled to get her own work recognised. But on the outside she was friendly enough, and Jilly was grateful for this opportunity.

They chatted about how the interview might go.

Then it was time for the prisoner to be brought in and Professor Love told her where to sit.

There was a bang on the door. Jilly held her breath. Then he was inside, standing in front of her, with his hands cuffed together in front of his body.

He was a big man with large blue eyes, which stared straight through her. He wore a grey tracksuit and had tattoos over most of the flesh she could see, except his face and head. He looked hard, as if he'd toiled all his life, and she felt a pang of shame as she realised she was judging him because of his worn appearance. She wondered if people looked like criminals because they *were* one, or they became like that because they had been condemned as one.

Professor Love made introductions and Jilly expected Lewis to ignore her at first, perhaps disinterested by the intrusion. But he didn't. He was warm and welcoming, throwing her off guard.

'Hi, Jilly. Thanks for coming. Meeting someone new is the highlight of my year, or years, depending on how you look at it. It's a pleasure to meet you, and I want to help you any way I can.' His voice was calm, deliberate and endlessly soothing.

She watched him watching her and she felt examined like a virus in a Petri dish. Suddenly, she felt very aware of her age, her gender and her freedom. He pounced on every inch of her with his eyes.

Professor Love coughed.

'Thank you, Mr Lewis, I'm so grateful for this opportunity,' Jilly managed to say.

'Behave yourself, Lewis,' Professor Love said.

He smiled and looked back to Jilly.

'Call me Declan.'

Chapter 25

Gloria opened the small ornate wooden box.

She was used to being sent gifts from the biggest couture houses across Europe and America, as well as from less well-known ones in Asia and Australia. It was a perk of the job. The problem was where to keep them all. In current use, at last count, she had sixty-seven handbags, and that was after giving hundreds away. She only kept the ones she knew she'd use. She gave plenty to Jilly and her friends, and to charity shops in Virginia Water and Ascot.

She had a wardrobe built solely for shoes, so they could sit in pairs, in ranges of colour and season. Everything in her life was made easier by having too much of something. Make-up, hair appointments, flights, villas, tables in restaurants, VIP tickets to shows and theatres. She remembered dreaming of the kit she now owned and thinking how her life would be perfect if she could have this dress or that bracelet.

But the only thing she cared about right now were the two blue pills in the lacquered box, which she absently recalled was made in Polynesia.

None of her belongings meant anything to her; all she could think about was how everything she trusted and relied upon was fading away, slipping down a huge black hole, about to be sucked into nothing, and she must steady her nerves.

Life had been simpler when she had nothing. Yet there she sat, covered in couture purchased or borrowed solely for her, lathered in make-up and hairspray, disappearing under the weight of it all.

She froze.

The box was empty, and she shook it, not quite believing it. It was a tiny little snuff box from Tonga, hand-painted in exquisite design, but that was of little consequence to her right now. Instead, she contemplated the awful reality that she'd run out of pills.

The breakfast show would start in just over an hour, and she faced going on air without her usual pick-me-up.

She calculated in her head that the box being empty meant that she had taken eight yesterday and four already today, and it wasn't even seven o'clock in the morning.

Fear gripped her stomach, but she soothed herself by considering that it was only a temporary blip. She didn't need them, she wasn't reliant upon them, they just took the edge off, and she'd been going through a particularly challenging time lately.

A small tipple of what was under her dressing table wouldn't hurt. But she'd have to take it neat, because she didn't have time to walk to the cooler on the next floor. And she didn't have a spare water bottle. The voice inside her head was loud and it boomed just inside her temples. She wasn't a stranger to neat spirits, but not at this time of the morning.

All the other noises – the voices telling her not to do it – were silenced by the one which was the loudest.

She got onto her knees and searched for the box she hid the bottle in, quickly found it, and sat back, staring at it, toying with whether she should or shouldn't. If she could or couldn't. She grabbed it and twisted off the top, hesitating once before taking a quick swig. It was disgusting and hot, but it didn't take long for the rough edges of her mind to be calmed and she took another, and another.

A new, unwelcome voice entered her head, the one that told her that alcoholics start like this. Conversing with a slippery and silent demon, telling themselves they won't make it a habit and convincing themselves that the lies are real.

As if on cue, she told herself she wasn't an alcoholic or hooked on prescription pills. Neither label applied to her. She didn't rely upon them; she just needed a livener to make the shadows go away. It didn't hurt anyone, she wasn't in debt and she wasn't snorting crystal meth on a street corner and pissing her pants, or stealing from relatives.

She told jokes to herself, like women who have their shit together were allowed to do. Who'd want to be fully in charge of their faculties in today's world, anyway? If she was a yummy mummy in Chelsea without a care in the world, apart from lunch with other baby-makers and choosing the colour of a hallway chaise, then daily lunchtime drinking would be acceptable. If she was a journo from the nineties, it'd be the same. Time might change boundaries, but it didn't change desire. She told herself that a little flyer eased the daily grind, and nobody needed to know.

Another secret.

It was a blissful slowing down of nerve circuitry, and all she needed was to pick herself up and face the discerning British public. Vodka was just the same as Adderall in the end.

A quiet knocking at her door disturbed her thoughts, and satisfied she'd justified taking a few shots before breakfast, she beckoned whoever it was to come in, after putting the bottle down between two bags of dirty clothes. A young man poked his head around the door and showed her a bag of fan mail.

Suddenly, she wanted it to be Andy Knight.

But he was dead, and it was her fault.

It was a huge bag today. She thanked the young man, who opened the bag and arranged the letters expertly on her desk in front of her.

She stared at them as he left her alone again and half of her wanted to beg him to stay.

Vodka wasn't the same as Adderall after all, and she felt her brain slow down with melancholy and she cursed her immaturity.

She stared at the pile of letters, wanting to rip them all open to search for the thing that most terrified her. She sifted through them with a finger and sent them spilling onto the floor.

She stiffened.

There it was.

It was the same handwriting.

Gloria leaned over and picked up the envelope. It was the same colour as the last one, and it was as light to the touch. There was nothing substantial inside it; nothing that could hurt her, not physically anyhow. Except for perhaps a nasty bacterial infection from the outside.

It was grubby around the edges, and it made her stomach churn over. She couldn't recall the last time she'd eaten, and her belly creaked under the burden of neglect.

She slid her fingers along the crease and tore it open, reading it quickly and throwing it onto her dressing table when she saw the number '724', as if it had just burned her.

This one felt different.

It read different and handled different. His voice had changed.

He'd signed it '*special* friend' instead of just 'friend', and its tone was threatening.

He was escalating, and Gloria knew with every fibre of her body that she must report it.

He'd mentioned Jilly by name twice now and he seemed obsessed with motherhood. It was freakish, with too many references to her personal life. Her past. Her career and her choices.

What had she done to this man?

Would the police be even interested? They were busy, everyone knew that, and as a celebrity she should expect obsession and a lack of privacy, it went with the territory. Everywhere she turned, she tried to talk herself out of reporting it.

And each time she did, she felt a little bit more alone.

There was no one she could trust with the information. There'd be those who'd be secretly smug that she was being harassed, then there'd be those who would want to take over and expose the whole thing.

She couldn't risk it.

Little Miss Sunshine, Docker Street, Bare Bunny, and now Suite 724.

The number of Roger's Manchester apartment in an exclusive private block called Deansgate.

Her eyes darted to the door and she rushed to open it, peering along the corridor as if hoping to catch him red-handed. She slammed it shut and sat down heavily.

Suddenly, all the letters made sense, as if the fog she'd been wading through had cleared. And she knew whom he was referring to when he said *she'd* wanted a child.

Gloria had assumed, foolishly, that the letters were all about her because they'd been sent to her and she was the celebrity star who should expect these kinds of things being sent to them.

But now she realised she'd been wrong.

And it wasn't about Jilly either, not yet; that was a warning.

This was about a woman from her past.

A woman she'd let down.

A woman she knew from Docker Street and the Bare Bunny, and who should have been a mother.

The young woman who was squeezed between two huge men in her dream.

But it hadn't been a dream.

Gloria peered at the letter on the floor, the latest one of six now.

They were becoming more sinister. The author was turning nasty and impatient. Was he expecting her to work something out? Was she expected to have identified him by now and somehow arranged a meeting? Is that what he wanted? So she could say sorry for what she'd done? What she'd seen?

Separately, none of the notes made sense. But together, they made all the sense in the world and told a story only a handful of people knew.

At first, she'd been in denial. She'd told herself that Docker Street meant nothing to her, like the Bare Bunny nightclub, which was on that very street.

She had a sudden need to stay concealed in her dressing room and not go out. She hadn't felt the sensation of something akin to stage fright for years and it took her by complete surprise. She wanted to stay where she was, hiding away from everybody until it all blew over, until the notes stopped coming.

But she knew they wouldn't.

It was impossible, she told herself. It had all been taken care of. It must have been twenty years ago now.

What if the notes kept arriving? she asked herself and stared at her reflection in the mirror. Until what? She had no idea what the end could be. What was the purpose? Somebody was contacting her about her time in Manchester and what happened there because they wanted something from her. She was famous now, and rich, and that's what they wanted. Money. It was always money. She rubbed her temples.

She peered into her dressing-room mirror, surrounded by bulbs like those used by Hollywood royalty in the glamourous old days of sirens like Marilyn Monroe. She was no Marilyn, and she was thankful for it.

The white bulbs were always switched off because they hurt her eyes after a long session in front of the cameras, and now, in their inert state, they mocked her.

She noticed her phone flash and rushed to pick it up to see if it was a message from Jilly. She at least owed it to her daughter to report her tormentor. She was being selfish, she realised, by keeping it to herself.

And despite what Oliver said about Andy Knight, the poor staffer who'd committed suicide, it couldn't be him because she'd received two more letters since his death… But what if he'd posted them before he died?

It was plausible, but she had no idea why he might have had a fixation on her in the first place. She'd barely noticed him in the studio. Perhaps that was why. His invisibility left a gaping hole behind the camera yesterday, with the whole crew reeling from the news. The studio had been deathly quiet between segments, and she felt as though they all stared at her with silent accusations that she'd killed him herself. As if she'd put a rope around his neck and suspended him from the shower unit in his bathroom.

The thought of it made her sick.

But it also gave her an idea.

She stood up, straightened her clothes, as if checking them for places where doubt could creep in, and left her dressing room, jogging in stocking feet along the corridor to the lift, which she took to the top floor, where Roger and Elaine had their offices.

She burst into Elaine's office without knocking and stood breathless in front of her desk.

'What the hell?' Elaine said. 'I thought you were an assassin! Gloria, have you gone mad? It's too early in the morning to burst in on me like that!'

Gloria caught her breath back.

'Andy Knight, do you have a sample of his handwriting?'

'What?'

'You heard me. It's important, do you have...'

'Okay, I heard you. Why?'

'Does it matter?'

'Well, actually it does. There's an active investigation into his suicide, so his files, and everything in them, are sensitive right now.'

'Bullshit, Elaine, do you or don't you?'

'I'm sure we do, hold on, but at least tell me what this is about.'

Elaine typed on her computer, and Gloria went around the back of her chair to look over her shoulder.

Staff often filled in forms by hand and scanned them. It was a long shot, but she had to know.

Elaine stared at her.

'I'm all over the place at the moment, Elaine. Indulge me. If Andy Knight left a suicide note and accused me of bullying, then we can discount it by showing his real handwriting,' Gloria said.

Elaine scowled. Gloria knew it made no sense, but that was the only excuse she could come up with on the spot, and confusion bought her time.

'Right,' Elaine said, studying Gloria and assessing that she was indeed going insane. But Gloria didn't care what Elaine thought; she'd rather she believe something ridiculous than catch on to the truth.

A document popped up on the screen and it was a form on leadership from a workshop they'd done last year.

'Jesus, we keep this crap?' Gloria asked, scanning it. The writing didn't match that of her stalker.

'So compassionate,' Elaine said sarcastically.

Gloria ignored her and walked to the door.

Whoever was sending her the letters, she was pretty sure that it hadn't been Andy Knight.

Gloria got back to her dressing room and closed the door, leaning against it, and closed her eyes.

A loud knock behind her made her start, and she jumped away from the door.

'Who is it?' she breathed nervously.

'It's Elaine. The police are here.'

Chapter 26

Gloria stared at the door and didn't answer.

Elaine opened it and came into the room.

'Why are the lights off? What happened? Did someone die?' Elaine grinned and flicked on the main lights. 'Honestly, Gloria, why are you skulking about? What do you know about Andy Knight that I don't? One minute you're in my office asking to see his handwriting and the next, the police are here at seven in the morning, wanting to talk to you about him.'

Gloria stared at her producer, wide-eyed.

Elaine could be like a whirlwind sometimes, and it was a battle to catch up. It struck Gloria that she was behaving very calmly, considering the police's arrival, but she realised that she had no idea why. It wasn't to do with his handwriting, or was it?

'What do the police want?' Gloria asked.

Elaine leaned against the table and Gloria eyed the bags of worn garments in between which she'd hidden the vodka bottle.

'It's about Andy Knight. I've been assured that it's procedure. They want to interview everybody who was on set on Monday, and they've given their promise that it's routine and they can work around the breakfast show. We'll go in together – I've got your back. Coincidence, though, isn't it?'

'Christ. This is serious,' Gloria said, trying to be nonchalant and ignoring Elaine's direct question. 'Can they wait until we've aired?'

'Apparently not. I've got a pre-recorded segment to play and I've found a stand-in until eleven o'clock.'

'Eleven o'clock! The show is practically over by then. Tongues will start to wag, Elaine. People will say I'm avoiding exposure, that I'm running scared.'

'About Andy's death?'

'No! About Roger.'

'Oh.'

'Where are they?'

'Who?'

'The police.'

'They're waiting in the foyer on the second floor. They've been offered coffee and cake, and are enjoying the break, I reckon, as well as looking at the wall of fame.'

The faces of the guests who'd graced their studios adorned the entrance halls up and down the building, on every floor, and they were like magnets for non-famous people. Their portraits were signed with messages, mostly to Gloria, and they drew attention, even from the police apparently.

She got up and staggered a little.

'Jesus, are you okay?' Elaine asked. 'Fuck's sake, go easy on the pills,' she added.

Gloria glared at her.

'What? You think nobody notices?' Elaine said. 'Get a grip, Gloria.'

Her producer then walked out of the room and the door slammed behind her. It was fixed onto heavy hinges designed to close the door tight shut in case of fire, but they felt like prison bars some days, locking Gloria in. And other days, she never wanted to leave. Like now.

Gloria peered in the mirror, straightened her clothes and slipped her feet into stilettos. Her face was complete; she looked like a clown ready for the circus. Hair, Make-up and Wardrobe had excelled themselves and she felt as though she was morphing into a US TV anchor before her own eyes, complete with white teeth, high cheeks and today's answer to shoulder pads: a nipped-in waist worthy of a Victorian lady of leisure, and accessories that pulled her back down to a seated position. She took a full intake of breath and walked out of the room, catching Elaine up at the lifts.

Upstairs on Floor Two, she spied two coppers. She knew they were police because they weren't daubed in fake tan, and they wore drab, uninspiring outfits not seen since the studio had been used for *The Bill*. They weren't in uniform, so she knew they were detectives, and this made her nervous.

'Is Oliver aware?'

Elaine nodded.

'They've already spoken to him. He defended you and gave them a whole catalogue of Andy's mental health concerns. They seemed happy.'

Gloria wasn't usually tense around people, but these two keen-eyed hopefuls who stood up to greet her had the law in their pants and could sniff history like a professor at a private showing of *The Elgin Marbles: The Musical*.

The woman introduced herself as Detective Sergeant Lucy Holt and the bloke as Detective Constable Eddie Tate. Gloria imagined them eating breakfast in the car; half of it was stuck to Eddie's tie. Lucy was clearly in charge.

DC Tate stared at her, obviously a fan, while DS Holt was more officious.

Gloria wondered what they knew and if they were really here about Andy Knight's suicide, or something else. Like him being her stalker.

'Shall we go somewhere private?' Elaine suggested.

They nodded and Gloria offered her hand. They took it one by one; Lucy Holt first. Her hand was warm and strong. Then Eddie Tate, who lingered a little longer. He was smitten, she could tell. She was tempted to warn him off and tell him that he needn't bother pursuing her because she wasn't worth it, and he'd only be disappointed. Like Rita Hayworth said about men going to bed with Gilda but waking up only with her.

Elaine led them into a room that was empty. It was one of their holding pens for less distinguished guests. They'd had Kylie in the studio before and stratospheric acts like her got the full star treatment in a suite on the top floor, overlooking the Thames.

Elaine flicked on the light and asked them if they'd like more tea or coffee. Lucy declined, but Eddie looked parched. His eyes were tired and his skin pale, and Gloria betted his diet consisted of takeaways and coffee during the day and booze at night. She recognised the signs of a fellow high-functioning addict.

'I'm fine, thank you,' Eddie surprised her.

'How can we help?' Gloria asked.

They remained standing.

'Thanks for seeing us, Ms White,' Lucy began. They ignored Elaine.

'Call me Gloria.'

The female detective smiled, but not as widely as Eddie. His attention was helping to ease her nerves. She directed most of her eye contact to him.

'We'll try to make this quick – it's just an informality at the moment.'

'At the moment?' Gloria asked.

'We're interviewing the staff who were present on Monday when Andy Knight was escorted off the premises after an incident.'

Gloria looked at Elaine.

'I was unaware that he was sent home,' Gloria said. 'He spilled a drink over me, and that was it. He apologised, I told him it was fine, and I meant it. It really wasn't a bother. It wasn't something I even remembered until I received the news about him.'

'Of course,' Lucy said. Eddie nodded.

They were here for something else. Elaine glanced at her.

'The family is dropping the case against you.'

Gloria was stunned. First, she wasn't aware there was an official case against her, and second, she didn't understand how in the space of twenty-four hours, she could be faced with bullying allegations that could end her career and then not. It didn't make sense.

'We wanted to ask you if you've been approached by anybody making demands, or trying to bribe you with threats?' It was Eddie's turn to ask the questions and the switching up of their game puzzled Gloria.

The question made the hairs on her arms stand up and a shadow cross her body like a ghoulish draught.

'Approached by whom?' she asked. Her mouth was dry.

'That's what we're asking you,' Eddie said again.

'Not at all,' Elaine butted in. 'Thank you for your time.'

Gloria couldn't let it go that easily.

'Erm, it depends what you call threats, really. I get sent all kinds of weird stuff...'

Elaine glared at her.

'I'm sure you do. It's a major problem with celebrities – we spend hours chasing stalkers.' It was Lucy's turn. 'Notes?' she added.

Gloria's guts turned to stone.

She tried to remember the obvious tics and movements that indicated lying, as explained by a guest they'd had on talking about faking it. Her face felt flushed, though it wasn't hot in the room. And her right eye quivered slightly.

'What kind of notes? I get letters, cards, songs...'

'Like this?'

Lucy showed her phone and Gloria was faced with a screenshot of a piece of paper behind clear plastic. She knew that it meant the bag was evidence, but she didn't know where it was from.

'May I?' she asked. Lucy passed her phone. It was a photograph of Gloria, taken years ago, and underneath was scrawled, *I want you, always*. The writing wasn't that of her stalker.

'Where did you get this?'

The detective nodded and took her phone back, scrolling to another shot and passing it back. This time, it was a photo of her and Jilly, and her blood froze.

'We have reason to suspect that Andy Knight was more than a fan. We found over two hundred images of you on his personal home computer.'

She wanted to laugh, or scream, but the coppers were serious, and she wondered if all her worry about the notes being from somebody in her past was unfounded. What if it had been Andy Knight all along? Maybe he used different handwriting for letters. She thought back to Monday morning and how the accident happened, and remembered thinking that he was hovering around her before he spilled the coffee.

Relief spread through her body.

The police looked at her oddly, but they had no idea what good news this was.

'I had no idea, and no, I didn't receive any notes from him.'

'Well, it looks like he was somewhat obsessed with you, and losing his job here made him think he'd never see you again. The family is satisfied that this is a good enough explanation for his suicide. Together with his mental health record, we've come to apologise on behalf of the family for any distress this has caused. Here, this is the number of a charity that deals with unwanted attention like this. You never know, you might remember something you thought was unrelated. If so, give us a shout.'

Lucy Holt passed her a card and Gloria took it in disbelief.

One of their problems had just gone away.

'We also found several compromising photographs of Mr Knight. It would appear that he was a very troubled individual,' Eddie said.

Lucy turned to the door and Elaine was already holding it open for them.

Eddie turned to Gloria and lingered. 'You take good care of yourself, and anything that seems out of the ordinary, please contact us. It might seem the smallest thing.'

Lucy smiled warmly too. They seemed genuinely concerned for her, which made her think there was something else to it. She wondered if they were holding something back.

'Did you find anything else?' she asked them.

They looked at her suspiciously, and she could kick herself for almost blowing it, but she had to know.

'Such as?'

'Oh, nothing, I just… You've thrown me – I'm shocked, that's all.'

'And you're absolutely sure you've had no unusual mail?' Eddie asked.

Her reply was a second too late and Lucy clocked her hesitance, and she knew, with the instinct of a woman who saw distress every day of her working life, that she was lying.

'No,' she said, and they walked to the door.

Chapter 27

Jilly took notes and she felt Declan Lewis's eyes on her. It wasn't as if she was wearing anything revealing, but he made her feel like she was. She'd thought carefully about her attire because the professor had warned her about walking into a male prison dressed attractively.

Her nerves were getting the better of her. She'd already dropped her pen on the floor and she'd wanted the ground to swallow her whole.

But rather than take advantage of her and the situation, Declan Lewis soothed her anxiety and turned the conversation around to the trees he could see when he went into the exercise yard, and asked her about random news pieces and what she thought about them. She hardly noticed his handcuffs after a while, and he acted as though they weren't there. He held his hands down on his lap, so it was like he wasn't wearing any at all.

It was just his eyes that pierced through her soul, but she told herself that he was an incarcerated man who hadn't had sex with a woman in twenty years.

Every time she looked at him, she tried to figure out if he'd done it.

That was one of the reasons she was there.

She'd read about the bloody screwdriver, found a few streets away from Linda Wilson's flat, and the fact he'd run from the coppers when they were after him, and how Linda had told friends he'd beaten her before she disappeared.

With such a wealth of history, Jilly couldn't help but think Professor Love's questions for the convict dull and lacking penetration. Declan seemed to sense it and winked at her while the professor's back was turned.

The professor liked to be in control – all the time – but Jilly was enjoying getting to know Declan Lewis, after taking a while for her to settle.

Lewis was gracious – gentle even – and despite being incarcerated in awful conditions, he had a sense of humour. He'd been patient with her, and thoughtful, pointing out details for her that she'd missed in her notes. He was the one serving a life sentence and yet he'd corrected her annoying little mistakes.

'Jilly is an old-fashioned name. I don't mean it rudely – it's one of those names that reminds me of the 1960s. Are you named after anyone?' he asked.

Professor Love shot him a withering glance.

'Declan, you know you're not supposed to ask personal questions – let's keep it professional,' she said.

Jilly saw that he was amusing himself and he'd caught her off guard. She was getting used to how he played the game. He was interested in her because that's how he'd get under her skin. He was toying with her, and the professor knew it, but they'd expected it. It reminded her that her earlier assessment was perhaps a little too charitable.

The professor was growing more impatient as the minutes ticked on but Jilly reckoned it must be hell inside here, having nothing to do but think all day; it would drive her crazy, being trapped like that. Surely, she appreciated that conversation with anyone broke the monotony and, with someone who was actually interested, provided some form of pleasure. Jilly thought the professor spoke to Declan like a child and she knew there was probably some decent explanation for it, but it bothered her, and she found it patronising. It was both motherly and condescending, but it was indisputably demeaning.

'I don't mind,' Jilly said to her mentor. 'It's only fair that, in a normal conversation between two people, they each have curiosity.'

Declan stared at the professor, clearly satisfied with the mutiny. Jilly saw disapproval on the professor's face, but she let it go. She noticed Declan throw her a conspiratorial glance.

'I'm named after my paternal grandmother. She was a debutante and belle of the ball fifty years ago. Jilly was her middle name.'

Declan looked at her and nodded. Jilly saw the professor glare at the convict.

Don't get personal.

The small creases at the corners of Declan's mouth turned up and the professor folded her arms. He was in trouble.

'May I ask *you* a question?' Jilly asked him.

Declan glanced at the professor, who looked down at her notes. This part was planned. Jilly had sought permission for her questions before the meeting and now she was being given a free pass to throw them in. Declan sat back and nodded.

'Fire away,' he said.

'We've got permission from the governor to ask certain questions, Declan. If you have any problem with any of them, simply ask to move on,' the professor said.

'You could have given them to me beforehand, and I'd have given them more thought. I'm only thinking of Jilly's work and the time restraints on us. She'd get much more out of it.'

Jilly heard her professor snort quietly. She knew that the convict's charm was an act, but she was gobsmacked at how convincing he was.

'Well, Jilly isn't really interested in the re-offending statistics of all offenders, but more curious about first-time offenders of serious crime,' the professor eased them in helpfully.

Declan nodded, but looked distracted now the interview had taken a distinctly academic turn.

Most of the prisoners in HMP Franklin were serial offenders. Their lives were peppered with stretches at His Majesty's pleasure. But Declan Lewis was an anomaly – he'd gone from petty crime and a clean-ish record to murder overnight.

'The official reasons given all follow the same theory,' Jilly said.

'The inherent badness of criminals,' Declan said. 'We were born like this.'

Jilly looked up from her notes and caught his eye. 'Yes. That's what they say. What do you think about that?'

'Am I *allowed* to think? Surely they put people like me away to turn us into animals who they can forget. Just feed 'em and drug 'em.'

Jilly was growing used to his body language. She'd noticed that he moved his body when he made certain impassioned statements. But when he confirmed bland details about his life, he sat quite still. When he talked about prison, he opened his legs and tapped his feet. But when he spoke about something that clearly roused him on some deeper level, that he cared about, he folded his arms, which he did now.

'Are you drugged?' she asked.

'What she means is do you *feel* as though you're drugged,' the professor interrupted.

Jilly apologised and Declan smiled.

'Give her a chance, Doc – she's finding her feet. No, I don't feel drugged. It's a metaphor. We're enslaved and dumbed down in here, just like society wants. Isn't that the point of prison? To control us?'

'So, you're forgotten?' Jilly asked.

He nodded.

'And what impact does that have?'

'On me? Nothing, they can't touch me. But on them poor bastards out there? Most of 'em just get high on depression. It keeps them down. They become animals. Then they start behaving like 'em. Then you get your boomerang offenders.'

'So, if you say you're not like they are, will you not re-offend when you're out?'

'Never offended in the first place. I didn't do it.'

Jilly paused and glanced at the professor out of the corner of her eye, still staring at Declan.

'Do you want to talk me through that?' Jilly asked.

'Sure.'

The prisoner would have been fully aware that Jilly had read his case files, because she'd needed his permission, and the governor's, to go ahead with the interview. Jilly had read everything about his alleged crimes, and yet still, she came to see him. She knew that he'd never confided in anyone about that night twenty years ago, except to say that he didn't do it. The prosecution had no forensics, no motive apart from jealousy, which was unconvincing because Declan and Linda seemed to have been in a solid relationship, and there was the problem of his alibi. All this had been pushed aside by the prosecution and the jury had fallen for the story of Declan's past, as a career criminal with the *capability* to do something awful. The traces of blood on the screwdriver hadn't even been a match to him.

'What do you want to know?' he asked her.

'Why do you keep denying it? You were found guilty in a courtroom.'

Declan laughed. 'Come on! You were doing so well. I had you for an intelligent kid. Don't waste my time. You're not a lawyer, you're a journalist! Do your job. You don't believe in British justice, surely? That's not why I let you in here.'

Jilly glanced at the professor, who remained quiet; this was her learning curve. She must do better. He was right, she'd been clumsy. This was why she was here: to learn.

'I'm not expecting some kind of human rights warrior who might help me get parole, but jeez, you need to move from behind the belief-in-social-justice crap.'

She felt her cheeks turn pink.

Declan scratched his nose with one hand but brought up two and she was reminded that they were pinned together for a reason.

'Try again,' he told her.

Jilly took a deep breath and sat upright.

'Why do you think you were found guilty?' she asked him.

'That's better,' he said. 'Because of the human habit of judgement. I was a simple boy from the wrong side of the tracks and my girlfriend went missing on my watch. I didn't have the luxury of protection from rich parents, powerful family or media leg-ups.'

He paused and she winced. He'd hit a nerve. He'd just described her own family entitlement to a tee.

'I was perfect criminal material, even without a shred of evidence, but the true perpetrator is still out there, and one day I'll find them.'

'You'd stand a better chance of getting parole if you told the authorities where Linda's body is,' she said.

She held his stare and saw a flutter of respect behind his eyes. He wanted to be asked awkward questions because this was his chance to convince somebody other than his shrink of his innocence.

'It would mean lying, because I don't know where she is. I wish I knew. I loved her. I could easily make up a location, string them along.' He nodded to the window, indicating a generic judicial system of uniforms queuing up to find dead bodies. 'But I didn't kill her.'

'You'd rather stay inside for the rest of your life?'

'No, that's not what I'd rather do, but I'm not in control – nobody like me is.'

'What's the first thing you'd do if you got out?'

'You mean if my conviction was quashed for being unsound and I was exonerated?'

'Yes.'

'I'd go to this little beach in Norfolk, where the sand is white. I used to go there with Linda. She loved it.'

Jilly noticed his eyes wander away from her to the window again – a sign of his freedom one day, out there, not in here – and the corner of his mouth turned up. She guessed his face didn't do that much. The tragedy was that his chances of surviving in here, as a category A murderer, were getting slimmer by the year. Violent offenders were at the most risk of being savaged by other inmates, and sometimes killed. She'd read that Declan Lewis had suffered two serious incidents during his time here. Both had put him in the medical wing. He might not want to appear guilty, but it could save his life.

'I know Norfolk – where is it?'

'Near Sheringham. I've got a place there.'

She sensed Professor Love out of the corner of her eye cross her legs, but she couldn't look away from the prisoner. He appealed to her with his eyes and backed away at the same time, and she knew that he'd just shared something with her that was so precious to him that it exposed a vulnerability inside him that wasn't often on display, particularly not on the wing.

He sniffed and crossed his legs – the habit was catching – and Jilly knew it for what it was: one of the most basic movements of protection when somebody feels uncomfortable. She'd pushed him, but she'd found something out about him, and she wanted to know more. The beach in Norfolk was the place he went to inside his head when he wanted out of this hellhole, and it symbolised his freedom. His other self. The part of him he didn't share with anyone else. Except, perhaps, Linda.

Chapter 28

Dear Gloria,

Have you worked it out yet?

Poor Andy.

He was in love with you. How do I know?

Because everybody has a role.

What a mistress of fraud you are.

I spy a spider, full to bursting with her young. Her abdomen is swollen to five times the size of her body, such is her fertility. Us weak humans can only muster up the nutrients for one at a time, on average. Her life's work is her sac of offspring.

She's weaving.

The silver threads, almost too fine to spot were it not for the light of the moon shining on them from time to time, twinkle with the proteinaceous secretion pouring out of the mother's spinnerets. The extrusion is as fine as an artist's touch when he pauses over the still-life nipple he strokes and creates with a breath. Her legs work like a pianist's fingers, caressing the fibres of her product as she crafts her masterpiece. I can't tell which concerto she's playing, but it captures me, like any decent tune. I can listen for hours. She's a beast of her art.

I wonder at the effort she takes over her desire and instinct, and can only admire her.

It's her patience I watch and learn from. Her mission isn't complete until her babies are safe and stored in her silken cocoon, and for that, she needs sustenance. She knows this. Her DNA has told her so. There's no argument or dissent. She does as she's instructed by her genes, and she trusts their genius.

I am in awe of the tiny mother whose shopping basket is stronger than steel. The threads she bleeds may in future be used to make bulletproof vests, such is the quality of her protein.

But now I spy a fly entangled in her web. It's blind in its stupidity. It spent hours doing fly-bys of my walls and ceiling, buzzing around aimlessly without purpose or grand design. And now it's stuck. It can't get away. Not only the electromagnetism of the silk, but the neurotoxins within the secretion also conspire to stick its body to the bonds across its path. It struggles and wriggles and buzzes for leniency, but the mother has waited all day for this moment. The fly is simply an amalgamation of nutrients that will give her babies a better chance of survival. She doesn't see the struggle. The pleading goes unnoticed. It's a battle to the death. The victor will survive. And life will carry on.

But they were never equal adversaries.

The defeated is wrapped up like a body in a shroud. This one is suspended in a ball and unmoving, like a corpse, though I know that it is not yet dead. The mother has merely injected it with a toxin so potent that it can suspend all movement, giving the impression of death, but in fact preserving life so that the nutrients inside the body are kept fresh for consumption. She's a fridge manufacturer as well.

She'll sleep now and so will I; then I'll continue her work. My web isn't as delicate as hers, but it is fine enough to locate the tiniest movement. The vibrations have already started.

As ever,
Once your friend.

Chapter 29

Jilly unlocked the door and went inside to find Max eating a bowl of cereal at the kitchen bar. It reminded her of their student days together.

'How did it go?' he asked.

She put her bags down and flicked the kettle on.

'Fascinating. He's...'

'He's...?' Max copied her.

'I don't know.'

She wanted to say that he reminded her of her mother, but she couldn't explain herself. It was in the way Declan had talked about striving without complaining. Jilly had listened to the stories told to her by her mother of what it was like to struggle to read a degree as a woman in the nineties. Her mother had paid her own way and survived off student loans and grants, as they were called back then. The last century seemed tough in many ways to Jilly. Women weren't as encouraged to pursue their goals, and the predominant aspiration was to become a housewife and mother, which Jilly thought belonged in the Napoleonic Wars, not thirty years ago, but her mother assured her it was true.

'He was so accepting of his situation.'

Max shrugged. 'I guess he can't afford to wallow in it – it'd drive you mad.'

Jilly nodded, before glancing at the cereal box in front of Max. 'I'll make some eggs, want some?'

He nodded.

'He was... normal,' she continued.

'What does that mean?'

'He was a regular guy with mannerisms like you and me, and he was intelligent. I'd expected him to be controlled by Professor Love, but she didn't really have any authority over him at all.'

'What? You mean, she's human?' Max pulled a face of mock horror. 'No, don't spoil my fantasy.'

She hit him. 'Max, that's vile, keep your delusions to yourself. She's got to be in her sixties!'

'So is Madonna.' He grinned. 'What was she wearing?' he asked.

She moved away from him and screwed up her face.

'Seriously, though, it sounds like you've fallen for the oldest trick in the book.'

'I know, that's what I thought. I was watching out for him to manipulate me, but I hadn't expected him to make me feel something for him.'

'Sympathy?'

'Yes, but something else too. Respect.'

'Jesus, do you think he did it?'

'I don't know. I honestly don't know. You've read the transcript of the trial. It was appalling.'

'Did he sense your empathy?'

She thought about the question and busied herself cracking eggs into a bowl.

'Yes, I think he did. I asked if I could see him again, but the rules mean I can't for a month at least; it prevents any prospect of forming a relationship with him.'

'Which, it seems, you already have.'

She smiled. 'You know, the whole time I was there, I couldn't imagine him murdering her, with his baby inside her. It just didn't make sense.'

'That's what people said about Bundy.'

'He isn't a charmer like Bundy – he's modest and quiet.'

'Christ, Jilly, let's get you under a cold shower.'

She threw him a hard stare and whisked eggs furiously, grinning at him. 'He's also repulsively old and looks ill.'

'That's what they all say. I'm allowed my private dream about the professor, and I'll keep your secret about Declan Lewis the ganglord killer. You know what they say about women who fancy criminals…'

'Don't try and psychoanalyse me, you dick. You're a computer science graduate and I don't have daddy issues.'

'Really?'

Her smile vanished, and Max realised he'd hit a nerve.

He held his hands up in surrender and apologised. 'We all have some kind of hang-up,' he said, but the moment had passed, and he couldn't take the words back. Jilly heated some butter in a pan and threw the eggs in, stirring them quickly, and she kept her head down, avoiding his gaze.

'Do you think I have daddy issues?' she asked quietly.

She'd always been direct, and it was the one thing that brought them together as friends. Jilly hated bullshit. She sought to see through people's costumes and get underneath; that way she could work out who might be after her money or not. Max had passed the test and she respected his judgement. He looked at her.

'I think everybody does,' he said.

'That doesn't answer my question and you know it.'

'You want toast with that?' he asked, getting off his bar stool and getting bread out of the freezer. She nodded. Max continued, 'Where do you want me to start? A divorcee who buys his kid everything to show he loves her – but you know all this already, you don't need me to…'

'I do. I want to hear it from you. What do you see?'

'Look, I'm just as fucked up as anyone,' he said.

'I know, we'll get on to that in a minute. For now, it's my turn.'

'All right. Your father has projected his romantic failure onto you and hails you as a princess who can do no wrong to make him feel as though he has at least one relationship with a woman who is perfect.'

'And my mother, while you're at it?'

He folded his arms to wait for the toast and smiled at her. 'No problem. She yearns for your privileged life that she never had, and she's scared you've turned into a spoiled brat because she hates anyone who doesn't graft for what they have, like she did.'

She smiled and nodded, turning off the eggs.

'Pretty spot on,' she said.

'I wonder what your dad experienced with his father to make him so…'

'So?'

'Wounded.'

'Wounded?'

'It's as if owning people makes everything better, but what if he doesn't own them at all? Like you, for example.'

'What do you mean?'

She looked at him warily, and for a second, he made her feel so uncomfortable that she wanted him to leave. It was a new sensation she'd never felt before with him.

'Can we eat now?' he asked, moving on.

He buttered the toast, and she turned the eggs out on top, and they sat next to one another, in companionable silence. But she found herself feeling self-conscious and unable to think of something to say.

They'd agreed there was little point in her doing a sociology degree unless she was able to apply what she knew to herself. It prevented anybody else from doing it by surprise, later in life, and it resulting in a divorce or worse, a bloodbath. It was grounding to flag up one's generational curses occasionally, and she relied on Max to tell her when she acted out. She'd instructed him how, and he was a fast learner. She realised he was only doing what she asked.

'Now we've established that I fantasise about a working-class hero for a father—' she joked.

'Like Declan Lewis,' he interjected.

'Like Declan Lewis,' she acceded. 'I think I might have to face up to the reality of who my grandfather was too.'

'You sure?' he asked.

She nodded and ate her eggs. Their spat was over.

'I could tell in my mother's voice when she tried to change the subject after those newspaper stories came out. Her mind is primed to sniff out people's flaws and she has been there, rooting around in the dross, fighting for her future. My dad wanted her to have nothing after their divorce – I found the letters between their lawyers.'

Max raised his eyebrows.

'They're careless and think I'm stupid – they left them lying around. He wanted to punish her and leave her with nothing. She's known that fear.'

'So why do you think she's avoiding the issue of your grandfather if she knows he's guilty and was an old pervert?'

She shot him a look and he held his hands up.

'Sorry.'

She softened.

'But I think he was more than just an old pervert. Have you read the articles?'

He nodded.

'So, you know what he did. I think she's protecting me, and I must tell her she doesn't need to. I'm not her baby girl any more.'

'But if she did that, and she knows something about the women, then she could be used by them as a witness.'

'Exactly. The whole Wade Media Group depends on her and she's protecting me and it's just plain wrong.'

'How sure are you?'

'I'm not, it's just a hunch, but my mum has a habit of behaving a certain way around me.'

'Demand characteristics?' Max suggested, referring to the efforts of study participants to validate a researcher's hypothesis if they know what the study is about. She'd made Max help her revise it for her finals.

'Exactly, and she's a master at it. Interviewing people on TV is just like a therapist's couch, and hers is orange. I've seen her manipulate people to lie as well as tell truths they've kept hidden their whole lives. Why do you think I studied sociology?'

Max laughed. 'These eggs are so good.'

'Thank you. I'm manipulating you now.'

'Because you put a roof over my head, I'm more likely to believe your theory?'

'Exactly, and it's why you're going to help me, else it's onto the streets with you.'

'And what exactly am I going to do?'

'We're going to go and find the women who were hurt by my grandfather.'

Chapter 30

Gloria stared at the framed photo of Jilly that she kept on her dressing table.

Curiously, it grounded her. Having a child was like running from crisis to crisis in a dazed, sleep-deprived world, and she was thankful that she only had one to worry about. A flicker of tragedy reminded her that some women couldn't have any. Kids didn't see the terror and the physical pain of being a parent, but that was the point. The child ran towards fear and the parent shielded them. Invisible and silent.

She recalled being nine months pregnant with Jilly and feeling ready to pop, as if her skin couldn't stretch any more over her belly.

Oliver still liked to party when she was carrying Jilly. Her pregnancy didn't stop him; it just meant he got to attend more events alone, and that had been part of their decaying relationship, although it had begun to fester much earlier than that, before Jilly had been born.

Oliver's distance grew gradually. There had been a time in her early pregnancy when he couldn't get enough of her and found her swollen body alluring and irresistible. They'd made love right up until her third trimester. Oliver's hands on her heavy breasts used to make her feel as though he was holding her very soul, and she let him caress her even when she felt tired and fat.

It was one of those nights, laying on their bed overlooking the lights of the city of Manchester, when he told her they were relocating to London. He'd just come out and said it. There was no debate, no consultation, just simply an order that the offices had been re-leased, and they'd found an ideal location in London. Manchester had its day, he'd explained, and the future was in the capital.

It had been Roger's idea.

She'd cried, as pregnant women tend to do, and said she couldn't possibly move home and work. She'd told him they'd have to wait until the baby was born, and then until it had its jabs.

But there was no negotiation.

It was at that point that she'd realised what marriage to Oliver Wade really meant.

This morning's show had gone by in a blur. The guest who was accusing Gary Chambers of 'inappropriate behaviour' (that was all they could call it until he was charged with anything) had been difficult to draw out, and Gloria had felt like pulling teeth might have been easier. Especially with the mood she was in after the police left. She understood that the woman was exposing herself and it was a huge risk, but she'd agreed to the interview and sure as hell made Gloria work for the snippets of information she gave. The legal department watched their every move, and the interview had been like dancing around a cheap handbag at a disco; nobody really wanted to pick it up.

Surprisingly, the vodka had given her a fuck-it edge that she rather enjoyed, and she'd managed to get through the whole show without thinking about her pills. Now, as she sat at her dressing mirror, with the bulbs off, she made a promise to herself to pull herself together.

For Jilly.

But she sensed it wouldn't be as easy as simply deciding to take control of her life. The sentiments didn't match reality. She sensed impending doom, and with Oliver at the helm, coming into the studio and hovering over her shoulder at every turn, she doubted she'd last. At least the Andy Knight case had been dropped before the news channels had got hold of it, but the whole thing still bothered her. It disturbed her that he had hundreds of photos of her on his personal computer and she shuddered to think that the police thought it was weird enough to consider that he had the potential to cause her harm. Were they holding back on something? Had they found something else?

She racked her brain for some link between the letters she'd been sent and tried to marry it with what little she knew about Andy Knight. She'd pulled his employment file in an attempt to discover who he was and find out more about his background and whether it crossed hers. But the guy was in his twenties and had never worked in Manchester, as far as she could tell. He was too young to have known her there. He'd joined the network a couple of years ago and was a technician. He had no association with the news desk or HR. He was a lackey. Insignificant.

It just didn't add up.

The female detective knew she was lying. She was like a fellow lioness who sniffed fragility, and for a few moments, Gloria's balance had been knocked off kilter by what she'd been told, and Lucy Holt had seen it.

The bloke, Eddie, had been oblivious, and happy in his ignorance because he'd shaken the hand of Gloria White, and lingered a little too long over it. But the woman was a wily fox. Gloria went through the letters in her head, one by one, and tried to find a link between them and Andy Knight.

Had he worked in a bar, perhaps? Had he known Oliver? How did he get his job at the network? Maybe that was it. Oliver had a habit of interviewing people in clubs and suggesting them to his father for employment – it's how he'd done 90 per cent of his business in the early days. To give him credit, they'd found some of their best people like that. But she'd read through Andy's job interview notes with Elaine, after he'd succeeded through the initial rounds with HR. And she'd asked her to recall the onboarding process for the young technician, and Elaine hadn't brought to mind anything memorable. She'd looked at her oddly when Gloria had asked if Oliver had hand-picked him, which told her he hadn't, but Elaine could always be lying because she'd been told to.

Gloria was becoming paranoid and she trusted no one, not even herself lately.

She felt in between the two bags on the floor and found the vodka bottle and told herself that it was a temporary stopgap until she could replenish her stock of pills. However, she had to admit that, without the drugs, her head had been clearer and her focus sharper this morning than it had been for some time.

She took a swig and her head started whirring again.

What if Andy hand-delivered the letters and it wasn't him who wrote them but somebody he knew? He could have easily slipped them into the postbag downstairs before work and gone unnoticed. But why? What was his motive? She'd never know now, because he'd been found dangling from the door of his shower room on Monday.

It was tragic and awful, and she couldn't help thinking that he must have had something else going on, something bigger. People don't get told off for screwing up at work and go home to hang themselves. There must be a bigger picture. The thought of him sneaking around the studio, slipping the grubby envelopes into the postbag, made bile rise in her throat.

She got up and put the vodka bottle at the back of a drawer, where it was safer than in between two washing bags, and paced up and down, thinking about everything and nothing. Her head hurt and Oliver wanted to see her. She knew that he'd want to know what the police had come for. That bit was easy, but she didn't want to tell him about the photographs and their general concerns over Andy Knight. She'd told Elaine as much. She wasn't to worry Oliver and was to keep it to herself.

A light tap on the door broke her spiralling negativity. It was Elaine again and Gloria wasn't sure that she could stand another conversation with her. The producer came in without being invited to and plonked herself on a chair.

'Do you think Andy Knight was a perverted stalker?' she asked.

Gloria sighed. 'Jesus, how do I know? They're two-a-penny nowadays. I'm surprised the police were even interested – usually, they don't give two fucks if a woman is being coveted by a sicko.'

'It's a great topic for the show – we haven't done stalkers for a while. Isn't Jilly into all of that? Women getting bumped off by men who think they're entitled?'

'Femicide,' Gloria said. 'Yes, she's written a few articles on it.'

'Let's get her on – mother and daughter! Genius!'

Gloria stared at her. 'I don't think Jilly would want to.'

'Why not? I thought Oliver was priming her to take over the empire?'

Gloria felt a crushing in her guts and had visions of all her worst nightmares coming true. The last thing she wanted was for Jilly to live the life she had.

'Well, for one, it's poor taste, given what her grandfather is accused of, and second, I think she's more, erm... academic.'

'Oh, please! She'll learn when she gets no interest in her intellectual claptrap. She needs to talk to real people. Besides, there's no money in being clever, is there? We know that.'

Gloria felt her eyes being drawn to the drawer where she'd put the vodka bottle.

'I've got a headache,' she said. 'And don't forget the accusations against Roger are still live. At some point the police will return to take statements about it. Doing a programme on the abuse of young women in the media at the same time is crass.'

Elaine suddenly looked concerned.

'Are you okay? You haven't seemed yourself lately. Stupid of me, I know – it's this Roger business. Maybe you should take some time off.'

'I'll be fine, I just need a minute.'

When Elaine showed no signs of leaving the room, Gloria continued. 'You don't really think he was fixated on me, do you?'

'Andy Knight? Is that what's freaked you out? What the police told you? It was unusual. You know you asked me about his interview to join us?'

'Yes,' Gloria said.

'Something bothered me about it, and I couldn't put my finger on it.'

'What was that?'

'Andy Knight was gay.'

Gloria was puzzled.

'Let me explain. I don't go around making people's sexual orientation my business, I'm really not interested, but what I do remember, distinctly now because that's how my brain works…' Gloria wished she'd just get on with it. 'Roger called him a "poofter" and I challenged him on it, you know, I pulled him up. Gently, of course – we all know how he was.'

'So, Andy Knight knew Roger personally?'

'My point is that Andy Knight's interest in you wasn't sexual – it must have been something else.'

'So why did you tell Oliver he was fixated on me?'

'I don't know! I went along with him.'

'Why would Roger notice a technician? That wasn't his style. When was this anyway?' Gloria asked.

'A couple of weeks before he stopped coming into the office. I remember it because when I sacked Andy Knight on Monday, he told me that if Roger was still alive, it'd be me losing my job.'

Elaine chuckled at the very thought of the young technician's insolence, but Gloria felt her neck turn hot.

Chapter 31

Oliver was jumpy.

Gloria thought she'd never get used to sitting in Roger's office with Oliver behind his desk, with his boots resting on top, acting as if he was born to rule the empire.

She had to get away before she was pushed.

'I've been contacted by the Met again. They've been instructed by the CPS to investigate the charges against my father posthumously.'

'Oh fuck.'

Gloria sank into one of the comfiest chairs by the window.

'You look tired out,' Oliver told her.

'Thanks so much,' Gloria replied in the most sarcastic tone she could muster.

'When I spoke to the police commissioner, he assured me that it's just a formality. They are compelled to investigate every claim and he was certain it would all be forgotten this time next week. They receive harassment accusations every week and they've got to work through them one by one, even when it's against somebody like Dad.'

'I would have thought *especially* for somebody like your father.'

'Now, hold on a minute – let's not trample on his grave just because he's gone,' Oliver said.

It was typical of the family, she thought, to have a personal hotline to the commissioner of the Met Police, at a time when such perks were themselves being investigated. The commissioner himself could be put on the ropes if this went public, but it wouldn't. It was still an old boys' club, and when his female predecessor had been sacked – and given a golden handshake of three million quid – men like Oliver had partied in the streets, or at least, their private wine cellars. It was the same system that had made sure Roger hadn't ever been investigated. Until now.

'Come on, Oliver, open your eyes. You know what I'm talking about.'

'Not here,' Oliver said.

She took a dramatic intake of breath, obviously exaggerated, and her teasing him felt good. Oliver brought a certain tension to the office and she realised that it had become maudlin since Roger's death.

'You think the office is bugged?' she asked him, still smiling.

'Fuck off, Gloria, I'm just careful, that's all. You know they are likely to turn up here asking questions.'

'The police?'

'Yes, the police.'

'They've only just left.'

'You know what I mean.'

Gloria thought for a while. She turned towards the huge window and surveyed the city beneath them and wondered how Roger must have felt being at the helm of all this power. No wonder he thought he could get away with anything. He was a boy with endless toys and no limits to the playground. It had always been so. It was no coincidence that the stories had broken now he was dead. And the fact that he'd left his mess for them to tidy up after him was galling.

'And you want Jilly to be a part of all this?' she said, more to evoke a response rather than expecting an answer. She was being incendiary, but she felt reckless.

'Leave her out of this.'

'How can I when Elaine tells me you want to prime her to take over this place? How can she possibly take ownership of this legacy when it's rotten to its core?'

'Isn't that a tad dramatic?'

'You really think so? You let her drift into this industry, Oliver. I never wanted her to go anywhere near it. You've encouraged her and given her contacts and seen to it that her articles are read by the top players, all the while pretending to her that it's all on her merit and not because her father used the Wade name to gain access to the toughest publications.'

He glared at her.

'You didn't stop her,' he said.

'I tried – you didn't support me. Every time I pointed her in a different direction, she ran to you, and you appeased her because it helped you score points against me.'

Oliver got up off Roger's chair and leaned on the side of his desk.

'Is it true?' she asked him.

'Which part? Sorry, there were so many insults hurled that I need help picking one out.'

'Stop it, Oliver. Have you offered her a job at the network?'

'What's so bad about it if I have? She has nothing to worry about – our lives were made in these walls. Don't tell me you regret having all this at your fingertips? Why don't you want it for her too? Are you going to go all Prince Harry on me now and whine that you would have preferred a normal life?'

'Maybe. What's so wrong with that? Look how it's all catching up with us now. We agreed we never wanted this for her,' she mumbled under her breath. She'd already said enough, and she turned to the window again.

'What did you say?'

'Nothing.'

'Yes, you did. You said it's all catching up with us. What did you mean?'

'Nothing.'

'You're lying. I can tell because you suck at it.'

'You don't know me well enough to accuse me of lying.'

'Don't change the subject, Gloria. What's happened?'

'Nothing.'

'This all comes out now and you asked me about the Bare Bunny the other night – I haven't forgotten, you know, and I wasn't drunk like you tend to be most of the time.'

'What?'

She stood up out of her chair.

It was a cheap shot and Gloria wasn't used to putting up with Oliver's abuse any more.

'Who told you that? Because it sure wasn't something you worked out for yourself!'

'Elaine mentioned—' he began to say.

'What? Jesus Christ, everybody in this building is a snake!'

'Are you denying it?'

'Denying what, exactly?'

'You're drinking too much, Gloria, and whatever it is you keep in your handbag – I presume sleeping tablets. If I know they're there, then others have noticed.'

'Did you threaten her for that information?'

Oliver smirked and she thought he looked like a little boy who'd been caught stealing pennies. Oliver loved getting his teeth into a fight and she checked herself, determined not to give him one.

'Are you calling her a liar?'

'Hell, yes! She'll say anything to get on your good side. That's not how you run this office, Oliver, through fear. Everybody will end up scared of you. It'd be better if you weren't here.'

'So, that's what you're really worried about? Me taking over. That's why you're bringing up the past and trying to rattle me. You didn't happen to notice that the Bare Bunny was being knocked down, you made it up. You're trying to set me up.'

She turned to leave but stopped. Did he actually believe that she'd brought up the past just to rile him? His obsession with himself was just what she needed. She spun around.

'You know what? I am always pissed because of the prospect of seeing your face every day in here, ruining what we've built, what your father built—'

'What do you care about my father? Don't even speak his name. It was you who threw him under the bus yesterday and said he was guilty as hell of everything he's being accused of. How dare you! After everything he did for you.'

'Exactly, and I don't want it. Sack me. I'm a drunk, and a liar, and utterly faithless to the Wade family cause.' She lowered her voice. 'Because he did do it! And more.'

He stared at her, and for a second, she thought he was going to strike her. It's what all Wade men did for kicks. She braced for the impact of his fist, but he turned away.

'Remember Dad's flat?' he said.

His voice had broken.

She was puzzled. 'His flat? Where?'

'Manchester? The one in Deansgate. The one that cost a million quid back in 2003, a year after it was built.'

'Suite 724,' she said lightly so he didn't hear.

'What?' he turned around.

'Suite 724,' she said, louder.

He nodded. 'How did you remember that?'

She shrugged. She hadn't. She'd been reminded.

He went to say more but she stopped him.

'Don't, Oliver. Don't tell me.' She knew he wanted to unburden himself of something. He'd done it before.

He nodded and went back to his chair – Roger's chair – and sat down heavily. He'd forgotten what they were arguing about, and that's exactly what she'd intended. He was back to himself, trapped inside his tiny world with him at the centre, and he'd forgotten that there were other stories at play, with other main players and walk-on parts.

'Elaine said she was concerned for you because she recommended a doctor who prescribes privately, and she thought—'

'Don't worry, I'll handle Elaine,' she said.

'I didn't mean—'

'I know.'

'We can't allow these stories to take a hold,' he said.

'They won't.'

'But how do you know?'

'You're doing everything you can. You've got the commissioner on side, your PI is getting on with his job, and soon he'll unearth something unsavoury about those women to discredit them. The news is fickle. Every other woman from here to John O'Groats has a story about being abused by somebody; we'll bury it underneath somebody else's shit.'

Oliver smiled and she knew the explosive outburst had been forgotten, along with her mention of the Bare Bunny.

Whoever it was sending her notes, she was 100 per cent certain that it had nothing to do with her ex-husband, which left the question: who else was it likely to be?

Chapter 32

Gloria felt as though she was on a hamster wheel that was never going to stop. Her house looked the same, it smelled the same and was the same, because she was never there long enough to make it look like she had ever set foot into it. Only her bed showed signs of being hers, because she could smell herself on the sheets, despite them being laundered daily by the housekeeper who was still paid for by the Wade estate.

Had Roger really loved her, or was he still buying her silence from the grave?

Roger Wade had done nothing in his life that wasn't for profit.

Her denial of this fact had allowed her to stay within his grasp all her career and had made her responsible for anything that was done in the Wade name. She wasn't blameless and she couldn't pretend she was.

The first thing she did when she was inside her house was search for a new packet of Adderall. She went to her bathroom and opened the cabinet next to the bath, where she kept a key. She left nothing visible for cleaners or cooks to nose around in. She trusted no one; Oliver had taught her that. They'd caught plenty of staff stealing from them over the years, and sadly, she'd come to realise that it was endemic when one had anything valuable that others coveted. Anything in her home that was worth something to her, which wasn't much, was hidden away. Clothes, bags, jewellery, gifts and trinkets could all be replaced. She had no photos on display, because it was all too tempting for people to try to sell images of her family. Anything personal was either locked in a safe underneath two floorboards in the utility room, or hidden in the panels inside cupboards, which is where she kept her pills. It depressed her to think that they'd become one of her most valuable possessions, but it was the need for a private space in which to be herself that had driven it, not her addiction to them, which she was convinced she could control.

The panel slid off and she reached her hand in, finding a fresh packet of prescription tablets, and she breathed a sigh of relief. She popped two out of the little silver foils and threw them down her throat.

She sank to the floor, sat beside the bathtub and leaned back on the wall. If her fans could see her now, in a place of safety, where she felt no one could get to her, leaning on the side of a toilet – a clean one, admittedly – praying for sleep, would they think she was mad? Or might they feel sympathy that she was hounded so? Or would they laugh at her for being ridiculous? Did she imagine their obsession with her?

She'd stopped caring.

All she knew was that her dressing room and under her duvet, with a few places in between, were the only spaces she trusted herself to let go and allow the layers of fakery to peel away.

Underneath it all, she had no idea who she was any more, but she did have enough sense left, even after a couple of pills, to know that whatever was coming wasn't going to be easy to get out of this time. Roger's past was threatening to emerge, and with him gone, it was down to the rest of them to shoulder the fallout.

Whichever way she looked, her life with or without Oliver was about to collide into something bigger than both of them and there was little anyone could do about it.

She remembered the night he'd taken her back to his place for the first time, to his mansion in the Cheshire countryside. She recalled the familiar feeling between her legs, as they'd giggled and she held onto his leg as he drove, thinking that what they had would last forever.

He'd been drinking. He always had, but she trusted him, and it was different back then. One couldn't be a serious journalist without a long boozy lunch and then a drive in the country after sex with a colleague. Anyway, if he ever had an accident, there weren't many models that could knock a Bentley off the road, that's what she used to tell herself. The evening had been beautiful, and it was summer, like now. The Bentley purred as Oliver accelerated into the fast lane as if he'd just won an Olympic gold. She'd only ever known him drive the luxury cars. He'd been pleased with himself. She had been once impressed with his masterful hand on the wheel, and his left thigh muscle, under his trousers, as his foot pressed the pedals. The gentle waft of his expensive cologne floated in the air and the heat of his body made it radiate outwards so it filled the generous space.

Everyone at work knew she'd left with him, even if they hadn't seen them go.

Luxury vehicles weren't uncommon in the city, thanks to the footballers, but a Bentley always drew attention.

Soon, the entrance to the private complex loomed and he'd turned off between huge trees, pulling up in front of two enormous iron gates, pressing a key fob in his pocket. The gates had swung open majestically and they'd passed through as they closed behind them. He'd swung the car behind the back of a house that she'd thought was a hotel, not his home, and her feet had crunched on the gravel when she got out. The main doors were huge and made of Welsh oak, but they were prone to sticking in the heat and it made Oliver cross.

She recalled the sound of his keys in the porcelain bowl — where he tossed them before he turned his attention back to her — as if she were stood there in his hallway all over again. She felt her nerves jangle with the noise.

'Drink? I can order takeaway.'

'Takeaway? They deliver here?' she'd asked innocently. He'd laughed.

But she couldn't get the noise out of her head; the clanging of the metal against pottery as his keys had missed the bowl and landed on the floor. She'd watched him pick them up and it was as if she could see them now. The bowl had cracks in it, no doubt from Oliver throwing his keys at it every day. And she noticed its beauty and realised that it was a habit of the very rich: using expensive things as trinkets, just because they could. She had to pull herself together.

She needed a drink.

It wouldn't be long before her key fob – which was as plain as day to her in her mind now, as if she could touch it – sat in the bowl, with his, for all those years. They used to joke that keys to a Bentley, or sometimes his Aston Martin, sat alongside hers to a VW Beetle, quite happily, as if they were meant to be bed partners.

The fob had been a small metal disc, on which was a cartoon of a character which she'd thought funny at the time because it was what Oliver called her.

He'd bought it for her from a market in Liverpool when they were in love and they'd thought they could never live without each other. She'd lost it years ago.

It had said, *Little Miss Sunshine*.

Chapter 33

Gloria woke on Thursday morning wishing it was Friday. She had no idea what time she'd dozed off after checking in with Jilly. Maybe that's why she'd slept for a few hours, because she knew that her daughter was safe. The further away she was from the shitstorm that was coming, the better. Jilly had reassured Gloria that she was happy anonymously enjoying the sunshine in Durham with Max, and Gloria believed her because she had no reason not to. Life seemed fraught with danger, but for her daughter, more so, because everything they did was in the public eye, and in that place, there were people waiting around every corner for you to fail and trip up so they could stand back and laugh, and point, and say, 'Look! They're not that special!'

Jilly had seemed happily distracted last night, and not for the first time, Gloria had wondered whether her daughter and Max were a thing. He was a handsome kid. She still thought of him as a kid because when they'd been introduced, he and Jilly had been eighteen.

Youngsters were a strange breed these days. She couldn't think of any other reason for Jilly to enjoy Max's company so much other than being interested romantically, otherwise, what was the point?

But her daughter was fiercely private when it came to Max.

She sensed the familiar fogginess of a deep sleep when she needed more, but it was nothing a stiff coffee couldn't fix.

Then in the car she'd add a little something stronger to it. Day drinking was only frowned upon when it came out of a brown bag and went down the throat of somebody who was unemployed and desperate. If it slid down the gullet of a professional, who needed a pep-up occasionally, it was acceptable. At least that's the way it was explained by the voices in her head.

She went to her bathroom and stepped under the shower, ignoring her phone as was her usual morning routine. She could tell the sun was up already, or at least trying to climb over the horizon. It was the best time of year. There was nothing like getting out of bed in the darkest winter, sky pitch-black and air freezing cold, to make you feel as though you were in the wrong job.

The water woke her up a little, and she set about getting dressed and gathering what she needed for the day, going downstairs to make coffee and grab some water from the fridge.

She blinked at the fridge light and sensed something was off, so mentally retraced her steps from the stairs to the kitchen. Something was missing, and she went through her morning routine again to see if she could figure it out.

Then she realised the security alarm light hadn't been on when she'd come downstairs. She thought she was going mad and had one of those moments where you check yourself just in case you are actually still asleep and inside one of those terribly sterile dreams where you're doing the washing-up or hoovering. Not that she'd done that in reality for years. But she could still dream of performing mundane tasks occasionally, and it usually meant she was overworked.

She retraced her steps and found that she'd been right.

She wasn't going mad, and she wasn't still inside a dream.

She tapped the console, and nothing happened. Then a creeping feeling spread across her chest, and she looked around for signs that somebody had broken in.

There were none.

But there was an envelope on the floor near the front door, in the hallway.

Which was odd because the driver picked up the post in the afternoon, from the box outside, and brought it in.

She knew the envelope hadn't been there last night because she would have stepped on it when she came in. And she remembered setting the alarm code before she went to bed.

So, two things had happened.

One, her alarm had been disconnected.

Two, somebody had got access to her driveway, opened her postbox and posted this envelope through the front letterbox.

Both facts made her shudder.

Her eyes darted around the hallway and then she ran upstairs, checking every room, cursing the fact that she had such a large house, which she didn't need. She ran back downstairs and checked each room down there too.

There was no one there.

Was it yesterday or the day before she'd said to herself, to reassure herself, that whoever was sending the letters knew her work address, but not her home address? She was trying to be rational and sensible in order to relieve the panic building in her body, but she was failing. Of course he knew her home address, he'd been watching her, waiting, biding his time for the right moment. He'd planned this timing all along. He was weakening her, wearing her down, preparing to pounce.

Her feet moved towards the front door and she stood helplessly over the envelope. It was small, like the others, but there was nothing written on the front. She stared at it.

She scoured her brain for who had a key to the front gate. The letter hadn't floated over the wall by itself. Perhaps the cleaning company could have slipped something through her door, or the driver could have put it there, telling her he was sick today, or some other excuse?

She bent down to pick it up and she felt something inside. It wasn't a letter, and she was relieved. Her body let out a sigh.

Whatever it was, there would be a perfectly logical explanation, and she ripped open the envelope to see what was inside.

A USB stick slid into her palm, and she stared at it. Inside the envelope, though, there was a letter, and her heart beat so fast inside her chest that she thought she could hear it.

The cleaner wouldn't send her a message via USB, and neither would the driver. Work, then? No, they'd send her an email. Elaine? She'd call. Jilly would call...

She went through all the people she contacted regularly and dismissed them one by one. Then she checked her phone.

Apart from a kiss goodnight from Jilly by text, nothing looked vaguely interesting or important, nothing that would indicate anything was amiss.

But something was amiss.

He'd been here. He'd slid the envelope through the door while she slept.

Don't be stupid, she chastised herself and told herself to be reasonable about it.

She held the letter in one hand and the USB in the other. A peek inside the letter confirmed her worst fears.

It was from him.

She threw the USB across the room, but then went to it and got down on her hands and knees to retrieve it from under a table.

She marched to the kitchen and plugged it into her laptop.

There was one file on it, and it was unnamed. She clicked on it.

Her hand absently felt behind the computer for the bottle of red she'd left half-drunk last night – or was it this morning? – and she poured some into a coffee cup, then drank it in one.

The screen was blank for a few seconds, then it filled with a grainy shot of a street. Gloria creased her brow and, for a moment, thought it might be a mistake. But the street looked familiar. It was like any other in a UK suburb, or at least a pretty one. It was an attractive street; one she'd like to live on if she had her time over again.

She noticed the cars parked outside the pretty little houses and a couple more drove past. Then a youngster on one of those new e-scooters that killed pedestrians every week on Britain's roads flashed across the screen, weaving in and out of parked cars.

Idiot, she thought.

Her attention was brought back to the houses, which looked a hundred years old at least and had small walled gardens out front. But somehow, they still managed to look unloved, as if the neighbourhood had faded from its glory days.

That's when she realised she knew the street she was looking at.

The camera panned back and forth, and Gloria covered her mouth with her hand and breathed into it. 'No.'

Her hands shook and she didn't know what to do first. She picked up her phone and hammered in a contact number. It went to voicemail. She tried again.

On the screen, the film homed in on a small cottage at the end of the terrace, all on its own. It was detached and grander than the others. Then a door opened, and Gloria's legs turned to stone.

The camera shook slightly, suggesting the footage had been filmed on a mobile phone. She knew cameras, had worked in front of them for three decades.

She studied the trees and decided that it was spring. Blossom clung to the branches and sprinkled the road with white confetti. The film had been taken months ago.

Then a figure emerged from the pretty cottage and stepped out into the sunshine.

It was her daughter, in front of her house in Durham.

A sob escaped from her throat and she felt as though she might throw up, but she couldn't stop watching. She tried Jilly's number again, but it went to answerphone again. Then Gloria realised that she didn't know what she'd say to her even if she picked up.

She'd see the missed calls when she woke up and be worried. How would she explain herself? Somebody filmed her coming out of her house in spring?

Gloria tried to calm herself down and think straight.

Should she ring Oliver? No, that was the last thing she should do.

The police? No, she needed to get a better perspective before she involved them. What would they do anyway? Anybody could find out with a bit of digging where her daughter went to university, and it wasn't too much of a stretch from there to deduce she probably had her own house in her second and third year, and that gave her an idea: perhaps it wasn't recent footage after all.

It was spring, but what year?

She paused the film and studied Jilly closely. She looked at her hair and her clothes, but then her heart sank. Gloria had bought the bag she carried for her graduation present – a Prada. It was Jilly's favourite and she carried it everywhere.

So, it was this year.

It still didn't mean Jilly was in imminent danger.

Gloria watched her daughter on screen as she stopped in the doorway to bend over and retrieve something from the doormat. As she did so, her Prada bag fell off her shoulder, and she slumped over as if disappointed that not even something as simple as a shoulder bag would stay where it was put.

Gloria smiled. It was an intimate moment, and she could hear her daughter sigh, but then she realised that she was sharing it with a stranger, and she had no idea why they were interested in her daughter and why they were communicating with her like this. And why now?

On screen, Jilly picked up her bag and walked to the end of her driveway to her car and got in. She slammed her door and started the engine, which Gloria couldn't hear but suddenly wished she could so she would know that Jilly was okay, despite the film having been taken months ago.

But then she realised the point of the film.

It was a message.

It said: *I know where she lives, and I can go there any time I please.*

Maybe he was there now.

She grabbed her phone and called again.

No answer.

The film cut, and Gloria thought she'd pressed something by accident, but then it appeared back on screen. But the lighting was different; it was a different time, a different day, a new season.

The person filming was stood in the same place, and she watched her daughter's house from the same perspective. The cars parked on the street had changed and she realised that the students had gone home for the holidays, and it was likely filmed during a quieter month. Sunshine reflected off the metal roofs of the cars and the bushes looked fuller. It was summer.

This summer.

Once again, she saw her daughter emerge out of her front door, but this time with Max. Jilly had her hair tied back and she wore a vest that Gloria had seen her in only last week.

Her ponytail swished in the breeze, over her shoulder, as she pulled it back off her neck, and she and Max laughed about something. On her other shoulder, there was a shopping bag, and they walked down the path towards the gate, oblivious they were being filmed. Screaming rage tore into Gloria's fists and she had a desperate need to hold her daughter. She saw the front gate crash onto its hinges behind them as they left and Gloria could almost hear the clatter of it, as well as the birdsong over their heads.

Her phone ringing made her jump so hard that she dropped it and stared at it on the floor.

It was Jilly.

She answered it and shouted her daughter's name down the phone.

'Mum? What's wrong? I've had five missed calls. What time is it?'

'Jilly?'

'Yes, Mum, you called me, is everything okay?'

'Jilly?'

'Yes, Mum.'

'Are you okay?'

'Yes, are you? You called me.'

'I know. You're in Durham?'

'Yes.'

'You need to come back to London.'

'What? Mum, it's four o'clock in the morning—'

'I know, you must come back, get up and... Is Max still there?'

'Yes.'

'Who has he spoken to?'

'What?'

'Who did he tell?'

'Mum, not this again.'

'Drive home now. Come straight to the office, don't go anywhere else, drive straight there. I'll explain everything when you get here.'

Nowhere was safe any more. He knew her home address and he knew Jilly's.

'Mum, what's going on?'

'I'll tell you when you get here. Don't worry, it's nothing serious, I just need you to come home. It's important.'

'What's happened? Tell me now. I can hear it in your voice – something is wrong.'

'It's nothing, I just need you to come home.'

'If it's nothing, then why the panic and why four o'clock in the morning? Is Dad okay?'

'Yes, Dad's fine. I'm sorry it's so early, I didn't notice. You know what I'm like this time of the morning – I'm up for work and expect everybody else is too. Promise me you'll come home.'

'Mum, you're scaring me.'

'Sorry, love. It's just I think you might have a leak at the flat.'

'What?'

'Come straight here. No, not here, to the office, there's more people.'

Gloria kicked herself. It was a pathetic excuse, but she couldn't think of any other reason to get her back to London and not panic her.

'Let Max drive – go and pack. I'll see you about nine?'

'Yeah, all right, Mum. See you later.'

Jilly hung up and Gloria stared at the phone. Then she looked at the computer screen and a series of stills of her daughter were flashing across in collages, as if somebody had put together a presentation of her daughter's life and they were playing it to an audience. One that loved her and wanted to remember her. Because she'd gone already.

Chapter 34

Dear Gloria,

Your face has changed.

Something goes missing behind so much make-up. It ruins you. And you've had surgery on your nose. That mouth, which looks the same but isn't, speaks no lies, but does. You sit there on your mighty sofa, giving advice to people you don't know, and all the while, they have no idea that you are as broken as they are. They watch your mouth, like I do, and look for answers, and they trust you. They want you to approve of them, to tell them what to do with their shattered lives. The lad you had on yesterday begged you with his eyes to help him tell the world that it's all right to fail all your exams because worth is on the inside, isn't that right, Gloria? Value isn't skin deep, you told him. So, why did you change yours? Your face stares back at me, only me, and lingers, and your eyes twitch like they used to when you were scared. What are you scared of now, Gloria?

Failure follows you everywhere. The paint on your skin won't mask it, just like the straight nose and white teeth won't armour your castle, and the red nails and silk blouse won't stop the rain getting in. Your soft, pale skin is porous just like the rest of us. The chemicals from your toxic mind seep into it and into your heart, killing it – if there's any of it left.

You're talking to a young lass, who's from the ghetto, just like me, and she's pleading with you to legitimise her giving up her baby because she was raped. I've seen this one before, it's a classic trending on YouTube and it's years old. You look a lot younger. You assumed life would be kind to you because you're rich and powerful and protected by the Wades, but it hasn't worked out like that, has it?

The young girl is crying, and you're trying to, aren't you? You're scowling and grimacing, and your mouth is turned down, just like they teach you to for the telly. But your eyes are dry, Gloria. You don't feel it in your heart, do you?

The lass has hundreds of viewers call in with messages of sympathy, and you read them like you're told to, and you try to look as though you feel it. But you don't. You can't ever know those emotions because you're dark and empty like a pit. I know where those emotions went, Gloria. They were killed off by greed. Your black, shrivelled heart doesn't beat like everybody else's.

You've got no love left.

Least of all for a poor baby who's sobbing on your velvet sofa, dripping all over the cushions and causing a mess that won't clean out; not like your shiny new boots and the silver bracelet around your wrist: pristine in their perfection. Does it jangle against the others and remind you of something else?

Shackles.

The prison keys you got rid of when you escaped to the bright lights that hide everything else.

I know where you're from, and I know where you're going, and now I know where you live.
Yours,
No more a friend.

Chapter 35

The car to London crawled through traffic as soon as they hit the outskirts of the city. Despite the early hour, taxis, executive cars and joyriders were all out, trying to beat the sunrise. But the golden orb was up already as they inched towards a set of traffic lights.

Gloria had called Jilly every half an hour and now she wasn't answering. Gloria had made her angry and she knew she couldn't blame the girl. She wasn't making any sense and refused to tell her daughter the truth, so she sounded like a madwoman.

But at least she was packing to come back to London – Max had been on the phone and promised Gloria he'd get her daughter back safe.

Mum, stop calling, I'm coming home!

Jilly had texted.

Gloria had told no one of the USB.

She couldn't.

She had no choice but to keep it to herself.

She'd run through all the options, one by one.

If she told Oliver, he'd fly off the handle and demand close protection for his daughter all the way down the A1, or at least a helicopter ride home. He'd make a fuss and blow everything out of proportion, and he'd strong-arm the police into launching a surveillance team. The story would take perhaps twenty-four hours to leak, and it'd be all over the news, so then she'd never know who was threatening her family, and he'd never be caught.

She had no faith in the coppers.

Which was why option two – getting the police involved – was out. If she called them, they'd turn up and take the USB and file it inside a brand-new envelope marked 'evidence', then wait until somebody died.

She couldn't tell Elaine, because she'd go straight to Oliver.

She couldn't take her driver to Durham and investigate herself because she didn't know where to start and she'd raise suspicion not turning up for work, and her driver would likely tell somebody anyway – mouths have a habit of blabbing when they have something to share, and any story that gets tongues wagging was worthy of sharing.

She toyed with notifying the private investigator Oliver had hired to investigate the women who'd made allegations against Roger. That was the most sensible option, but Oliver paid the PI's wages – he answered to him, not her. She'd have to hire her own, but that was risky too, because Roger had been right when he'd told her not to trust anyone, not even her husband, the day after he'd given her the most lucrative anchor position on TV and Oliver had sulked for months.

Trust no one.

Her head whirred as she tried to work out who could be sending her the notes. They'd planned it for a long time and had been watching her daughter for months. And they knew her home address.

And whoever it was knew about what happened in Manchester. She tried to narrow it down by thinking of all the people connected with the Bare Bunny twenty years ago.

There were dozens of possibilities. But not that many when she put all the letters together.

So he was no longer her friend.

The latest letter confirmed it.

What do people usually want? she asked herself.

Money, at least that bit was obvious.

What did extortionists usually want?

Payment for something.

For what? She had no clue. Silence perhaps? Or a confession. But first they had to negotiate. She hadn't been told what he wanted, and she hadn't been told how she could contact him. Kidnappers usually demanded something, unless they weren't planning on taking Jilly at all, just hurting her. Or simply scaring her mother.

If they were serious about harming her, or Jilly, they would have made contact and demanded what they wanted by now.

Unless they want nothing.

But who wanted nothing?

Those who have nothing to lose.

Or somebody who'd had everything, then lost it.

The car stopped and she found her eyes closing and the back of her head going soft and mushy like liquid, as her exhausted brain begged her to allow it some rest.

In the video footage, Jilly had seemed distant to her, and this was what terrified her more than anything: never seeing her daughter again as her daughter, but just as a memory. Gloria had downloaded it to her phone and couldn't stop watching it, to memorise every frame, perhaps for the police, but more to see if she could catch the person behind the camera. People always made mistakes. Perhaps his reflection was shown somewhere without him knowing. Perhaps there was a clue to his identity.

Jilly looked like any ordinary young woman going about her business, unaware that anyone was watching and hunting.

The car jolted and Gloria almost dropped her phone, realising she'd nodded off again. She must have slept for a few minutes only, and she put it down to mixing a small nip of vodka with her tablets this morning. She'd forgotten the last time she'd had a dose, so she might have doubled up on them.

A face filled her vision, but it wasn't Jilly's. It was another around the same age. She wore more make-up and looked rougher, not as tended to or loved as her daughter.

She'd first seen her when she'd come into the Manchester office for an interview. It was years ago but she still reminded

Gloria of her daughter. It must have been the age, or perhaps the sense that she was being watched but unaware of it. There was a tragic innocence to her. A sense of impending doom.

The young woman had waited patiently for her name to be called, and Gloria had walked past her, noticing that she was dressed more for a night out than an interview at a reputable TV network. Gloria surmised she must have been going for one of the pop magazine segments. She wore tight trousers that showed off her slim legs and Gloria remembered feeling like the woman wasn't safe dressing like that in the industry. It was as if she was trying too hard. She looked out of her depth and Gloria felt as though she'd wanted to dress her properly. But most of all, she'd checked who was conducting the interview, and she'd felt momentary panic when she read that it was Oliver.

The woman's cut-away top was skin-tight, and she seemed to wear it like a second skin, as if oblivious to the messages it gave off in an environment like a media office, which back then was dominated by men. The testosterone in the air was as thick as the cigarette smoke and should have come with health warnings to alert women to beware or go get another job, like cleaning or being a dinner lady, or an air hostess.

It wasn't that Gloria had been a prude, but it had stuck in her mind. It was only after her interview, when she'd got to know the young woman, that her infectious enthusiasm explained her attire. The young woman was bursting with ideas and dressed how she felt. And she felt like a radical. She predicted seismic shifts in the industry and Gloria remembered thinking what a breath of fresh air she was. The young woman had left school with three GCSEs, but good ones. And she had a voice, one that needed hearing. She'd blown them away with her desire to deliver stories, with hare-brained ideas of going undercover and exposing corruption and venality wherever they could be found. It was cutting edge. She'd told them she'd grown bored with old men dominating the news scene in the eighties and when Kate Adie had come along, she'd known she'd found her idol. Women could do anything they wanted, she'd told them. The Spice Girls had, and so had Madonna. Life was there for the taking, and that's exactly what she intended on doing.

Gloria had been reminded of an image of diamonds that were cut from rock after thousands of years of being surrounded by shit. Balls and grit had got her on TV, why not this girl?

Gloria had followed the young woman into the interview room and Oliver had scowled at his wife, questioning her move, but she'd insisted on staying for the whole interview. The young woman had something that Gloria wanted. Her make-up was cheap and her face sweated underneath it; she had animal hair on her jacket, and her perfume made Gloria want to sneeze, but she was given the job.

Once they knew why she was there, and what she had to tell them, they'd given her the position in a heartbeat.

Oliver hadn't seen her potential, only her sexual allure.

He called her Lynne.

'My name is Linda,' she'd told him proudly. 'My name is Linda Wilson.'

Chapter 36

'You look like shit.'

'Thanks,' Gloria said.

Oliver had arranged a meeting with the private investigator, who had some news for them, and he wanted Gloria there. But she'd have to propel herself somehow through the morning show first. They walked to the lift together.

'It's been a long few days,' she continued, by way of explanation.

'Quite. What's this about demanding Jilly drive home?'

Gloria stopped dead in her tracks.

'She called me. She said you were raving like a lunatic. What about our last conversation? You seemed to persuade me you were in control and Elaine was wrong to call out your habits – now I'm concerned.'

She stopped herself from taking the bait.

'You have no cause to be concerned about me, Oliver.'

They had other, more pressing, troubles.

He was here early, she observed, and he'd caught her in the corridor going to the lift. Staffers, researchers and camera technicians went about their business at this time of the morning, which was the busiest time of the day, and nodded greetings to them as they passed.

'Gloria, what's going on?'

She couldn't answer. Her mouth went to let it all out, to blab everything to him about the letters and the videos but her brain kicked in at the last moment to stop her.

'I changed my mind. I think she should be close to us, if anything else blows up.'

'Anything else? What else have you got to worry about? You're in the clear over that technician who hanged himself, and you've got it off your chest what you really feel about me being here. And yet you're still keeping something from me. I can tell.'

The lift arrived.

'I'll take the stairs,' she said and went off in the opposite direction.

The White Report went by in a blur, and she was vaguely aware of Elaine scowling at her from the business end of the camera, warning her to stay on track. The terrible strain of keeping secrets was wearing her down, and she scraped her way through the show like a snail slithering across glass.

It hadn't been pretty.

Elaine had raised her very large tattooed eyebrows several times in her direction when she'd lost her thread, but in the grand scheme of things, it hadn't been all that bad. But she was teetering on the edge of a precipice.

Months ago, she'd told Jilly to enable the tracker on her phone, but she hadn't done it and now she was mad at her.

She was mad at everyone.

Max had at least checked in as they stopped for coffee at a service station on the A1, so she knew they were on their way home. But Gloria had heard nothing for a couple of hours, and she was getting jumpy.

She toyed with telling Oliver all morning but held on to the notion that it was better for everyone if he didn't know. She'd hear what the PI had to say and then make a call on it.

After filming, she made her way to her dressing room and drew a deep breath, before planning her approach with Oliver.

All she really wanted to do was get into a car and go to Jilly, to hold her and make sure she was unharmed.

But detectives were coming back today to take statements about Roger and what they could remember about his employment of five females in Manchester between 1987 and 2001. Gloria could safely say, with her hand on her heart, that she knew absolutely nothing, because she had only just met Oliver in 2001. That was her off the hook. It was comforting to know that she didn't have to lie. She felt as though the untruths were snowballing into a giant avalanche that nobody could stop, and the feeling of being imminently buried alive had taken hold of her and wouldn't let go. Before going to work for his father in 2000, at the age of thirty-one, Oliver had worked in London, and so he was prepared to say the same thing.

He knew nothing.

But they'd both heard the rumours, even though they'd been closed down by an army of warriors guarding Roger at the time. It was one of those corporate mysteries that everybody knew about but nobody discussed. Like Nanny McPhee's warts, they sat festering on the face of the company, until somebody was willing to do something about it. Eventually, they all thought they'd disappeared, cut off by a surgeon's scalpel. But they hadn't, it seemed, and now they were here to haunt them. It was typical of Roger that he'd dropped a fart and left the room.

She wondered if Oliver would still be angry with her. Or would he have forgotten and be more concerned with the detectives? She hoped he'd be his usual self, too wrapped up in himself to notice that her skin was slipping off.

When she'd waved at the waiting photographers this morning, outside the studio – the regulars who snapped her arriving every day – she'd posed without worry, like she always did. But she'd sensed a seismic shift in her place there. Her image was everything and she must appear as though she always looked ready for the cameras, even though inside she was shrivelling up into a tiny mess.

She felt as though her normally lizard-thick skin had been wearing thinner lately and becoming more porous, as if she was melting away.

She was used to evisceration by the press.

Gloria's Wardrobe Horror! Gloria's Wardrobe Malfunction! Where is Gloria's Classic Chic?

Her very moral fibre hung in the balance between approval and disapproval.

But this was different, this was personal.

All she could think about was Jilly, but she couldn't show it.

What she thought mattered.

What she said mattered.

She mattered.

And yet the yawning emptiness was getting worse.

She felt rudderless.

And through the fog was the ever-present voice telling her that she was making an almighty mistake.

She was a terrible mother for not going straight to the police.

What will you choose?

Will you choose her when you have to?

His words taunted her. It was as if he knew what was going to happen before it did, and he even knew how she'd react when it did. He was orchestrating the whole thing and she felt lost.

Her body craved something to calm her down. She could no longer do it alone and needed chemical help but even that had been spotted by both Oliver and Elaine. And if they saw it, who else had? Shame burned her cheeks, and her brain told her in an unforgiving cycle of cravings that she needed a tablet, or a quick swig of vodka. She felt as though they were laughing at her because she no longer knew what she was doing, but they also didn't know what she was keeping inside.

And she couldn't possibly tell them.

She must face this head-on, alone. What was she so scared of? She'd been battling alone her whole life. She'd never needed anyone before, so why would she now? It was ludicrous to think anybody else could benefit her or save her daughter from what horrors Gloria imagined she was threatened with. No, this whole situation needed a clear head for her to think through it, so she could protect her daughter. She was the only one who could do it.

Meanwhile, she remained the jolliest woman on TV.

It was only when she'd led a segment on drug addiction two years ago, interviewing a teenager who'd been prescribed pills for ADHD, that she'd taken an interest in what Adderall was, and she realised she'd been taking amphetamines. They'd been magic at first, and no wonder, it was like taking crack every day. But their sorcery was wearing off.

She looked at her phone.

Jilly should be here by now.

'Gloria!'

She jumped as Elaine burst into her dressing room.

'Jesus Christ, don't you fucking knock?'

'What happened?' Elaine asked.

'When?' A creeping sense of contrition entered her head and she felt pinned against a wall for a second. Then she realised she was talking about the breakfast show. Maybe her missing a few cues and losing her way a few times had been noticed more than she thought it had.

On screen, her mouth had moved and she'd formed the right words, but the faces of her guests and those behind the cameras had been like blobs of paint on a canvas, nameless and nondescript. She'd followed the autocue and had managed to finish the sentences, thinking nobody had clocked that she was crumbling inside. She'd fixed a smile onto her face like a cartoon transfer tattoo, and her muscles had got used to it. But then she recalled Elaine's arms flailing about and that's when she'd first realised she was off topic. She'd been daydreaming and she'd remembered the double dose of Adderall.

Her words had slurred, but only Elaine could tell she was failing live on air.

It had been worse than she feared.

She remembered now.

Everybody else's heads were down. But Elaine threw her hands up in the air, indicating she was going off script again.

Then others noticed. No one knew what to do. They froze, staring at her, then looking to Elaine for guidance.

Gloria was falling.

She was known for taking risks live on air and it made pure TV gold. It's what got her paid so handsomely. It was her free ticket to anywhere. It was a condo in the Hamptons and a backstage pass to meet Taylor Swift...

But this morning had been different.

Elaine had cut her for the first time ever, live on air.

'Let's go to Susan from Essex,' she'd read the prompt.

Susan from Essex droned on about her brain fog and the menopause, and she'd pretended to listen, but her mind had wandered to a vision of a man hanging by his neck, inside a shower cubicle, shit running down his legs. And why he had photos of her.

The crew had their heads in their hands.

They went to a commercial break.

Several people came to her aid, but she'd batted them away.

But now she realised that Elaine's thunderous entrance to her private space wasn't to chastise her about her performance. She wasn't there to admonish her about her confusion on air. This wasn't just about her or her meltdown.

'The news about Andy has broken on other channels. They're milking it and running with the bullying story,' she said. 'We're trending for being heartless bastards for carrying on as normal with today's show.'

'What do we do?' Gloria asked.

'You're asking me? Gloria, what the hell is wrong with you? I came to ask you. I've had ideas thrown at me by everybody but you. You hide in here as if it's your pit. You need to wake up and realise what's going on. I'm announcing a public apology. I'll explain we're respecting Andy's privacy. You need to do it.'

'What?'

'I have no idea what has got into you, but you need to pull yourself together. You are this programme. If you go down, we all do. Hear me? We're going on air for a special in two minutes, and I've got a statement coming from HR. Act normal – well, act *Gloria*, at least. I'll give you a feature, then we'll cut to a recorded piece on mental health in three minutes. Got it?'

'Got it.'

Gloria felt as though she was sliding into a dark cavern full of unknown monsters wailing and clawing at her to tear her to pieces.

'Then you'll read a prepared statement about Andy's sad passing. We'll cobble together something on depression and addiction or some shit like that.'

'Right.'

'And go easy on the fucking pills, Gloria.'

Elaine flounced out of the dressing room in the same manner as she'd come in. Gloria was stunned.

Two admonishments from her producer in the space of as many days told her to watch her back. The ship felt unsteady. Like they were sinking.

Elaine's little speech sat heavy on the air. *'You are this programme. If you go down, we all do...'*

Was she going down?

Another loud bang on her door pulled her out of her reverie and she rushed to put her shoes back on and check her make-up. She left the room.

'Here,' Elaine said, handing her an iPad as she entered the studio. On it was a statement from HR, which she read eagerly, trying to get into the spirit of what was being asked of her.

> Andy was a much-loved member of The White Report. He began working for us as a keen young graduate three years ago...
>
> Our thoughts are with his girlfriend, Freda, and his parents at this difficult time...

She'd thought Elaine said he was gay...

'Girlfriend?'

'It's the line the family is taking. I heard a whisper he was being blackmailed over gay photos.'

'Really? Blackmailed to do what?'

'How the hell should I know?'

Elaine stood over her, waiting. 'Well?'

'Of course, it's fine. I can do it.'

'Good.'

'I don't know what happened this morning. I'm sorry.'

Elaine ignored her and counted them in. The studio fell into a hushed silence as the final few seconds disappeared and Gloria faced the cameras.

Chapter 37

Private Investigator Pete Young was a stocky man; Oliver called him Mr Grey. He was ex-special forces and blended in with any background, which is why he was the best in his field. Oliver trusted him implicitly; Gloria wasn't so sure.

His handshake was firm enough and he held eye contact, which was encouraging, but Gloria had a fundamental mistrust of anyone associated with Oliver on a financial basis.

Anybody could be bought. And furthermore, he'd once been paid by Roger, which was equally worrying.

Just because Oliver paid top dollar for the man stood in Roger's office didn't necessarily mean that he was good at his job. But it did mean he was unscrupulous. She reckoned she had a good idea of the sorts of things he'd done for Roger.

Gloria sat facing the window, listening to them speak. *Keep it in the family.*

She turned when they shared a joke and Pete looked pleased with himself, and Gloria was reminded of a wolf's smile when the pack closes down their prey. She hoped Oliver never set Pete on to her. Maybe he already had. She certainly wouldn't put it past her ex-husband. On that note, she listened to what the PI had to say.

'I've managed to find out a few things that help us. First, several gifts and payments made from your father to four of the women – this always looks good in these cases for the defendant because it makes the girls look like gold diggers, and the public don't like that.'

He waited for their approval. Oliver nodded. He moved on.

'Also, three of them were booked into hotels to stay with your father on several occasions, all logged; again, this looks good because it shows they were willing.'

Another nod.

'On top of this, one of the women's sisters is willing to go on record and say that her sister told her that Roger Wade was an easy touch and she stood to make thousands out of him.'

'When was all this?' Gloria asked.

'Between the years in question,' the PI said.

'Great work. Anything else?' Oliver asked.

'Legally, the Met is obliged to investigate, and they've been told to.'

'We know – they're due to pay us a visit imminently,' Oliver said.

'I'd have a lawyer present,' Pete said.

Oliver nodded. 'Will do.'

'The burden of proof is on them. In my opinion, there's no value in the CPS pursuing these cases because they're unlikely to get a conviction, not least because your father is dead and it would be simply for the public record. That's a big expense for something that's not black and white.'

'Good. Case closed,' Oliver said.

'Case *virtually* closed,' the PI said. Pete spoke as though he had previous experience of cases like this one, and Gloria shuddered to think what that might have involved. She couldn't help feeling that the three of them gathered in Roger's office were there to collaborate and ruin women's lives, further to the pain they'd already suffered, but neither of the men in her company was interested in that. And to be honest, her mind was elsewhere.

'Two of them have filed spurious cases against men before, and the cases were kicked out.'

'Excellent,' Oliver said.

Gloria's attention was absorbed by a seagull flying outside the window and she was reminded that London had once been a port. It still was, of course, but not like in its heyday, when ships from across the globe would clog up the docks with goods, and women waited for the sailors to relieve their stresses so they could make enough money to feed their children; women providing a service for men with cash to pay.

Not much had changed.

She missed the rest of the conversation but was aware when Oliver showed Pete out, thanking him and shaking his hand. She turned and thanked Pete too, before he left. He was resourceful and professional, she gave him that much.

Oliver closed the door after him.

'That was positive,' he said.

She nodded weakly.

'Do you need a break?' he asked her. He kneeled in front of her and looked into her eyes, and suddenly she felt examined, and wary. He took her hands. 'I'm worried about you,' he said.

His gentle attention was jarring, and she stared at him as she would a total stranger. Then she looked down at her phone, which she'd been clenching all morning. The last communication with Max had been two hours ago and she'd heard nothing since. Now, neither Jilly nor Max was answering her messages.

She looked at Oliver, who stared up at her, waiting for her to respond to his concern. Her insides felt like jelly.

His face hadn't changed that much at all in the years she'd known him; he still possessed those piercing eyes that stripped her of all falsehood. His hands rested on her knees and she felt the heat through them. His closeness unsettled her and she suddenly felt naked. He saw through her. He saw everything. She couldn't keep it from him any longer.

'I've got something to tell you,' she said.

Chapter 38

Oliver's face turned purple with fury.

Gloria had witnessed plenty of Oliver's incendiary rages, but she'd never seen him like he was now. His eyes looked as though they'd pop out at any moment.

'How could you keep this from me?' he roared.

He'd squeezed her legs angrily before standing up and turning away from her.

She sat totally alone and terrified of what might come next. It was an unfamiliar sensation for her. She was always in control. She was always certain. She was always sure.

But now she floundered like a floppy fish out of water, writhing and twisting, trying to get air into its gills, but failing and slowly suffocating in agony.

And she'd only told him about the USB.

To Oliver, she'd kept it from him for a few hours and his anger was because she hadn't come to him straight away. She dreaded to imagine what his reaction would be should he know the truth about the letters and them mentioning Jilly by name.

'Have you got it on you?'

'No, it's in my dressing room,' she said.

He slammed his finger onto his iPhone screen and called Jilly time and time again, each attempt only getting voicemail.

'Fuck, Gloria! Hours matter! What if she's been taken by somebody who wants to blackmail me about Dad?'

It was all about him.

Typical.

'I didn't know what to do. She promised she was coming straight here – she'll probably be in an area with no signal.'

'If she hadn't called me, I wouldn't even know she was coming back to London. You intended to keep it from me, didn't you? You had no intention of telling me at all! I caught you out and now you're panicking because she's not answering her phone. Jesus, Gloria, it's our daughter!'

Guilt trickled through her body. He was right. Her decision to keep him in the dark was selfish.

'Fuck!' Oliver kicked the table and missed, so his shin went straight into the hard wood and he howled in pain. He charged out of the office. She called after him, thinking he'd gone to run around the streets of London shouting their daughter's name, such was the madness of the morning, but he came back in under a minute, with Pete – who hadn't yet made it out of the building – and slammed the office door.

'Tell him,' he demanded.

'Don't speak to me like that,' Gloria said in a controlled tone.

Pete stared at her, then Oliver.

'A new development?' he asked.

Gloria took a few deep breaths and began speaking. She told Pete everything about that morning since receiving the USB. But she held back telling them both about the anonymous letters from 'her friend'.

'I need to see it,' Pete said.

Gloria nodded and left the room. Her whole body shook as she approached the lift and it took her less than five minutes to return with the USB. When she went back into Roger's office, the two men hushed their chat and she eyed them suspiciously.

They played the device on Oliver's laptop and Pete studied it. Oliver had to look away several times and Gloria found it difficult to watch her daughter on the threshold of her home, looking so carefree and young. Her life was in danger because of them. What Gloria had always feared – that her life with the Wade family would never leave her – was happening right now.

'What time did you receive this?' Pete asked her.

'I don't know – it was there when I woke up at four this morning.'

Oliver looked at his watch. 'And she left Durham at six?'

Gloria nodded. 'That's what she told me.'

'What do you mean, "what she told you"?'

'She was annoyed – I couldn't tell her why I wanted her home – and she thought I was being awkward. I'm not sure she even took me seriously. Which is why she phoned you.'

'Is Max with her?' Oliver asked.

'Who's Max?' Pete asked.

They both turned to him and noted the change in his voice.

'Her flatmate, her best friend. He's travelling with her,' Gloria said.

'You've tried her phone?' Pete asked.

'Ten times in the last fifteen minutes,' Oliver said.

'Car reg?'

Oliver gave it to him.

'I'll make some calls.'

'We've got to call the police,' Oliver said.

Gloria felt her whole world giving way beneath her and she stared at him.

'What if they make it worse?' she asked.

'How could it be any worse?' Oliver bellowed.

'We don't know where she is yet.'

'Why are you being so obstructive? I don't get it. I know you are a heartless bitch, Gloria, but this is your daughter.'

She glared at him. *Mother or child?*

'What are you not telling me?' Oliver asked.

She looked away.

Pete finished his call and addressed them both.

'I've got a mate at the Met searching for her car. She should get a hit in the next hour. If Jilly is on the road, she'll let me know. You need to report this, but there are ways to do it to get maximum attention. For one, I'd forget the lad, say she's alone.

Second, have you had any other contact from unusual sources lately? I know you guys must get all sorts of nutters contacting you, especially you, Gloria, but did anything stand out?'

Gloria looked away; Oliver noticed.

'Pete, can you give us a minute?' Oliver said.

Pete nodded and left the room.

'What is it? You've had previous? What the fuck? Gloria, you better tell me or I'll—'

'You'll what, Oliver? Let me think, for Christ's sake.'

'No! Goddammit, Gloria, tell me now!' He slammed his hand down on Roger's desk so hard that coffee spilled out of a mug, but Gloria didn't flinch.

'Sit down,' she said.

Oliver glared at her and she repeated the command.

Oliver did as he was told and waited. 'Well? I'm sat down.'

Gloria took a breath, then told him about the letters. All of them. Every disturbing detail, including all the references to their time in Manchester together, when Roger was at the height of his power and influence, and women were discarded from the Wade Media Group with the same frequency as day followed night.

He sat down.

'This isn't about Jilly,' he said. 'It's about us.'

'And Linda.'

Chapter 39

When Oliver asked Pete to come back into the office, he'd had a return call from his contact at the Met. Jilly's car had been spotted driving down the A1.

As promised, she was coming home.

They breathed a sigh of relief with the news.

But Pete's face didn't reflect their joy. In fact, it did the opposite.

'That was an hour and a half ago. A member of the public called in to say that a car was found abandoned near junction 10 of the A1.'

Oliver and Gloria stared at him.

'It's Jilly's car. There's no one inside.'

Gloria's world fell away beneath her, and she collapsed into a chair.

She couldn't speak. Her mouth had lost its muscle memory and the mechanics that make the bundles of nerves and muscles function seemed lost. She stared at her phone and called Jilly's number again. Her fingers felt numb as she heard the call end.

This time, Jilly's phone was switched off.

'We haven't got time for that,' Pete said.

Gloria looked up at him in a daze. Pete's face was sympathetic, but he looked hard, like his military roots. He spoke softly, though, and brought Gloria a moment's calm, before the waves of dread hit her again. Oliver slammed something and it made her nerves shout out for him to stop.

'That won't help either,' Pete said, turning to him. 'I'll drive the route of her last known movements. By our reckoning, she would have been at the junction where her car is abandoned around eleven o'clock. That means she's been missing for under two hours. I need to get going.'

'What about the police?' Oliver asked him.

'Involve them, but don't expect anything to happen fast. Jilly is one of thousands of missing persons.'

'But she's not just anybody! She's my daughter!' Oliver boomed.

'I know who you are, and so does the rest of the country, but to whoever has taken her, and whoever took that video, she's prey, which makes her just like everyone else. And that's why I'm leaving now.'

'I want to come with you,' Gloria said, trying to stand.

'That won't help either,' Pete said and left the room.

The door closing left the two of them in a finality that was impossible to accept.

Oliver went to Gloria and kneeled in front of her. He looked as if he was appealing for something. Forgiveness? Liberation? His hands held her knees in a vice-like grip and she was reminded of how small she was, not just in stature, but in importance. She looked at him. She didn't have experience of this sensation… this endless notion of helplessness. Before the last few weeks, Gloria's life had been on track, but now it had derailed. It had happened that quick. The feeling gripped her like a stranglehold, and she felt as though every muscle in her body had just turned to concrete. She knew she was in shock, and she thought about the vodka and the pills in her dressing room. They'd take the edge off and help her cope with the sudden blow to her nervous system. That's what she needed, she told herself. She launched herself upright and went to leave the room.

'Where are you going?' Oliver asked her. He was like a little lost boy appealing for somebody to take notice of him.

'My room. I need to get my things. We need to go and look for her. She's out there and we're in here, and we can't stay here, Oliver, we can't.'

He went to her.

'Breathe, Gloria. Come on, calm down. That's right. In… Out…'

He stood in front of her, holding her and breathing with her, and she felt air start to enter her lungs, but she still thought she might suffocate.

'I'll come with you and then we'll go to the police. I'll call them as we walk.'

'Lucy…' she said.

'Lucy?'

'The detective who came about Andy Knight. Call her. She's good. She knows…'

'Knows what?'

She didn't answer, but instead concentrated on getting her feet in the right order as they walked to the lift.

She was hit by a swell of emotion and a sob caught in her throat, and she realised she didn't even have the breath to cry. They got into the lift and Oliver pressed the buttons. He called the commissioner of the Met.

'Ask for Lucy… Holt,' she told him. Oliver shrugged and relayed her message. They spoke for a couple of seconds and Oliver hung up.

'Come on,' he said, as the lift doors opened and they emerged onto the lower floor where her dressing room was. People walked past them and murmured hellos but they all merged into some strange underwater concerto to her. They reached her dressing room and she went straight to the drawer where the vodka was and, finding it, she pulled off the cap and took a swig. A box of pills spilled out across the floor as she did so.

Oliver appeared next to her and ripped the bottle out of her hand.

'What the fuck is this?' he seethed.

She stood staring at him, not knowing what to say or do. Her body had folded like a cheap cardboard box, and she had no idea what to do next. He stared at her then took her into his arms and held her tight.

'Jesus, Gloria, I had no idea it was this bad.'

It was his turn to allow his emotions to burst out of his body and he shook with pain. They held each other for what seemed like a long time, and she felt her muscles relax for a few seconds.

'Adderall? Elaine told me but I didn't believe her.' He looked at the blue tablets on the floor.

She said nothing because she felt nothing.

He pulled away and sat on a stool. She kneeled on the floor and scraped up two pills into her fingers and downed them with another gulp of vodka. He held out his hand and she passed him the bottle. He took a few gulps and winced.

'One of us needs to remain sober. That'll keep me going. What do we do?' he asked.

He wiped his face with some tissues from her dressing table and she packed a few things into a holdall. She needed time to think. She changed quickly into comfortable clothes and didn't give a damn about the photographers outside waiting to pounce.

'Whoever took the video, we need to find them. Who'd do that? Why Jilly? I don't understand,' he said. 'We need to search for clues in the letters. Have you got them here?'

She nodded and pulled them out of a drawer. They were folded together, having been straightened out once they'd been screwed up in anger. She'd collected them together for something, perhaps knowing they wouldn't stop coming until it came to this.

He scanned them and his face turned to horror and disgust, and she wished she'd told him earlier and felt desperate stupidity for thinking it could have been him.

Gloria hadn't heard Oliver's voice so broken since the day she'd told him she was leaving him. It had taken him by surprise. He'd cried, like he was doing now. It wasn't often she saw his heart, but she could see it now, if she looked close enough. It had shocked her then and it rocked her now.

'Lucy Holt told me that Andy Knight had photos of me in his apartment.'

'What?' he said.

Her mind was clearer now. Her body was still struggling to function, but the booze had helped. She felt more focused, and she was determined to drive the energy of her trauma into something useful. They had no time to lose.

'Never mind. This isn't about Andy Knight, not directly, at least. It's about who he knows. It could lead us to Jilly.'

She stood up, satisfied that anything she didn't have with her she could buy. She packed the vodka and the pills too, then zipped up the bag.

'If I'd known, Oliver…'

Oliver stared at the letters.

'Christ. It can't be *him*, can it?'

Gloria didn't respond straight away. Memories from long ago assaulted her head and she realised her stupidity.

'I thought you took care of it,' she said.

'I did. Jesus, let me think.' He paced up and down her dressing room, running his hand through his hair and waving the letters around as if it would make them reveal their author.

'Little Miss Sunshine?' he asked her.

'My key fob – we used my car, remember.'

'Who the fuck would know that?'

'I have no idea. Somebody on the inside?'

'No, they wouldn't have waited twenty years. Why now? This is personal. And you said Andy Knight had photos of you?'

She nodded. 'And Elaine said it was odd because he was gay, or so she said, so why would he have pervy photos of me? It doesn't make sense.'

'Because he was gathering them for someone else, for money. Didn't he have financial trouble? I feel so fucking useless,' he said.

Gloria realised that Oliver had a naturally investigative mind. He was right.

'I was such a fool, Oliver. I should have told you, I'm so sorry.'

He looked at her.

'There's no time for that.'

Tears sprung from her eyes then, originating from deep down in her chest, and they simply fell down her face. She'd never been a fan of criers, thinking them self-indulgent and dramatic. But now she couldn't shut her own supply off. Oliver's phone rang.

'Yes?'

He nodded and told whoever it was that they were here at the studios and that they'd wait. He ended the call.

'That was DS Lucy Holt,' he said.

'That was quick,' she said, finding a tissue and blowing her nose.

'I knew the commissioner wouldn't let me down – he owed Dad a few favours.'

'I'll say.' It was a lighter moment, if only a tiny flicker of good humour, coming after her darkest hours, and she noticed her breathing had become easier. Adrenaline – and amphetamines – had kicked in and she was ready to kick some butt and find her daughter. Roger Wade might have made secrets disappear for the commissioner of the Met Police, but his own were coming back to haunt those he'd left behind.

Chapter 40

Dear Gloria,

Jilly gave me your personal number.

If you want to see her again, do not show this to the police.

If you do as I say, then you'll see her again.

Once she digs her way out.

Down in the ditch, your little mole tunnels away.

But she has no claws, so what does she do? She makes noises like a little mouse, but mice cannot survive down here. Do you remember that feature on the oubliette, Gloria? I hadn't heard of it until I saw it on your show. You tried to come across as sympathetic when you stumbled across the story of the poor girl who was locked in a dungeon by her cruel father, but I saw through your fake horror. You didn't care. But perhaps you will now Jilly is with me and underneath the ground, locked in her own hole in the mud. The French named it the oubliette, you know. Because it means 'to forget'. In medieval times, it was simply a gap between a wall, just big enough to fit a human body. It had a locked grate above it and was typically situated in the basement, close to the kitchens. Victims were locked in there and forgotten, able to smell the food cooking for the lords. Meanwhile, those locked away starved and dehydrated to death.

Live entombment.

But you've been doing that for years. Hiding away what is dear to you.

There are lots of different methods of immurements, of course, not just physical. You can be trapped by fear, for example, like you are now.

Jilly's succumbed to it quicker than I thought she would. Her perfect face went pale so suddenly, and she's transformed from belonging to a member of the ruling class to one from the underclass.

She is suffering.

Like you.

On the sofa this week you haven't been your calm, collected self. Is it the shock of that young technician's suicide? Why would you care about that?

No, it was something else. Things are slowly unravelling for you, Gloria.

You're in trouble, aren't you? I can feel it.

Your day will get steadily worse, I promise.

I've only seen you scared once before and I can't wait to look into your eyes and see it again, but this time there'll be no one else there.

Just me and you, Gloria.

I can hear her screaming. Her throat is dry.

I sit above the grate in the ground and stare at her, which makes her worse.

'Mummy isn't coming,' I tell her.

She's whimpering and clawing at the mud on all sides of her.

She's got fight in her, your little girl.

Chapter 41

Gloria couldn't breathe.

She passed her phone to Oliver, who read the text message and squeezed the handset so hard, his knuckles turned white.

Knuckles...

'There's no number, I can't reply... I can't...'

Letters were intrusive and personal, but a message on her phone was suddenly so much worse. It was a medium of familiarity that one used with friends, family, lovers... not stalkers.

So this was how it would be from now on. He could message her directly whenever he chose and she would be waiting next to the phone like a coiled-up spring, at his beck and call, locked in dreadful anticipation.

'Look at me,' Oliver said. 'We will find her. I've sent Pete copies of the letters and I'll send him this too. He might be able to trace it. Whoever this is, they want something. Jilly is worth something alive. Where's Gloria White? I need her right now. I need her to fight.'

Gloria nodded.

'Let me handle DS Lucy Holt. I'll do the talking,' he said.

'I'm okay,' she said, recovering. He was right. She must pull her head out of her backside and concentrate. She was no use to Jilly if she gave up.

'I have faith in Pete,' he said.

'We can't tell the police about the letters,' she said. 'He said he'll hurt her...'

He nodded in agreement.

'It's too risky. If this bastard finds out, there's no telling what he might do.'

'Agreed.'

'But we'll show them the USB.'

They were sat in a recording suite on the ground floor, waiting for DS Lucy Holt to arrive. They'd been informed that a DCI had been appointed in charge of their case, but DS Holt would take preliminary statements. And so began the prehistoric sluggishness of the police machine. *No wonder criminals are always three steps ahead*, Gloria thought. But their daughter was only a priority to her parents, not to the general public, and they had no evidence, yet, that she had come to any harm. Pete had talked them through the steps the police would take, and what to expect. In the meantime, he had a head start and had already left London.

DS Lucy Holt and her sidekick, Eddie, were shown into the studio and they looked sombre.

Introductions were made and sympathies passed on, as well as assurances they were doing everything they could – and would do – to find Jilly. Gloria couldn't help feeling as though the cops radiated a judgemental pity stare of 'I told you so'…

'An angle we're looking at is the link to Andy Knight and his suspicious behaviour before he died, namely, the images he had of you, Gloria,' Lucy kicked things off.

Gloria nodded. It had been decided that they should give a press release to the public to go out on the news channels, including the Wade Group's, to maximise the chances of finding Jilly.

They still hadn't informed the police that she'd been with Max.

It was one of Pete's theories that Max was involved, and although this idea was horrific, they couldn't rule it out.

How well did they know him, really? Could he want money? He wasn't from the same background as Jilly and had sponged off her from the moment they met. He lived rent-free, he drove her car and he'd been with her when she vanished. Pete was looking into it.

'We suggest you both remain here for the rest of today,' Lucy said.

They were virtual prisoners at the studios anyway, since the news had broken. Some news sources were reporting that they'd staged the whole thing to divert attention from the suicide of one of their employees and the stories about Roger Wade. It was sickening but logical; it's what Wade Media would have reported if the tables were reversed.

Gloria listened to Lucy and Eddie speaking, but the sounds coming from their mouths merged into one gelatinous mass and Gloria didn't hear the individual words or statements, just facile promises to do all they could. They were noting down all the information they could give them, like what Jilly was wearing, her probable route and the time they left Durham, as well as the last contact from her. Gloria wondered if this is what all parents were told when their babies disappeared. She'd had the parents of missing children on her orange couch before, but she'd never empathised like she did now. Shock had turned to despair and despondency, and her body felt numb. She was aware of Oliver nodding and answering questions.

When the two detectives watched the footage from the USB, she heard Lucy suck her teeth. Eddie scratched his head and smiled sympathetically. It was an awful reassurance because Gloria felt as though it was one of those smiles that is given by executioners just before certain death.

'And when was this sent to you?'

'It was put through my door last night.'

'You didn't see by whom?'

'I was asleep. They disabled the alarm and the CCTV camera.'

'And you warned Jilly?'

Oliver and Gloria glanced at one another. 'No, we didn't want to scare her. I just told her to come home,' Gloria said.

It was Eddie's turn to suck his teeth.

Gloria felt wretched, as if it was her fault. She should have warned her daughter. She should have treated her like an adult and told her the truth, and then maybe she would have been more vigilant. They should have driven up there themselves and told her to barricade herself inside the house until they arrived. A thousand other scenarios played through her head, all but the one she actually chose.

'We've had her car towed to a compound where it will be processed.'

'How long will that take?' Oliver asked.

'It depends on the compound. We can't promise anything, but forensics usually come back within a few weeks.'

Gloria felt an overwhelming desire to take the female detective by her hair and force her head down onto the table in front of her with such force that it smashed her face in.

She smiled instead. Pete had been right about them being slow. She wondered how he was getting on.

Oliver's phone buzzed and he excused himself and left the room.

'We've assigned a liaison team to help you through this,' Lucy said.

'A what?'

'It's a victim-support service. Sometimes it's good to have professionals around in these moments.'

Gloria set her face into an awkward grimace. Oliver came back in the room.

'All right, sir?' Eddie asked.

'Yes, all good. Just work.'

Something in his tone told Gloria that it was no such thing and probably an update from Pete. She was desperate to get rid of the police. They'd taken their notes, and Jilly's case would be thrown into the churner of public priorities.

'Well, we'll leave you two alone now. The liaison team will be here soon – they're with another family at present. And we'll keep you updated,' Lucy said, standing to leave.

They shook hands and Gloria saw them out of the office.

Oliver turned to Gloria once the door was shut.

'That was Pete. Max has been found.'

'Where?'

'Somewhere on the A1. He was found by a member of the public and taken to a local hospital near Stevenage.'

'Has Pete spoken to him?'

'He's there now. The police haven't been informed yet because Max was seriously injured, and he hasn't been communicative.'

'Injured? How badly?'

'Pete didn't say. He's working on it. He told them some bullshit about Max having mental health episodes and running away from home; they bought it, I guess they're too busy to care.'

'He's with him now?'

Oliver nodded.

'We need to see him – he saw who took her.'

'Hold on,' he said.

She was up and ready to go out of the door, but he held her back.

'It'll take two hours to get there, by the time we get through London traffic. Meanwhile, we have no idea where Jilly is; she could have been taken closer to London, or further away, we just don't know. It's best to stay put and wait for Pete to report back. That's what he told me to do.'

'How can I stay put?' she yelled at him. 'Oh, God, Oliver, I can't… I must do something,' she said.

'I know, I feel the same way… Fuck it. Let's go. We can't just sit here.'

Chapter 42

They left through the back entrance and told no one except Elaine, who was instructed to deflect any questions. The front was chaos. Since Jilly's disappearance had hit the press earlier, there was a rumour circulating that Oliver Wade and Gloria White were scheduled to deliver a press statement together. It was potential TV gold.

Elaine said there must have been a hundred photographers and reporters outside the studio. Oliver had a car brought to the back street and had chosen one of the Mercedes limousines with blackened windows. He drove. He said it would give him something to occupy his mind. As they pulled away and left the studio behind, Gloria felt as though they were finally doing something. The movement beneath her body and the growl of the car's engine told her that it was doing its best to propel her forward, and it kept her in check. She leaned on the seat rest and stared out of the window. Their mobile phones were plugged in to the console and switched to loud, in case anyone called.

In case Jilly called.

They had to keep hoping they'd find her unharmed. That all this was a dreadful mistake. That Jilly and Max had an accident and Jilly would be okay. Anything else was out of the question.

Gloria's mind wandered to when Jilly was a baby, and before that, when they'd first moved to London.

The estate in Buckinghamshire, chosen by Roger, was beautiful. It still was. She'd spent hours wandering through its rooms, adorned with treasures from around the world, witnessing the testimony to Roger at the height of his wealth and power.

The drawing room was where guests gathered and were entertained, but it stayed mostly empty, except for the luxurious sofas, vases from China, rugs from Persia and paintings from all over Europe, probably stolen at some point by the Nazis, making their way from the murderers' hands, via Switzerland, into private collections owned by the victors of war, and sold on for millions. But Roger had millions to spend, and he bought countless precious artefacts to fill his new home. Money had never impressed or changed her, but she loved it nonetheless. To her, money was about freedom, not about things.

The house was full of rare vases, lacquered antique mirrors from Italy and replicas of Michelangelo's Sistine Chapel paintings. Money bought history.

Roger purchased the whole estate before they moved from Manchester, and it was decorated to his taste in under a month. That kind of power took her breath away back then. Some would say money and history were power, and that's what Roger believed too. Without it, he would've been just another businessman hustling to make a living wage. Success was so fleeting and relative; for every Roger, there were thousands who never made it.

The sitting room – called a parlour in the old days – stayed empty most of the time too, and Gloria realised after living there for some time that the whole estate in Buckinghamshire was a shell, where people existed rather than lived, and that's why she and Oliver had eventually moved out to the lodge.

After Jilly was born.

Images of her baby filled Gloria's head, and she felt as though she were carrying her in her arms as the car sped north on the A1, past Borehamwood, creeping northwards.

The nursery at the Wade estate had everything Gloria and Jilly could possibly need, but it wasn't what she wanted. The house had always been deathly silent, with Oliver and Roger in London all day, and Gloria spent hours alone watching her daughter sleep. A baby who had no idea what she'd been born into. Bottles, blankets, toys and soothers surrounded her, appearing without asking from the silent staff who moved around the house without footsteps. Time stood still there, and it drove Gloria half-mad. She was supposed to rest. To enjoy a break from the frenetic press meetings at their new offices in London. It was a total migration to the capital, after the national experiment of provincial posturing failed.

But *she* wasn't back in the capital. She was in rural Buckinghamshire, with no role but mother. She was a bystander in everything there, and the change in her status was made clear to her everywhere she looked.

The only thing she insisted on doing herself was bath time. Jilly smelled like soap and powder when she was bathed. For those precious minutes, the baby was all hers. At other times, she wandered the corridors, checking on her daughter to see if she was still breathing. Sometimes she panicked when she couldn't hear her. She'd walk into the hall and peer up the grand staircase and feel the need to check on her. She'd climb the stairs and walk quicker towards the top, gripped by sudden panic and questioning her sanity. Sometimes she sat in one of the bays along the first-floor hallway overlooking the vast land to the south, with Buckingham in the far distance. The view was only disturbed by the huge monolithic testimony to Roger's ego that was his burial tomb over the pond, and she'd never understood his desire to build it. Surely it reminded one of death? Be that as it may, Roger admired it, but Gloria loathed it.

One time she'd checked Jilly's room and found the door closed. Locked even. She'd grabbed the handle and twisted it, and finally it had opened. The room had been dark and airy, and the only light was from under the curtain, which billowed in the breeze. Her eyes grew accustomed to the dim vision, and she'd spotted her baby in the cot. She was a lump of white, swaddled in soft blankets from Fortnum & Mason. She'd walked to the edge of the crib and peered over, holding on to the side rail.

Jilly had been a wonder of biology and Gloria recalled having no idea how two people could make such a perfect thing. Her tiny nose stuck out from over the blanket and her cheeks peeked out like two soft bread rolls, round and plump. Gloria reached out her hand to stroke her daughter's cheek but pulled away, dazzled by its softness. She was a marvel.

Then Gloria recalled a door slamming and jarring her senses, and she'd left her daughter and peered out onto the balcony above the staircase.

Oliver stormed through the hall below and his father shouted after him.

'Son, please! We did all we can. You have to be patient.'

Oliver turned, and she dipped down beneath the rail.

'No, Dad. This needs to go away. She can never be found, or else… you know what.'

Gloria heard Roger rather than saw him. His breath was short because he refused to take his inhaler when he needed to. He wheezed and she felt his fear.

'If I go down, then so do you.'

She'd heard it before, but not from Roger. She'd never witnessed him threaten his son, and it made her worry for her Jilly.

'I told you I'd sorted it. The case is closed. The club will be investigated and closed down,' Oliver had reassured his father, but Gloria had noted the tension in his voice – had it been fear?

Gloria saw the grubby façade of the Bare Bunny reflected in her window as they sped past signs for the approaching A1. But it wasn't there; it was inside her head, where it had been decaying for twenty years.

In daylight, it had been more like a warehouse down a back alley, but at night, it buzzed with the promise of escape. But it had only been when a petite local girl walked into their offices in Manchester asking for a job that they began to see the club in an entirely different light. There was talk of it being at the centre of the high-end Manchester drugs scene in the nineties, but that wasn't news. What was of interest was that the girl told them she knew the owner, and she had a story to tell that could make their names.

Gloria recalled Oliver's interest being aroused and his attention towards the girl being a little too forced. She'd felt the first slithers of jealousy beginning to form as she watched her husband shape a slow-burning infatuation with the young intern, and she understood how the girl had managed to get close to one of the North of England's most notorious criminals.

Chapter 43

Jilly stared at the brown mud on the wall of her tomb. It was cold down there. She tried to keep some semblance of calm, which she failed to do when the bastard who took her came to gloat. She squinted up towards the sunlight to see him, to try to remember details of him that might be useful when she got out of here.

Not being found wasn't an option.

It had been so easy. Laughable almost. The guy had stopped them at the services on the A1. He'd said he was starving and wanted any help they could offer to buy some food. Jilly had taken pity on him and offered to buy him lunch. He'd given her some fake story about a little girl in the back of his car and had persuaded her to go with him to check on her.

All it had taken was a threat to her mother to make her do as he said and convince Max to do the same. Then they'd swapped cars along a country lane, near a little place called Newnham to get rid of hers, along with any evidence. She and Max had been forced into the boot, threatened with a hammer, then about ten minutes later, they'd stopped again, and Max had been ordered out of the car. She'd listened as Max was assaulted and then he stopped making any noise. Her heart had jumped out of her body, as she'd believed him dead, killed by the lunatic who wanted something from her, and knew who her mother was.

Of course he knew who her mother was.

Jilly felt foolish, but it had all happened so fast. She'd read in countless papers that abduction happened in stages, and if you got into a vehicle, you were 60 per cent closer to being murdered. But compliance had been their only option. The stranger carried two knives as well as the hammer, and one looked big enough to gut her with one swipe. Her nervous system had seized up and she'd gone from Jilly to victim in seconds. It was terrifying.

Now, in this disgusting hole in the ground, guarded by the slimeball who threw taunts and insults down to her whenever he felt like it, she'd revived and found her voice. But she'd called and screamed so much that her throat was raw and burning.

She'd refused to get in at first, but he'd punched her on the side of the head and she'd fallen down, then he'd pushed her in and she was lucky to have landed the right way up. It was a squeeze. But she could just manage to stand up and turn around, keeping her feet moving and hugging herself.

Night was falling and she feared for her sanity and her body. She reckoned she'd freeze to death, but then her rational brain told her that the evenings were falling to about twenty-three degrees at the moment. She might be uncomfortable, but she would not die.

Not in this hole.

Without her mother.

She couldn't touch the grate above her, and neither could she climb to it; the walls of the pit were too slippery. She'd managed to get a footing onto the side a few times but had slipped back down as she neared the grate, each time landing in a heap at the bottom. There was nothing on the floor of the pit, which was about two feet wide, and she reckoned ten feet deep. What sort of maniac did something like this? Dig a cavity in the earth to fit a young woman, to torture her there and let her die a slow agonising death?

Mum had warned her of nutcases who stalked her and sent her weird stuff at work. She'd suffered it her whole career. But Jilly hadn't really listened to her. It was like being told about the bogeyman, who came to prey on little girls when no one was around. Those stories worked for a while, sometimes, and they kept little girls away from strangers and out of cars, but what happened when they dressed up as normal people?

This had been planned, Jilly realised with a shudder.

She screamed again. Then stopped and told herself to fucking pull herself together. Max was probably dead – and it was her fault – but the last thing he needed was for his death to be in vain. She couldn't fail to get out of here because she was so immature and lacking in self-control that she drove the nutter to become even more nuts with her cries.

She had a stern word with herself and took a few deep breaths.

Think.

There was no use trying to work out what he wanted, so all she could do was look out for opportunities to either escape or manipulate him.

Mum knew there was something going on. Her voice when she'd called at four this morning and demanded that Jilly get back to London as soon as she could gave it away. She'd expected it.

Damn. And she hadn't told her. She'd treated her like a child and tried to protect her from the threat, but in doing so, she'd left her devoid of vital knowledge that could save her life.

A tiny worm wriggled in front of her face, having had its permanently dark home destroyed and carved into. Before today, she might have recoiled in disgust at the thing, but now she felt her nerves calm as the worm struggled to dig in and find a new tunnel in the mud.

It was alive.

And so was she.

Chapter 44

Max struggled to lift his hand when Gloria and Oliver walked into his hospital room.

'No, don't,' Gloria soothed him. It was as if being close to him made her feel she hadn't lost Jilly entirely. The clothes he was wearing, and the weak smile he gave them as they pulled up chairs close to his bed, were the last images Jilly saw and Gloria wanted to hold him to be as close to her daughter as she possibly could.

Pete had fobbed off the hospital staff with a story about Max being a relative. Oliver had also made a few phone calls to an old contact who was high up in the Hertfordshire NHS Trust and pulled some strings. Two of the Wade Group bodyguards had followed them up the A1 and were stood outside the door to prevent members of the public from cottoning on to who they were and spreading the word before they could take control of the situation. So far, they hadn't caused a stir, but it was only a matter of time.

One of the nurses had definitely been star-struck when she'd come to check Max's vitals. Oliver had been able to smooth-talk her into silence, for now, by asking her on a date. Gloria had never thought Oliver's penis would ever be so useful.

Max was able to talk, and that's all they wanted: information. He'd been the last person to see their daughter alive and he'd taken a severe beating for it. Pete had already done much of the work for them and he'd generated some leads. But nothing could have prepared them for what Max was to tell them next. What he'd waited to tell them in person.

Gloria stroked his hand and listened to his patchy description of the man, imagining him hunched over paper, writing letters to her.

Max had already told them he didn't get a good look at the man because he'd been inside the services, getting chocolate and coffee. When Jilly had told him of the guy with a sob story, he hadn't paid much attention either. That was the difference between an old soul and a new one, Gloria thought. Degrees of innocence.

'How tall was he?'

'Tall. He was dirty. He wore a hood.'

Grimy like the author of her letters.

'Did he say anything?' Pete asked.

'I was looking at the knives. I did what he asked and got in the boot.'

'You poor thing,' Gloria soothed. 'We need to update the police.'

'I've already done it. I updated Lucy Holt,' Oliver said. 'I told her that Max contacted us after being found. I told her we didn't know he was with her.'

'Why did you do that?' Max asked.

'It's a long story,' Oliver said.

'So, you wound up in the boot of the car?' Pete asked him.

Max nodded, trying his best, but he was clearly in a lot of pain. 'Jilly was beside me, but she wasn't moving, then the car stopped, and he put something over my head and dragged me out of the car, kicked me a few times and left me.'

'Is that unusual, Pete?' Oliver asked.

Pete stroked his chin. 'Depends. How big was he? He must've been pretty strong to carry you.'

'He didn't carry me, he dragged me. That's when I broke my ankle – I felt it snap as it was dragged over the lip of the boot.'

'Ouch,' Gloria said.

'Did he say anything?'

'No, he just left me and drove away. I stayed there for ages, thinking he'd come back.'

'And the woman who found you?'

'She's a farmer. I was blocking the access to her field – she thought I was a pile of rubbish and nearly ran me over.'

'Have you had any prior unusual contact to this recently? Missed phone calls from wrong numbers? No caller ID? Your phone acting strangely?' Pete asked.

'No, I don't think so,' Max said.

'Is the car being processed?' Pete asked Oliver.

'Apparently, it's been sent to a compound,' Oliver said.

'Do you know where?'

'No,' Oliver said. 'But I can find out.'

'Is there anything else you remember?' Pete asked, turning back to Max.

'Like what?'

'Did she meet anyone she hadn't met before in the run-up to this morning? Something out of the ordinary? Did you have a chance encounter with a stranger that might not have been by pure chance? That sort of thing.'

Gloria listened to Pete's questions and realised he was a professional, the sort that Lucy Holt talked about. It was chilling to compare the service you could get if you paid enough for it. Oliver had just told her he'd informed the police of Max's link to their daughter's disappearance, and still nobody had visited the hospital. It was as if they were updating the police out of courtesy rather than because it made any difference at all.

But the police didn't know everything and the guilt still tore away at her. If they knew about the letters, maybe that would change their investigation and focus them more, although Pete had said not.

'Erm, there is one thing,' Max said. 'It's probably not important.'

'That tells me that it is,' Pete said. 'What is it?'

'She visited Frankland Prison yesterday.'

'What?' Gloria and Oliver said in unison.

'Our old criminology professor arranged it. She was writing an article on lifers.'

'Lifers?' Oliver asked.

'People serving life sentences,' Max said.

'Yes, thank you, I know what a lifer is. Why was Jilly allowed inside a category A prison to meet a dangerous criminal?' Oliver asked.

'She told me her professor worked there, but she said nothing about going inside,' Gloria said.

'It's not unusual for academics to interview inmates if they get permission, and Professor Love is his rehabilitation officer,' Max said.

'Whose rehabilitation officer?'

'I can't remember his name,' Max said, rubbing his head and lying down on the pillow behind him.

'Have you got this professor's number?' Pete demanded.

'Look in my phone. She's on WhatsApp.'

Pete scrolled through the phone.

'Why would she be so reckless?' Oliver said, but Gloria remained quiet. She knew her daughter's hunger for a story; and not any story, one that no one else was writing. She'd been that person herself many years ago. She'd put the story before everything else and had taken risks, even with her life. They all had. It was the only way to get noticed.

'It's all right, Max, it's not your fault. You've had enough, I can tell,' she said.

'But—' Oliver butted in.

'He needs to rest, for God's sake, Oliver. We haven't even informed his parents. Leave him alone.'

'I remember now,' Max said, and Gloria turned to him and suspected she'd been hoodwinked; had he known all along? Was he playing them? Had he kept it from them because he knew Jilly was in deep, deep trouble? Whoever it was must be a real class A thug. Suspicion rested upon Max again and she couldn't help wondering if he was part of the plan. She shivered. Who had the reach? It couldn't have been a serving convict who'd taken her, because he was banged up, but somebody had done his dirty work for him. A beautiful graduate playing around at amateur psychology would have been too tempting for a hardened criminal to resist. Jilly had walked straight into a trap.

'You remember his name? What's he in for?' she asked him, less sympathetic now.

'Murder.'

'Jesus,' Oliver said.

Gloria felt sick.

Pete got through to the professor and their attention was drawn away from Max to him. Gloria and Oliver listened to his quick conversation before he ended the call. They looked at him expectantly.

'She's pretty shaken up with the news. She's going to contact the Met herself. I said I'd text her a direct number to DS Holt.'

'So, who is the professor's muse?' Gloria asked.

'Someone called Declan Lewis. Yesterday was their first meeting. She is adamant that he had nothing to do with what's happened, but she extends her sympathies,' Pete said. 'Which is not in any way helpful but nice to know, I guess. I'll investigate his contacts, who visits him, what his background was before he got banged up.'

Pete was met with silent stares.

'What have I missed?' he asked.

Chapter 45

Gloria sat in the lounge of Jilly's London apartment. They'd got back to the capital at seven in the evening. It was gone nine o'clock now. So far, they'd managed to avoid the press. Elaine had done a good job. It would seem that no one knew where they were, but that wouldn't last for long. The story was still all over the news. DS Lucy Holt and DC Eddie Tate had joined them at the flat and promised this would be the final round of questions. Gloria held one of her daughter's cuddly toys; she'd had it since she was a baby and it had been a bedfellow in her first cot at the Wade estate, in the huge nursery that Gloria came to hate.

Her face stung with the tears she'd cried. Holt and Tate sat on chairs in front of her and asked incessant questions.

'If you two are in here firing questions, who's out there looking for Jilly?' she asked.

'We appreciate your frustration, Gloria, we do.' Eddie spoke to her as though she were a child, but she sensed that he was enjoying calling her by her first name. 'We've got dozens of officers out looking and working the leads. We recommend you stay here now and don't move around. We're having a job keeping the press at bay as it is. We'll be out from under your feet soon – we have several lines of inquiry to pursue.'

They were being told off and ordered around, and Gloria couldn't stand it. Inertia would be what killed Jilly if they didn't get her back soon. She'd been gone for over twelve hours.

Max had given a formal statement, the processing of Jilly's car had been fast-tracked and Declan Lewis was going to be interviewed as soon as possible the next day.

She thought she'd heard the last of his name.

'She interviewed a murderer this week – isn't it obvious what's going on here?' Oliver spat out. He couldn't sit and he couldn't settle. He'd been used to getting his own way all his life. He wasn't used to relying on others whom he couldn't pay to go faster.

'We appreciate your desire to piece things together, but the footage was first filmed in the spring, wasn't it? There's no evidence that Jilly even knew about Mr Lewis then, but be assured every angle will be explored,' Lucy said.

They still hadn't told anyone about the letters. They'd agreed that it didn't matter any more. Jilly being taken was clearly linked to Declan Lewis, they just didn't know how, and paltry details from twenty years ago weren't going to give them an address.

It made sense now that whoever wrote them was connected to him somehow. Declan Lewis would know all the details they contained. What they couldn't work out was what benefit they served him.

And why now, after all this time?

The police were working on a list of Lewis's known associates.

So, too, was Pete, and Gloria and Oliver had no doubt who would come up with answers quicker.

Lewis wanted something.

She twisted the stuffed animal in her hands, wringing it as if it was sodden with her tears. She'd forgotten all about Declan Lewis – almost – and she had no idea where he'd been incarcerated. Would it have made any difference if she had?

What are you scared of now, Gloria?

Several times, she'd considered blurting everything out to get it off her chest. She wanted to tell the detectives the truth about all the lies and the lies about all the truth.

But she knew that neither would help.

Lewis would let her go when he was done.

But done with what?

Gloria buried her head in the soft toy and hid.

Surely he wouldn't hurt her?

Layers of lies were coming back to haunt them, and she felt them creeping out from under the furniture as she sat idly on Jilly's sofa.

She got up to go to the bathroom, grabbing her bag as she went, and the officers watched her. She felt as though she had spiders crawling all over her and she couldn't wait to get to the privacy of the bathroom. As soon as she did, she threw two Adderall down her throat.

She'd become her own headline.

And she hated it.

The press had set up camp outside their houses, the offices and now Jilly's apartment, and Gloria's phone hadn't stopped ringing for comments and sound bites. People she considered friends, associates, trusted and respected colleagues had all called, trying to get information out of them.

When she returned to the sitting room, the detectives were asking Oliver questions about Declan Lewis and if he'd ever heard of him, and why Jilly might be interested in him.

Oliver looked at her, then back to the police officers.

'We had a few brushes with him in Manchester, back in the day, before he was caught,' Gloria answered for him.

Lucy Holt looked at her partner and Gloria could see their police brains whirring. Their case had just got a lot more interesting.

'What kind of brushes?'

Chapter 46

Gloria stared into the bathroom mirror and felt a mixture of regret and disgust. Regret at having ever met Oliver Wade, and disgust that she had raised a child with him. The anger she felt just under her skin was threatening to burst out through each and every pore.

It was his fault.

All of this was his fault.

He'd been smitten with the girl. She'd known it from the moment his behaviour shifted, and she also knew he'd slept with her.

Gloria remembered it like it was yesterday.

'So, what do you have for us, Linda?' Oliver had asked breezily. But the girl's smile told Gloria that they had shared intimacy. She recalled the girl's smile, because she was so pretty when she smiled.

They'd been sat in Oliver's office.

It was perhaps then, or later, she couldn't recall, that Roger had come in and met Linda for the first time himself.

'Hello, who do we have here, then? A new girl? When were you going to tell me? My, you're pretty.'

The nineties wasn't the time to attend workshops on toxic masculinity and inherent corporate sexism.

Roger was the boss.

End of story.

'I can get you Declan Lewis,' Linda had told them.

And the world stood still. Rivers stopped flowing and rain stopped hammering on their bleak Manchester windows. The clouds ceased their journey across the sky, and they held their breath.

'Declan Lewis? *The* Declan Lewis?' Roger had asked.

Gloria recalled watching her husband's face, and it was distinctly post-coital. The small, unassuming girl with the captivating smile had given them a gift that no one else could give them, and that made her more valuable than anyone in that moment. More valuable than Gloria.

That was when she knew Oliver had already slept with her.

People had been trying to nail Declan Lewis for years. Cops, journos, bankers, other dealers, competitors, the lot. And nobody had.

'This is a dangerous business, Linda,' Gloria had warned.

If only they'd stopped then.

'She has a point.'

Thank you, Roger.

'Do you know what you're getting into?' he'd asked her.

Linda had nodded confidently.

'She's been inside his circle for some time,' Oliver said.

They already had several regulars reporting from the Bare Bunny, from where Lewis ran his empire, but Gloria hadn't heard of Linda before.

'Under your own name?' she asked her. Red flags waved at her from behind her husband's head.

Linda nodded again.

As a couple, she and Oliver had been invited to the Bare Bunny club on many occasions, as was customary for those wishing to impress anyone of importance in the entertainment industry. The worlds of organised crime and recreational hedonism had been happy bedfellows for decades. It was where most celebs came unstuck, and where any good journo would hang out.

The first time she'd been inside, she'd felt out of place. It had been pulsating and dark. She'd felt old at thirty and instantly uncomfortable. But she'd relaxed a little and begun to enjoy herself when they were ushered into the VIP area and served expensive champagne. A large man with broad shoulders, a tempting smile and bright blue eyes, sporting a beard and an aggressive demeanour, approached them, and Oliver pinched her, indicating that it was Lewis himself. He'd sidled right up to her, with the bravado of a mountain bear, and shouted into her ear. They were ushered towards a roped-off area where she spotted footballers and *Coronation Street* stars all quaffing champagne. New Order throbbed over the sound system and made her body vibrate. Then she felt Declan's arm around her waist. He was strong, and electricity shot up her arm. But Lewis wasn't just a powerful man with a fearsome reputation; he was a modern-day mafia boss who was alleged to have killed over twenty people, although, of course, there was never any proof.

Like the Kray twins, they'd have to pin something else on him to get him behind bars.

'I don't rate newspapers,' Declan had told her.

They were privileged to be guests in his club.

She recalled looking at him and feeling his breath, two inches from hers, and asking herself how badly she wanted this story.

Not the story he thought they were telling – the story that had got them inside the Bare Bunny – the one about him donating half a million quid to send a local Mancunian boy to Italy for life-saving cancer treatment.

A different one.

The truth.

Next to them, a man bent over a glass table and snorted white powder off it through a rolled-up banknote. When he was done, he threw the note on the floor.

They were memorable times, lost inside a vacuum of otherness that Gloria thought she'd never have to face ever again.

But here they were, and she found herself dragging things up from a past she thought had been flushed away with the little white packets, and the grime of bodies rubbing up against one another, and all the things they'd done to get the story. And the way she felt when Declan Lewis put his hand on the small of her back.

Chapter 47

Dear Gloria,

Your daughter looks just like you when she's angry.

I grew up around strong women. I broke my mother's heart when I ruined the suit she bought me to work for Mr Lewis. It cost her a week's wages.

What a privilege it was, driving the main man, she told me. I wore my dad's only tie – a purple one with a green stripe – and felt like one of those models in a magazine. He paid me well but still tipped because that's the sort of boss he was. I can still feel the twenty-pound note he pressed into my hand, folded up into three like a fan. Three weeks before that, I'd been on remand inside Haverigg Prison, waiting for news of my case from my snotty lawyer. I got caught with a seven-inch knife two days after my eighteenth birthday. Prison was no place for a boy and Mr Lewis understood that.

He gave me a job.

Mam stopped working and I bought my own suits.

I paid my way, not like your spoiled brat. She's weak and delicate like a butterfly that I catch with one hand in the summer, but she has no wings to fly away.

She's a handful, though. Just like you, Gloria.

I told her as much when I shouted at her down in the hole.

I told her, Mummy isn't coming.

She's got a mouth on her, like her mother.

She's a lively one, as Mr Lewis used to say.

Old Mr Wade said it too.

I told her she's trending on social media. You and her both.

But not from down in the hole. It's not picture-perfect down there.

I stood in there when I dug it, and it was humid and smothering. Like a mother's womb, I imagine.

You were fearless once, Gloria.

You believed in what you were doing.

Before you sold us out.

Chapter 48

Gloria had received the new text fifteen minutes ago. But she was in game-face mode now. She was in control of her body and when it told her it wanted to shake, with anger and repulsion, she overruled it. They must maintain composure in front of Lucy and Eddie. Instead, she created a diversion.

'What happened to Tommy?' Gloria asked no one in particular.

The two police officers made intermittent phone calls, checked statements from their phones and relayed details back to them to see if any kind of pattern was emerging. Apparently, the coppers had software now that could do the work of twenty officers.

But what good are twenty coppers when none of them know what's going on?

'Who's Tommy?' Eddie asked.

Oliver looked at Gloria and answered for her.

'He was the manager of Lewis's club in Manchester, the Bare Bunny.'

'Tommy Fawcett. I have no idea what happened to him, but he was very close to Declan Lewis. He could be the kind of person who'd do his dirty work on the outside,' Gloria said.

'And why do you think this might have something to do with Lewis's club?' Lucy Holt asked. They'd filled in the coppers on how the nightclub scene around Declan Lewis used to be the place to land big stories. They hadn't elaborated.

Good question. Gloria thought quickly. 'These organised-crime sorts stick together, don't they? You're not telling me somebody like Declan Lewis gets sent down and simply stops being the head of an organisation like his, just because he is kept within four walls. If someone is doing his dirty work on the outside, it could be Tommy Fawcett.'

'This is the sort of information we can work with and look into,' Eddie said. 'Can you tell us why somebody connected to Declan Lewis might want to bring harm to your family in particular, if this is a targeted attack, which we have to assume it is.'

'Couldn't it be about money?' Gloria asked. 'Everybody knows Roger Wade just died and it makes Jilly a very rich young woman.'

Lucy tapped something into her tablet, which was more like a padded briefcase. They called it a Toughpad and Lucy had tried to lighten the atmosphere by telling them that coppers had to use them because they were notoriously clumsy.

Not with lives, Gloria hoped...

'Tommy Fawcett, here we go.' Lucy had a hit on her Toughpad and Gloria was impressed but appalled at the same time.

'He's got a long criminal record. Inside for seven years, in HMP Frankland, alongside our friend, Mr Declan Lewis.'

Eddie whistled. It was quite a moment, but rather than sit and piece together bits of the puzzle, Gloria was impatient for real results.

'He ran the office above the club,' Gloria said. 'There was CCTV everywhere, as far as I recall,' she added.

Eddie nodded and Gloria watched him read a police history of the club manager from his phone, which had updated from Lucy's tablet.

'He withheld CCTV footage that could have implicated suspects in the Linda Wilson murder case,' Eddie said. 'The footage was never recovered, which was inconvenient for Lewis, because he said it could have exonerated him. Awkward... Perhaps they weren't pals after all.'

Oliver and Gloria glanced at one another. Oliver answered his phone after it buzzed in his pocket and everybody held their breath, thinking it might be Jilly.

It wasn't.

Oliver apologised and left the room. Gloria watched him, wondering if it was Pete. Moments later, her own phone pinged and they suffered the same cycle of emotions again, only to be disappointed once more. It was a text from Oliver in the next room.

> Pete has spoken to Professor Love. She's due to attend Durham police station to give a statement later today. He thinks she set Jilly up with Lewis.

Gloria tried to react in a controlled manner, but her blood was boiling. Jilly had been thrown under the bus by her own tutor. Gloria had suspected as much all along. She hadn't liked the woman from the first moment Jilly had described her. She felt sick. Eddie eyed her suspiciously.

'Everything all right?' he asked.

She nodded and got up to pace the room.

'I really need the bathroom,' she said finally, disappearing into the hallway.

She bumped into Oliver.

'If I could get my hands on that bitch,' Gloria raged about the professor. 'What will she tell the police? Does she know where Jilly is?'

'Let's not get our hopes up. Pete is looking into it. It's more likely that she just arranged the meeting to get Declan close to Jilly.'

Gloria turned away. She felt suddenly very old, as if she'd aged ten years in the last few hours.

'I feel so helpless waiting here,' she said. 'I can't bear the thought of her in a hole in the ground.'

'Stop, you're torturing yourself. Now he's got your number, he's tormenting you. He's trying to make you desperate. The hole is a ruse to make you crazy.'

She went to her bag and got the bottle out, taking a gulp of vodka, at the same time as peering towards the door. Oliver came to her side and took it off her, throwing back a couple of sips. The most recent text message had shaken them.

'Want some of these too?' she asked him, showing him her Adderall.

'No thanks – slippery slope.'

'Christ, Oliver, you're a two-faced prick. I can't think how much you've snorted up your nose – probably enough to pay off the debt of a small nation.'

'We pick our poison. There's something about a prescription that puts me off. It's too… clinical.'

'I know what you mean, it's not fun enough. It's not naughty.'

He smiled. 'Yeah, I like that, it's not naughty.'

'Well, they work.' She popped two out and threw them back with more vodka.

'If your *Blue Peter* following could see you now,' he joked.

'Jesus, what do we do? This is hell. What if the police ask for my phone and they find the messages? We must tell them – it could help.'

'Stop that. It won't help. Pete has connections – he's our best bet in finding her.'

Gloria stared at him.

'Connections like the Met Police? Are you sure you trust him?'

Oliver went to her and put his arms around her, and she let him.

'We need to keep our heads. She'll turn up, we'll find her.'

She pulled back. 'Are you sure about that?'

He nodded. 'The alternative is unthinkable.'

'Do you think Tommy could be involved?' he asked.

She shrugged. 'He and Declan were joined at the hip.'

'It sounds like they did time together.'

'We should tell Pete,' she said.

'I already have,' Oliver said.

They walked back into the kitchen together and made coffee. The two detectives looked up from what they were doing, and Gloria felt exposed and her skin tingled. The conversation in the hallway had disturbed Gloria and a terrible thought was forming inside her brain. What if Oliver didn't want the police to be involved for a reason other than he believed Pete was more competent? He was so insistent that they shouldn't tell the police. What if he was limiting their knowledge to benefit himself in some way? To make sure they didn't discover something about him that could see him thrust into the spotlight. She thought about it hard. Given the choice between his own skin and his daughter's, what would he choose? Hadn't the author of the letters asked her the very same thing?

'Tommy Fawcett led the police a merry dance, and he was a violent thug, there's no doubt about that,' Eddie said.

Oliver appeared behind her and they listened carefully. They knew all about Tommy Fawcett and what he was capable of.

'He was Lewis's tech whizz and had us going round in circles for years. He's the chief reason we could never pin anything on the main man. It's skills like his that the Met searches for in recruits to keep ahead of criminals now,' Eddie said. He was proud of his job and Gloria felt a ripple of respect for him and what he was trying to do.

But they were so goddamn methodical; at this rate, it'd take days to find Jilly.

However, what Eddie said struck a chord with her; if Declan Lewis was ever looking for somebody to run his business on the outside while he was banged up, then Tommy would be the man to do it. Tommy had been way ahead of his time with computers and had advised Gloria and Oliver to buy shares in a company called Apple, which had split its stock in 2000, telling them that information technology was the future. She'd never forgotten it. If they'd done as he said, a thousand pounds would be worth about half a million now. Gloria felt a stab of nostalgia as she recalled Tommy with fondness, but it soon turned to fear. Tommy was close to Declan. He'd do anything for him.

'Can't you just go to Frankland Prison and interview Lewis and get him to tell you where she is?' Gloria said.

'It doesn't work like that. We don't just walk into prisons – it's out of our jurisdiction. We have to get the permission of the governor. And plus, prisoners don't just cough up details. They're already incarcerated so they play games to try to cut deals. There are ways to talk sense to them, but that's not our main problem where Jilly is concerned, because inside prison, Declan Lewis can't hurt her. However, Tommy Fawcett was released five years ago, so you could be on to something.'

'Oh God, no,' Gloria said.

'If it is Tommy who has got her, I know him. If you could find him, I could talk to him, negotiate perhaps,' Oliver said.

'Why would you do that?' Lucy asked.

'Because it's my fault his boss went to prison and his life was destroyed.'

Chapter 49

The next day, Lucy Holt and Eddie Tate were happy to have a change of scenery, even if it involved a four-hour drive.

Jilly Wade's London flat was becoming claustrophobic, and there was little they could do to move the investigation forward from there. They had enough information to be going on from what Jilly's parents had told them. Now, it was the turn of the liaison team to assess the family.

They chatted about the case as Lucy drove a steady seventy up the A1 to Frankland Prison.

They'd been given permission to interview Declan Lewis for a whole hour, starting at midday.

'Back in 2005, Manchester Police reckoned the cause of Linda Wilson's death was sharp force trauma, from the blood spatter analysis, but the kill site wasn't located until three weeks after she disappeared. It's a nasty one,' Eddie read from the archived file on his phone.

'Nice bloke, then.'

'She was his girlfriend.'

'They usually are.'

The disappearance of a local woman might have gone unreported in Manchester in 2005, especially one who was reportedly a working girl on the club scene, but Linda Wilson, though allegedly moonlighting as a call girl at night, was a trainee editor at the Wade Group newspapers, and her boss, Oliver Wade, was the one to raise the alarm when she didn't show for work for two weeks.

'When questioned why he'd waited so long, Oliver Wade said Linda was freelance and only checked in about once a week. That's what he meant when he told us it was his fault that Lewis was eventually caught. So he could be right, this could be about a grudge, but why wait until now? It's much easier to kidnap a small child, why wait till she's twenty-one?'

Eddie shrugged.

'It was a pretty big story,' Lucy said. 'She was pregnant.'

'Was the baby Lewis's?' Eddie asked.

'It's unclear. The prosecution against Lewis argued that was his motive, that the baby could have been somebody else's.'

'Did they find out whose?'

'Nope. Her body's never been found.'

'Unusual to get a life sentence at a murder trial with no body.'

'Yep. And there was no forensic evidence either. The kill site was assumed to be her flat, because of the blood spatter, but there was no physical evidence linking Lewis to her murder.'

They both fell silent.

The rest of the journey was spent discussing whose turn it was to buy coffee at the services and which junction was best to take to the small hamlet of Brasside.

'I wonder what it's like to live near a prison. It's the only thing the town is famous for. It's quite depressing really,' Lucy said as she searched for signs to the category A facility.

'Terrible reputation too,' Eddie said. 'Geordie playground for thugs.'

'And that's just the guards,' Lucy finished the joke for him.

It took them half an hour to park, get through security and collect lanyards for their visit. They'd been allowed recording equipment, but that didn't mean that Declan Lewis would be compliant. He was under no obligation to tell them anything. He was already serving life, with parole coming up next year, which was a possible leverage point, but really, he could tell them as much, or as little, as he liked. If only life meant life, like it did in the USA, Lucy thought.

'His parole hearing will probably be suspended because he's never told anyone where he put her body,' Eddie said.

'*If* he killed her,' Lucy said.

They were shown into a visiting area and Lucy was reminded of a school hall. The atmosphere wasn't as benign, but the chairs were plastic and far too small for adults. It was done on purpose, she thought, to keep visitors uncomfortable so they had to sit upright at all times, making it harder to pass contraband.

Declan Lewis was escorted in, and he was cuffed. His legs dragged as he shuffled awkwardly, but the precaution was necessary; category A prisons didn't mess around. He sat before them and made the most of his little excursion away from his cell by stretching and putting his arms – locked together – high above his head.

The coppers introduced themselves, and Declan yawned.

'You from down south? What you doing all the way up here?'

'We've come to ask you to help with our inquiries about a missing woman,' Eddie said.

'Cat got your tongue?' he said to Lucy.

'No, I'm fully capable of speaking, when I'm ready.'

She knew that the law was detested by the men inside these walls. It was responsible for taking away their freedom. Police, lawyers, barristers and judges: all were equally hated.

'Who might that be, then?' he asked.

'Jilly Wade,' Eddie said. 'She accompanied Professor Love to one of your sessions on Wednesday.'

'No way? Really? She's missing? Nice girl.'

Lucy couldn't read him. He was play-acting for sure, but they'd expected that.

'She's the daughter of Gloria White and Oliver Wade – heard of them?' Lucy asked.

'Gloria White off the telly?'

'The same,' Eddie said.

Declan whistled.

'You knew them? Back in Manchester, when they were reporters over there. They came to your club, the Bare Bunny?'

'Did they?'

'Must we play this game, Declan? You know very well that Oliver Wade was the person who reported your girlfriend missing. He changed your life.'

'Oh, and you think now I've nicked his daughter to teach him a lesson? Bit late, aren't I?'

'Or one of your associates?'

'Such as?'

'Tommy Fawcett.'

Declan watched the detectives, and Lucy got the impression he was sussing them out, and he would only do that for two reasons: either he knew where Jilly was because he was behind it and was buying time, or he didn't know where she was and wasn't involved at all, but was simply enjoying the sport. Either way, he wasn't giving them anything.

'You've always enjoyed Tommy's loyalty and he's been here visiting you in the last couple of years since he left. Good pals?'

They'd discovered the information on their journey north.

'You're sure to ask him when you drag him into one of your friendly chats,' Declan said.

'We'll be asking for an interview with him, yes.'

'Have you considered that the parents are making it all up?'

Lucy hesitated.

'There's no shame in it, making a mistake. I mean, you lot do it all the time. That's why I'm in here – you were bought by Wade money.'

'Why do you say that?'

''Cause it's true.'

'Okay, so tell us why the Wades would spend money on seeing you go down for murder.'

'Just a theory. I'm trying to put myself in the shoes of the father of a missing child. I don't know how that feels 'cause mine was never born.'

'Was it yours?'

'You fuckers.' Declan lunged across the floor space with lightning speed, but the guard was quicker and restrained him, forcing him back in his seat.

'You want to carry on?' the guard asked Lucy, who nodded.

'Tell us what really happened, if you're hanging on to the story that you didn't kill Linda.'

'Of course I didn't kill her, you stupid fuckers. I loved her.'

Lucy held his stare. She'd put money on him telling the truth, but what did she know? All the cons in here were slimy bastards who couldn't tell the difference between fact and fiction. They'd hang their own mothers to get what they wanted.

'Did you pay Professor Love to fix a session with Jilly?'

Declan smiled.

'Nope.'

Now Lucy saw his lie.

'That's curious, because ten thousand pounds was credited to her bank account last week.'

'Lucky girl – she's on shit wages. I have no idea why a good woman like that does this job.'

'So don't you understand why we're a little concerned that last week you paid a criminologist to get close to a woman who is now missing, and whose father you blame for your girlfriend's disappearance?'

'I don't blame Oliver Wade.'

'Who do you blame, then?'

'Look, if I'd wanted to get to Gloria and Oliver, I'd have done it by now. They stitched me up, sure, but they didn't kill Linda.'

'So, you blame Gloria too?'

'I didn't say that.'

'Yes, you did. Just now, you paired them off. I didn't,' Lucy reminded him. 'And how do you know Linda's dead?'

He glanced at them with a mixture of surprise and condescension.

'Have you seen the photos of the blood spatter under fluorescent light in her flat?' he asked.

'Yes, we have.'

'She's dead.'

'And where is she buried?'

'You're asking the wrong person – I have no idea.'

'Do you think the same person who took Linda has taken Jilly Wade?'

'No.' Declan sniggered.

'Why is that such an outrageous supposition?'

He didn't answer.

'Gloria wrote an article on you back in the day, when she was based in Manchester. It was one of the things that made her who she is today, set her star rising.'

'Did it?'

'Keep in touch?'

'No, I don't like journalists.'

'Why did you want to meet Jilly?'

It was the first time Lucy had seen him hesitate and he looked down. Lucy thought he was going to tell them something, but when he looked back, he was smiling. The interview was over; he'd given them as much as he was going to, the rest of it would just be sport to him.

'What was she like?' Lucy couldn't help asking.

'Who?' Declan asked.

Lucy stared at him. He knew who she was talking about.

'Linda.'

He swallowed. He looked away and back to them, then to the window.

'Twenty years is a long time in here. Why have you never appealed?' Eddie asked.

'What's the point? Once you're stitched up by those fuckers in wigs, you're never getting out. It all fitted into place. They fucked me from the word go, and their money was behind it.'

'The Wades?'

'Aye.'

'So why don't you tell us what they did.'

'It won't make no difference to me.'

'But it might make a difference to somebody.'

'There are people who think they were behind it.'

'But you said they didn't kill her.'

'Aye. But I didn't say they didn't pay for it. Or at least the father did.'

'Roger Wade?'

'I'm done.'

'Declan, has Tommy Fawcett taken Jilly Wade on your bidding?'

'No.'

'Do you know who might have taken her? Declan, this isn't her fault – she's an innocent woman. She doesn't deserve to be discarded and thrown away, just because—'

'I know that! Don't you think I know that? If I knew who it was, I'd tell you. She's a nice girl. A good girl.'

'Like Linda?'

Lucy saw Declan's eyes mask over with something – regret? Sadness? Loss?

'Yes. Like Linda. If you want to know where she is, you need to look closer to home. That's me done.'

Chapter 50

Gloria held her phone close to her body all night. When it ran low on battery, she plugged it in and checked again. She'd spent the whole of Friday doing it and the days seemed to be passing her by. Her head felt like it had when she, Oliver and Jilly had gone scuba-diving in the Red Sea. She'd hated it and her ears had felt as though they were exploding. Jilly and Oliver loved it. The wetsuit had made Gloria feel like a whale stood next to Jilly, whose own diving attire fitted perfectly around her pubescent body and made her look like a slender sports diver who'd been doing it all her life. Gloria had ended up snorkelling instead, hovering above them, watching their shapes glide effortlessly in between rocks and giant fish. She'd felt as though she were spying, and it was a snapshot of something so beautiful, she shouldn't watch.

Gloria moved out that autumn.

She woke with a start, with tears in her eyes.

She rubbed them, and the wafer-thin skin covering them dragged across her eyeballs like a fine silk sheet over gravel. She reached over to the bedside table and took the glass to drink some water. Her mouth thanked her for the hydration, but her head still complained of no sleep and a punishing litany of self-loathing.

She was in Jilly's bed; Oliver had taken Max's room.

The pillow smelled of her daughter and she turned over to bury her face in it, sniffing the lingering after-scents of the Hermès perfume they'd bought together on Bond Street. It hadn't been a birthday, or any other special occasion, it was just a gift.

She'd give them all back just to see Jilly.

They'd wandered down to Burlington Arcade and Gloria had pointed out a pair of ruby earrings in Michael Rose. They'd laughed at her reflection in the glass because she wore dark sunglasses and a baseball cap when she went into London. Jilly said she looked like a *French and Saunders* impression of a peeved teenager.

The fragment of remembrance stabbed at her like a shard of glass, and she screwed up her face and covered it with angry fists.

Rage stirred unwelcome guests in her head, and she saw Declan's face suddenly on the pillow next to her.

She'd done it to get back at Oliver.

She'd known that Linda was his girlfriend. She'd known the lengths she was going to get her story. So, by the time she fell pregnant, everyone assumed it was Declan's.

But only Linda's corpse, with the foetus inside, could confirm the paternity of her child.

A feeling of stiffness spread through Gloria's belly as she dared to contemplate who else could have been the father, and why Linda's remains had never been found.

She shook it off, but Declan wouldn't leave her alone. He sat inside her brain like a computer chip, feeding her information.

He'd surprised her. His touch had been astonishingly soft. His attention was something she'd never received from Oliver, even in the early throes of their relationship, shagging like rabbits and being wonderfully reckless, doing stuff like eating food off their naked bodies and finding places to make love outside like it said in all the women's magazines about novelty bonking. She closed her eyes and rested the delicate lids, and she felt Declan's hand on her back, stroking her as he whispered to her that everything was going to be okay.

She could even smell him; the scent was palliative, and she didn't want to be let go from its potency.

His bedroom, as she recalled, was clean and grown-up. Again, another revelation.

He had good taste.

She pushed away thoughts of what his hands had done, what they were responsible for, and how she'd ended up beneath him on his bed. They'd moved together, and he'd stared at her face, pinning her soul down so it couldn't move from the place he'd brought her to.

The memory of it was so powerful that when she rolled over, after dozing off into another snippet of a dream, she imagined seeing him standing there at the foot of the bed, asking her if she'd like waffles or pancakes.

'You're not faithful?' she'd asked him.

'Nope. You?'

He'd made her laugh.

'I've discovered that life is so short, mine in particular, in this game, that it's my mission to grab on to what I can. Whatever opportunity comes my way, I'll take it, because when I die, I don't want to be like my father, who withered away, a mess of bitterness and anger at the life he'd fucked up. He always blamed everybody else, of course – the government, his mother, his wife, the horses,' he said.

She'd listened to him for a couple of hours before she'd realised she must leave, but she'd wanted to stay and she hadn't felt like that about anyone in a long time. Oliver made her feel as though she wanted to vacate a room every time he was in it. His presence caused a stress reaction inside of her that she was only able to quantify when she experienced something so deliciously the opposite that it made her stop and think about everything. It made her consider time, like Declan said he did.

'You should enjoy life more,' he'd told her. 'Don't take it too seriously, because what might be here today could be gone tomorrow.'

A bang on the door startled her and Gloria regretfully turned her attention to today's reality. She tried to figure out what day it was. Saturday, she thought; it was Saturday. She felt as though she'd lost a whole day waiting for phone calls and updates, and time had melted into one mass of tension. Her stomach churned as she recalled the image of Jilly in a hole in the ground. Unless he was toying with them.

'Yes?' she shouted in a croaky voice.

'I've got tea – can I come in?'

It was Oliver. He pushed open the door with his elbow and walked over to the bed, before sitting on the edge and putting the tea down.

'How are you doing?' he asked.

'So-so. You?'

'Same.'

'Any news?'

He shook his head. 'Max is on the mend – he has no other broken bones except his ankle, just sprains and bruises. He'll be released today. But his description of whoever knocked him out and took Jilly doesn't match Tommy Fawcett.'

'Have they found him?'

'I haven't heard.'

'He could be mistaken – it all happened so fast.'

He nodded. 'Do you think Declan is behind this?' he asked her.

'It's the obvious theory, isn't it? I knew it'd never go away,' she said. 'If only Roger was here to face the music – instead he's six feet under, getting away with it like he always did.'

'We had no choice.'

'Are you fucking kidding me? He should have gone down for what he did. Why did he deserve protection when if you're an ordinary dullard without cash, you'd be publicly crucified and thrown in a cell for the rest of your life?'

'Let's not do this again,' he said.

'Why? Does it make you feel uncomfortable? You know what, Oliver...' she said, getting out of bed and stomping around, gathering her discarded clothes from when she'd fallen into bed. 'This is your legacy. This is what he really left you to enjoy. And for the record, I don't think Declan Lewis is behind this.'

'Keep your voice down,' he warned her. 'What makes you so sure?'

She gathered her clothes into a large pile on her arm and went to Jilly's bathroom, pausing in the doorway.

'I just know.'

Chapter 51

Lucy eyed the professor as Eddie set up the recording equipment in an interview suite in a police station in the city of Durham. It was a five-minute drive from Brasside and a welcome relief to be out of Frankland Prison. Police weren't the most favoured visitors inside prisons.

Professor Love was nervous and understandably so. She had some serious questions to answer.

'Professor, we've explained that this is an interview regarding an active missing person case. You are not under arrest, do you understand?'

She nodded.

'Is she okay?' she asked.

'We can't discuss the details of the case,' Eddie told her.

'If you'd like to tell us about your relationship with Jilly Wade,' Lucy asked her.

The professor nodded.

'Jilly was one of my students – one of the most talented I've had.' The professor broke off to smile, but Lucy wasn't impressed.

The smile soon evaporated.

'She received a first-class degree in sociology.'

'Very nice,' Lucy said. 'What about your relationship? How close were you on a non-professional basis?'

'Non-professional?'

'Were you friends?'

'No, nothing like that. I... thought Jilly was a nice person, obviously...'

'Why obviously?' Eddie asked.

'Well, Officer, some of the students we get through the university are a little arrogant, and so they should be. They're young and inexperienced. It's their confidence that keeps them alive, is it not?'

Lucy side-glanced at her partner. They had no idea what the academic was going on about.

'So, you think she's nice. What else?'

'She's very bright, and a gifted writer.'

'You know who her parents are?'

The professor hesitated and looked around the room.

'Erm, yes, I think I do. Her mother is on TV, isn't she?'

'That's right, Gloria White, and she has all sorts of strange people contact her, begging for favours. Is that what this is about? You thought you could earn some easy cash by selling Jilly out?'

The professor looked horrified.

'I didn't...'

'Let's not pretend, shall we? We have a transaction of ten thousand pounds into your bank account last week. The source is an account in Merseyside that belongs to a known associate of your client in Frankland Prison, Declan Lewis. Did Mr Lewis pay you to get an interview with Jilly?'

'I...'

'Professor Love.' Lucy leaned over the desk. 'You're being recorded. This interview would go a lot smoother if you simply told the truth. Yes or no. Did you receive funds from Declan Lewis to get him face time with Jilly Wade?'

The professor broke down. She nodded lamely.

'Yes. I never thought it would lead to...'

'Lead to what? Her kidnap? Really? What did you think it would lead to? A convicted murderer asking to get close to a young woman whose parents are extremely wealthy?'

'I don't know,' the professor said.

'For a professor, you're not sure of much, are you?' Eddie said.

'When did he first ask you to arrange it?' Lucy asked.

'He didn't,' the professor said.

Eddie and Lucy looked at each other.

'She asked me to try to arrange it.'

'Wait a minute, that doesn't make sense. Why did he have to pay you, then, if she was willing?'

'Jilly was desperate to interview a convict. It didn't enter my mind to suggest Declan Lewis until after he'd told me about her.'

'What did he tell you about her?'

'He told me that he respected her work and he'd only be interviewed by someone he trusted. He said he knew her parents.'

'How did you react to that? A convicted murderer telling you he knew a TV personality and a rich businessman?'

'I didn't believe him. I thought he was delusional.'

'Yet you put the safety of a twenty-one-year-old woman at risk for ten thousand pounds?'

'I know it sounds terrible,' said Professor Love.

Lucy rolled her eyes at Eddie.

'Did he tell you his plans to have her kidnapped?'

'No! Is that what he did?'

Lucy glanced at Eddie and he knew it was his cue to leave it alone. The strong-arm tactics had produced a result and Professor Love had given them a confession for her part. Now she needed to be treated softly.

'Did you tell Jilly that he knew her parents, when you arranged the interview?' Lucy said gently.

The professor looked down at her hands. She shook her head.

'Why not? Did you not suspect his motives at all?'

Lucy watched the woman. She was tremendously uncomfortable, but then that was the point. No one who had done the dirty on somebody, like she had, should be allowed to relax in comfort. But there was more, and now the penny dropped.

'You got more money because you promised not to tell?' Lucy asked.

The professor nodded once, firmly.

'Is this everything?' Eddie added.

The professor looked away.

'Did you meet anyone outside of Frankland involved in this arrangement?' Lucy asked.

They waited.

The professor blushed, and Lucy couldn't help thinking that the shade complemented her lipstick.

'No. My involvement was simply to arrange the meeting. The payment was done online.'

'Do you know who is helping Declan on the outside set things like this up? We're presuming he's done this before.'

Professor Love squirmed at this and they knew they'd hit a nerve.

'*You've* done this before,' Lucy said.

The professor looked at them and her face was crumpled in agony, but it told them everything they needed to know.

Chapter 52

Gloria marched into the kitchen and headed for the balcony.

She stopped just short of actually venturing outside because she knew that the press was camped on the street underneath, with their long-range lenses aimed at the flat.

The apartment was strangely quiet without the two coppers who she'd wished would leave but now, in their absence, she missed. Eddie was humorous and had asked her about fame and how she coped. She'd told him funny stories about times she'd dressed up to escape cameras. She felt, in a weird way, that she'd lost an ally, though with coppers, you never knew.

The detectives had been sent up north to interview persons of interest but she was only concerned by one of them.

Declan Lewis.

Was he behind all this?

She searched in the cupboards for some food and pulled out a box of Special K. She was ravenous and it took her by surprise. She felt ready to fight today for some reason, perhaps because she felt inert and helpless stuck inside this flat. She was desperate to leave. She got out a bowl and some milk from the fridge and made herself a huge portion of cereal and sat on the sofa and stared across London.

She realised that it was when she was alone and lost inside some sort of contemplation about her daughter that Eddie would ask her lots of questions, but now he was gone, it struck her that he was only pally with her to dig for information, and she felt a fool.

She was desperate to find out some snippet of information about her daughter. She'd been told they'd be kept up to date but the lack of news was killing her.

There were so many leads to chase and loose ends to investigate. She wondered if Jilly's car had been processed yet. Had they looked for blood? Or fibres? Had they found anything? The investigation was grindingly slow.

It was one reason they had private healthcare. Service was directly proportional to the money you paid for it.

Lucy and Eddie were paid their wages whether they solved crimes or not.

That made them below par on performance in Gloria's book.

Gloria found the police fascinating. They were so damned *measured* in everything they did. Gloria had spent her life in heels and make-up, with the latest handbags swinging off her arm, tailored belts paired with cute sandals – worn once – and big, floppy hats matched with silk scarves for summer broadcasts. Objectives were barked in the morning and attained by lunch. These detectives selected their clothes for function and ease. There were no flashes of flair, or any accents to tell anybody anything about their personalities. They didn't care for trends or fashion. It was alien to her. Gloria was so used to projecting a certain confidence through her clothing and her performance being bolstered by her image that she didn't know what it felt like to be appreciated for her work alone. By 'work', she meant graft and effort, rather than simply appearing at a party or being photographed.

Gloria yearned to know how it felt to make a difference to the way people felt, rather than what they bought, or who they talked about, or what they looked like.

The business of policing was about making criminals pay for what they'd done. In that sense, a detective's job was giving something to families, like hers, whose pain never seemed to go away, and that was true nobility. Gloria had no idea if either

Eddie or Lucy had partners, kids or others to go home to, but they were out all hours, and driving up and down the country for their work. To get her daughter back, if they could.

She felt guilty for keeping information from them. But at the same time she knew they wouldn't find Jilly any quicker than Pete.

The inside of Jilly's apartment had become Gloria's cocoon. In here, she didn't feel fashionable or current, but she didn't feel useful either. In fact, she felt impotent.

Oliver came into the room deep in thought. He flicked on the kettle and she saw from his expression that he was sulking. It was just like the good old days.

Here they were, sharing a flat together, not speaking, with something terribly important to do, but neither wanting to face it.

'It's been two days,' Gloria whispered. She put her bowl down on a table and stared at her ex-husband.

'Oliver, we have to talk about Linda,' she said.

'Jesus, Gloria, don't bring that up again.'

'Why? What are you so afraid of? You've seen the letters, you know what Declan is capable of, and we're not talking about the elephant in the room, which is what your father did.'

He came over to the sofa and sat next to her. His body flopped heavily into the seat and she faced him.

A gentle breeze flowed in through the open curtains either side of the balcony doors.

'Remember when we used to dress up to go out, in caps and wigs?' he said.

For a moment, she almost smiled at the memory, but the rock in her guts never let her forget why they were sleeping under the same roof again, even temporarily.

She scowled.

The balcony beckoned her. It was big enough for a table and eight chairs, which sat empty because journos would have rented spots opposite and would be waiting to take her photograph to publish above the headline: *Gloria's Heartache* or *TV*

Star's Sorrow. A bit of simple alliteration went a long way in her industry. Anything to sell copy. She wished them no ill will, the people who were desperate to get their hands on her story, because she would be doing exactly the same if it was a colleague going through this nightmare.

She could just walk over to the edge of the glass barrier and slide herself over and fall to her death. It would hurt but not as much as losing Jilly.

'Rack your brains, Oliver. He's a driver. He drove Declan, and he drove your father. Don't you recall anyone?'

Oliver shook his head. 'There were so many.'

She shook her head. 'No. We're missing something. Who was that one whose mum died? He was thin and wore a suit. He smiled all the time. Roger used him for late nights. I can't remember his bloody name.'

Oliver looked at her in confusion. She knew that he couldn't remember the man she spoke of, not because Roger and Declan used so many drivers, but because he never took any notice. Oliver had been cosseted from the moment he'd been born; he wasn't primed to see danger in every corner like she was.

She'd spent her working life avoiding men like Roger Wade, who'd wanted to rub up against her and give her promotions for favours. Not that Roger would ever have done that to her, but she knew he'd done it to plenty of others.

'I feel responsible for giving her a job. She looked desperate. So small and keen. I let her in. Why did I do that?' she looked at him.

'What are you talking about?' Oliver asked.

'Linda! I employed her knowing what she was walking into.'

'Don't give me that, Gloria! She was Declan Lewis's girlfriend – she wasn't exactly a shrinking violet. She knew—'

'What was coming? God, Oliver, you sound like your father. She was innocent.'

'No, she wasn't. She knew exactly what she was doing the minute she walked into our office. She was playing both sides, and Roger found out.'

'No! Don't you dare tell yourself that! She might have backed two horses, but if she did, it was because she was desperate to make her name. She was chasing the story! Don't you see? You refused to give her what she wanted so she went back to him, but it was too late.'

'Don't, Gloria. Don't say it.'

'Why not? Are you afraid if I do, it will make it real? Declan kicked her out and you didn't want her either, so she got into that car with those men, and that man was driving. For God's sake, what was his name?'

'Benton?' Oliver said out of the blue.

'Benton? Benton! Yes! That's him.'

Suddenly, they had a joint mission again, and they put their heads together to remember everything they could about the driver called Benton.

'But if he was driving when Linda went home with my father, then surely he's just as guilty of what happened to her as anyone?'

Gloria stared at him.

'Theoretically,' he added.

But it was too late. A nagging doubt in her memory, forgotten long ago – or rubbed out – clawed at her attention. Nobody had said anything about Linda going home with Roger, just that she'd got into a car with strangers.

There was no going back.

Oliver had just confirmed her worst fears: whatever happened to Linda that night, he knew more about it than he'd ever shared with her.

Chapter 53

Gloria sat in Jilly's bath and found it comforting somehow to use her daughter's bath oil.

Her body was exhausted and the warm water, along with the scent, conspired to make her drift off into a light daydream.

In those long-ago days, when they'd frequented the Bare Bunny, Gloria usually found Tommy leaning against the wall behind the club, smoking, whenever she'd gone to see Declan. He was the only one who suspected her of being there a little too often, even for a journo. The Manchester sky was always grey, she remembered, and it matched the plumes of smoke Tommy blew above his head.

The empty ground behind the club, sparse apart from the odd pallet or plastic bag blowing in the prevailing wind that whistled through the city, was where he'd seen Linda on CCTV the last time she was seen alive. It had been the footage he'd withheld from the police.

Behind the club, where Linda shouldn't have been that night, you could hear the rest of the world going by at the end of the alleyway, but not see it. Cabs, buses and the odd police car zoomed past the end and never bothered to slow down to peer down the alleyway where Linda Wilson had been taken into a car by two men.

Tommy knew. Declan knew. And she knew.

So did the man who'd been driving.

The only reason why Tommy would have withheld information that could have helped his boss was if Declan had told him to.

Linda had never been a drinker, and neither was she a club-goer, but she'd hovered around the place, hoping to get noticed by the gaffer.

Gloria recalled how Tommy looked at Linda. It was obvious he'd fallen for her the first time he'd seen her on the security cameras covering the VIP bar area. Linda had worn a small red tube across her chest and a tiny black skirt, with a white handbag slung over her shoulder. He'd watched her from the comfort of the main office, like he watched everyone, above the throbbing dance floor. Linda had ordered a water, and that had caught his attention. He'd told her the story when Gloria smoked a cigarette with him outside.

The computer system he'd designed kept tabs on the bar receipts and the order matched what she was handed. It wasn't vodka or soda or a cocktail, but just a plain old plastic bottle of water, and he'd known then that she was trouble.

Linda had confirmed the story of how she met the boss, and how she spied Tommy, Declan's tough guy, watching her with lascivious eyes.

Declan never saw it. For all his hardman image and boisterous bravado, he'd failed to spot the side hustle. Nobody walked into one of the most exclusive clubs in Manchester and stood at the bar alone with a bottle of water unless they were high on drugs, or a journalist. And Linda didn't touch drugs.

It had been Tommy's job to know these things, and he'd tracked her that night, on the cameras, talking to people, and watching. Always watching. And Linda knew it.

Linda knew the boss was smitten with her when she saw him approach her, flanked by two bouncers who doubled as his personal bodyguards, although more for show than because Declan was worried about anything. Declan Lewis didn't believe anything, or anyone, could get to him.

Which was why Tommy watched his every move.

Gloria joked that Tommy was Declan's shadow.

From the quiet of his office, Linda had watched Tommy watching her through the glass. He hadn't been able to take his eyes off her, all the while with his boss whispering into her ear and making her laugh. When she did, she threw her head back and opened her mouth, and she could see him staring at his boss when he leaned in and got close to her neck, staring at it as if he wanted to touch it and squeeze it at the same time.

An incident had torn Tommy away from the monitors that night and Linda hadn't seen him again, she reported back to Gloria. The next time was much later, months perhaps, when she was whisked straight to the same quiet corner and waited on by the same two heavies, employed to protect the gaffer.

Gloria had seen the footage.

The tape had been given to Oliver, for the head of Wade media. Tommy had trusted them rather than the police. Gloria didn't watch the footage but Oliver told her about it. The fact that it existed and how they weren't planning to use it to find Linda.

It had been a very different Linda on the monitor that night, in 2005, staggering about in the yard, lost and alone. She'd been intoxicated, Oliver said, and it was no surprise she'd attracted the attention of strangers. It was the night Gloria had watched Linda squeezed by two men, the one that came back to her in the middle of the night. She'd been suffocated between the two men, who'd touched her and pinned her against the bar.

Nobody had seen Linda again.

Meanwhile, Tommy conducted his own investigation into the two men but came up with a dead trail that led to nothing. That's when he trusted Gloria to help.

Gloria had made Tommy a promise.

A pact that she'd never give up trying to find Linda. She'd asked Tommy to reassure Declan of the fact, by message, as he rotted on remand awaiting his fate.

Then came the stories in the local media of Linda being a prostitute and her work at the Wade Group being a cover for her illicit role at the Bare Bunny. Her reputation was slurred and her history erased. And Gloria knew the Wade Group was behind it.

But she did nothing.

Tommy had known then whose side Gloria had chosen.

Chapter 54

Dear Gloria,

You called me loyal once, can you remember?

I remember it so well because people didn't often pay me compliments. And it's a saying lofty people use to describe those who work under them.

But you noticed me when I drove you around in Declan's cars. And then later when your father-in-law gave me a job out of sympathy, you recognised me, and when you said my name, my head burned with longing.

The night I took that girl home from Roger's house, you knew, didn't you? You knew she wouldn't make it. Not Linda – no, it was way before her – but she looked like her, didn't she? They all looked the same. Like your daughter. Jilly.

I carried her.

She couldn't even stand she was so drunk. I was told to leave her there, but how could I do that? You understood. You told me I was right to care, and I was right to tell you.

You promised to ask after her and let me know.

If she'd been driven to the hospital, she would've made it.

It's her clothes that I remember. They didn't look right. She was missing a shoe and her skirt was on the wrong way round.

My mother told me to always look after girls because they can't fend for themselves. She was right.

That girl was so small. Like a doll.

She smelled of perfume and vomit. And she had blood on her blouse. I propped her up against the door where her parents would find her.

I never knew her name until I saw it in the paper, and I knew you'd lied to me.

Have you made Jilly the same promise?

She's calling your name.

Down in the pit, she's looking so frail and weak, and I only see you in her.

If she dies it's your fault, Gloria. She looks too weak to survive the fight. She's quiet and slumps against the damp mud. Her face is stained with your mistakes. Her nails are full of the filth you said you'd never feed off, but you do.

You said you'd save a girl once.

But you didn't.

And I don't think you'll save this one either.

Chapter 55

'Mr Fawcett, this is a preliminary interview to help with our inquiries about a missing person.'

Lucy and Eddie sat in similar chairs to the ones they'd sat in when they'd interviewed the professor, the only difference was the police station. They'd driven to Yorkshire this time, but at least it was on their way back to London. They'd tracked Tommy Fawcett to a betting shop outside Skipton. Now wasn't the time to go into the business dealings of the man, though they strongly suspected that the shop, along with other joint ventures controlled by Mr Fawcett, was funded with money from Declan Lewis.

They weren't here for that. That was the domain of Financial Crimes. Their one interest was the whereabouts of Jilly Wade.

Fawcett was a portly man but with kind eyes. Lucy reckoned in another universe he'd have been a teacher or a nurse.

But that was life.

Fawcett had first met Declan Lewis in his teens, before his life took a predestined path to here.

'Mr Fawcett, what is your relationship with Declan Lewis?' DC Eddie Tate asked.

'He's an old friend. I visit him in prison occasionally.'

Of course, that took away the element of surprise at the fact they'd seen him visiting the prison on CCTV.

'Just friends?'

'We're not lovers, if that's what you mean?'

The man had a sense of humour.

'No, that wasn't what I meant. I wondered if you had business arrangements together?'

'I look after his family, what's left of them.'

'And do you know this woman?' Eddie asked.

They showed him a photograph of Jilly. He shook his head, then smiled.

'Is she in the news? No, wait, her mother is! Yes, Gloria White from *The White Report*. That's her daughter. She was assaulted by her boyfriend the other night.'

Cute. He was way ahead of them.

'And this man.'

They showed him a photograph of Andy Knight.

'Never seen him before in my life.'

Liar. It was their turn to get ahead.

'So the IP address you share with him is a coincidence?'

The colour drained from Tommy Fawcett's face. Eddie couldn't help but grin; they'd been passed the nugget of information just this morning.

'We have a dedicated IT department, Mr Fawcett. It's not just you who has technical skill. Why would you share an IP address with someone who works closely with Gloria White and was being blackmailed?' DS Lucy Holt asked.

'I have no idea what you're talking about. IP addresses can be easily misappropriated. It must have been shifted on to my landline by somebody, I have no idea why.'

Lucy couldn't prove one way or another if that was the case. All she'd been told was that the photographs of Gloria White had been sent to Andy Knight's computer from an identical IP address in Skipton and it had been traced to the address of Tommy Fawcett.

She hated coincidences.

'Did you use Andy Knight to communicate with Gloria White?' she asked.

'Nope. Why would I do that?'

'Old times' sake? A catch-up on your Manchester days when you managed the Bare Bunny club for Declan Lewis.'

'That was a long time ago. Are you telling me that Gloria White used to go there back in the day?'

'Are you telling us she didn't?'

'Ah, now I remember. She used to come in with that dickhead of a husband of hers – the one who was shagging the boss's girlfriend. Yes. I do remember now.'

Lucy and Eddie stared at one another and Tommy sat back on his chair with a satisfied expression on his face.

Chapter 56

Gloria's mobile rang and she fumbled with it as she searched for it under a towel.

She panicked. It might be Jilly.

She was almost dry, having stepped out of the bath reluctantly. She wrapped herself tighter in her towel and sat on the edge of the bath.

It wasn't Jilly's number.

No Caller ID flashed on the screen and Gloria answered it breathlessly, thinking it to be the police.

'Hello, Gloria.' Her body suddenly turned cold all over.

She knew his voice. It was an echo from a different world than the one she lived in now.

'Declan,' she breathed. 'This will be recorded.'

'Wrong, the British penal system really isn't that clever. They won't even pick up a signal. I know someone who's good at cell tower manipulation.'

Gloria didn't even know what that meant.

'You've got yourself into a pickle,' he said.

'How the hell are you calling me?'

'Mini handsets smuggled inside the most unusual hiding places.'

'Jesus. What do you want? Have you got Jilly?'

'No. Don't be silly, Gloria, I'm in prison… thanks to your husband.'

'He's not my husband.'

Her heart was beating so fast that she could feel it through her chest, and she clung on to it tightly beneath her towel lest it burst out and take her life with it, preventing her from ever finding Jilly.

'Do you know where my daughter is?'

'No, I don't,' he said.

She covered her mouth with a corner of the towel and hot tears stung her eyes.

She believed him.

'Does Tommy?'

'Well, if he does, he hasn't told me, and Tommy is a lad who is loyal. You know what I mean, Gloria? Loyalty is that thing that—'

'I know what loyalty is,' she hissed.

You called me loyal...

'Do you, though? I don't think so. I know what you did to stitch me up.'

'Nobody stitched you up.'

'Is that what they told you?'

'Why are you calling me if you have no information about Jilly? You paid that bitch of a tutor to get her into prison to see you.'

'Now, that's not fair, Gloria. Professor Love isn't a bitch, she's just on government wages, that's all, and you can't blame her. She's just like you – Jilly, I mean, not the professor. You're not on shit wages, are you? What does it feel like to have so much money but not be able to get that one thing you really want?'

'If you called to gloat, you can fuck off.'

'Don't hang up, Gloria, wait. I might be able to help you.'

Gloria held her breath.

'Can you?' Her throat threatened to betray her, and it tightened as she struggled to get the words out. 'I'm begging you,' she said, gagging on her own desperation.

He didn't reply.

'Are you still there?' she asked.

'I'm still here. I think I can, but it's going to cost you.'

'What? Anything. I'll do anything.'

'Will you testify against your ex-husband?'

All the pent-up fury that she'd been holding on to held her body so tightly that she thought she'd stopped breathing, but a huge gulp of air ripped through her chest, and she bit her lip to stop it blasting the phone out of the window.

'Yes, I'll do it. Just tell me.'

'I already knew Roger before I met you,' Declan said.

'What?'

Gloria's mind was befuddled. They were supposed to be talking about Jilly, but now he was telling her about Roger.

'I'm not interested, Declan. All I want is to find Jilly.'

'This is background, Gloria, you need to hear it. I'm not going to make it easy for you unless I can trust you, and I made that mistake once before, didn't I?'

'I'm sorry,' she said quickly. 'I had no choice.'

'Everybody has a choice.'

'Tell me where Jilly is.'

'You know Tommy's a genius. He actually had a certificate through from Mensa and everything. You should get him on *The White Report* – people would love it. Tough man from the wrong side of the tracks with a brain the size of the moon.'

'How do you know about *The White Report*?'

He laughed. 'We watch you every day in here. We're you're biggest fans. I have to make sure the lads control themselves, mind. You're just as beautiful as you were then.'

'You watch me?'

'Of course! The lads in here love you. With your tight blouses and bright lipstick, you're the middle-aged con's answer to freedom – they spend hours thinking about you in their cells alone at night.'

Gloria took a few deep breaths and realised what was going on. She had to play his game in order for him to release the information she wanted.

'That's a good story.'

'Back to Tommy. He's so good at what he does that he's even able to make sure there's an outage in power to the digital network recording calls inside several prisons across the North of England today. He has a network of computer science geniuses helping him up and down the country.'

Gloria almost missed it, but in her line of work, she was familiar with the way snakes paused before they struck.

Could he be talking about Max? Max was a genius in technology, just like Tommy... Glue spread through her gut. Could they have been working together?

She swallowed hard and held her nerve.

'That's what I've been trying to tell you. Trust me, and you'll get Jilly back.'

'So, you do know where she is? You bastard, give her back to me!' Her throat rasped as she tried to shout as loud as she could without making a sound and rousing suspicion.

There was a knock at the door, and she shouted she'd be five minutes.

'Gloria, are you alone? I heard voices,' Oliver said through the bathroom door.

'It's Elaine on the phone,' she said.

She heard Oliver move away from the door.

'Coffee?' he shouted.

'Yes please,' she replied.

'You're an expert liar, Gloria, but you do it every day, so I shouldn't be surprised.'

'Stop it, Declan. I'll do anything you want, just tell me.'

'I need to hear you say it, that you'll testify against your ex-husband.'

'I told you I will.'

'But you haven't asked what he's accused of. You're just appeasing me. You're agreeing to anything because you're desperate.'

'Okay. I'll do anything, but I don't know what you're talking about, I admit it. How can I testify? What has he done?'

'Now, that is a question, Gloria, which needs longer than two minutes to answer. I'm amazed you're acting as though he's straight out of a Disney ensemble. Everybody knows what Oliver is.'

'Is this relevant? Now?'

'Tommy brought me some treats last week.'

'Treats?'

'Cadbury chocolate is the answer to all my prayers in here – well, not all of them. A few bottles of shampoo, cigarettes, Fruit Pastilles, batteries, anything I can sell. Oh, and Attilus Royal Siberian caviar. Do you remember that?'

Gloria imagined his face now. It had been twenty years. She'd only known him in his late thirties, at the top of his game, master of his universe. He lived like a king before she knew what it was to have enough money not to care. She recalled taking a spoonful of the small black eggs from a gold tin, heaping them onto a slither of toast and chomping on it greedily, all the while laughing and chugging back champagne.

'Yes, I remember it.'

'He also brought me information.'

'On Jilly?'

'He bought me a new Bentley last week,' Declan said.

'So, he runs your business for you?'

'It purrs like a grand piano, but I'll never know how it drives because I'm in here and I can't use it. But I can imagine. I have a very good imagination. I've dreamed I've done lots of things in the last twenty years.'

'I'm sorry,' she whispered.

'Sorry for what? Gloria, are you telling me that it's because of you that I'm in here? No, don't be so hard on yourself. If your adoring fans found out, you'd lose everything. Maybe Jilly isn't worth everything.'

'You fucking know she is.'

'Really, though? Do you know what you're saying?'

'Yes,' she said.

She leaned over the toilet and grabbed her handbag and reached into it, finding a sheet of Adderall and the quarter bottle of vodka that was the perfect fit for the Chanel tote. She swigged the pills down with the drink and focused.

'The Wades liked their Bentleys, didn't they? Still do?'

Gloria knew that Declan Lewis never said anything in his life that didn't mean something, and she tried to rack her brains to work out what he was telling her, in riddle, to play the game. She knew if she'd been inside for twenty years, if she lasted that long, she'd want to play games too. But this was a play-off for her daughter. The stakes couldn't be higher. She thought about Roger and his love of fine things, including cars. His Bentley collection was still in the vast suite of garages back in Buckinghamshire.

She recalled him being driven around in them, and how he treated them better than he'd treated his wife. The only person reserved special attention, more than his cars, was his granddaughter...

'She was his most precious possession,' she whispered.

'Yes, she was.'

'You're punishing him. This is about Roger.'

'I'm not punishing anyone, Gloria. I'm in jail, I can't get out. I haven't got Jilly.'

'But you know who has.'

'It's a guess,' he said.

'Tell me.'

'I don't do anything for free. My time costs money, even in here. Especially in here.'

'You knew it was going to happen, that's why you arranged to see her, to see what all the fuss was about. To see if she knew.'

'Actually, I wanted to see her for something else.'

Gloria shuddered and daren't ask what.

'Such as if she knew what her family was really like. I confirmed that she doesn't. She's as innocent as the driven snow that I don't see any more. When it snowed in Manchester, we used to drive up to the Lake District and get a steamer across a lake and stare at the mountains. We used to rent some crazy places up there. God, I miss those days.'

Gloria stayed silent. She didn't know what to say about the passage of time to a man who had been incarcerated for two decades.

'You almost stayed, didn't you?'

'Stop. You know the police are onto Tommy – he'll tell them everything,' she said.

Declan laughed out loud.

'One day he'll invent a chip to put into people's minds and that'll change everything. The man's a genius, did I tell you that?'

Gloria tried to piece together what Declan had emphasised. She knew it had something to do with Roger being driven around, and technology.

'Stop fucking toying with me!' she spat. 'This is my daughter's life!'

'And what about my daughter's life?'

'She wasn't even yours, Declan.'

It was out before she could stop her mouth.

But before she could back-pedal and take it back, the phone went silent and a shot of fear pierced her chest.

'Declan?'

She heard his breath and knew he was still on the other end.

'She was mine.'

'The baby? Are you sure?' Gloria felt powerful suddenly and armed with knowledge. The pills and alcohol had made her reckless.

'I didn't kill her,' Declan said. His voice had changed. It was low, controlled and resonant.

'I know,' she said.

'Help me,' he said.

'If you help me.' Gloria took a breath. She had no choice. 'How can I contact you?'

'Check your emails. The spam. There's a number.'

'How?'

'I have ways. The authorities are stupid and lazy. Tiny Zanco phones are worth a grand a pop in here. Mine is top of the range.'

'Where the hell do you hide that?'

'It's about the size of a mini chocolate bar, so use your imagination.'

He hung up.

Chapter 57

When she'd dried herself properly and changed, Gloria walked back into the sitting room and took a coffee from Oliver.

She smiled absently at him. Her mind was elsewhere.

She knew what Declan had been trying to tell her.

He was leading her to recall his driver, and she knew she was right about Benton Cooke. Now all she had to do was find him. She felt emboldened but jittery. Declan had given her a few pieces of a puzzle and she had to work out what he'd meant by it.

But she had a good idea, or she thought she did. The last message on her phone took her a step closer to narrowing the possibilities down. She'd seen dozens of girls taken from Roger's private apartments in Manchester and then London, drunk and unable to walk. And she'd met several drivers, but Benton stood out.

A loner.

And he'd also worked for Declan. He'd been passed on from Declan to Roger after his incarceration; the recollection jarred her.

Roger liked him. He trusted him.

He kept him on.

She recalled his face, vaguely, and the way he stared at her from the rear-view mirror, but she couldn't remember the conversation about the girl.

'I told Elaine to leave us alone,' Oliver said.

He talked with his mouth full. He was scoffing down toast. He'd always done it. For somebody who dined in the finest restaurants in the world, he had repulsive table habits, but manners didn't automatically follow money.

'Don't be mad with her – she's doing a great job. She just needed to know where some things were in your office. Any news? Do we know how Max is doing?'

'He's at home now, recovering with his parents in Leeds. He's suffering from shock, but his statements to the police have been helpful, apparently. He's been cleared of any involvement in Jilly's disappearance.'

'His parents?'

'Yes, why?'

'Jilly told me he was estranged from them, that's all… It seems odd. That was a quick recovery.' She scowled. 'Has Tommy Fawcett been interviewed yet?' she asked.

Oliver nodded. He'd received the update from Eddie. 'He went into his local police station willingly. Tommy doesn't match the description Max gave, and Max also gave a definitive no for his ID. Tommy also has a solid alibi. It leaves them unable to detain him.'

'So, a dead end? Did he tell them anything at all? What about his association with Declan Lewis?'

Oliver stared at her. She knew she was expecting too much. They'd been warned that anger was the worst enemy when waiting for information, but a creeping feeling told her gut that Declan Lewis, Tommy Fawcett, Benton Cooke and Max were all working together in some way.

'I've got all this energy that I don't know what to do with,' she said, and Oliver nodded.

'I can't stay in here,' Gloria said.

'You can't leave,' Oliver said.

'Watch me – I'm sick of doing nothing.'

She paced up and down.

'Tommy Fawcett visited Declan Lewis last week,' Oliver said.

Gloria knew the information was an attempt to distract her. And she tried to hide her prior knowledge of the meeting, thanks to her phone call with Declan. All she could think of was Declan eating caviar in a prison canteen, surrounded by murderers, rapists and paedophiles.

'I know that wasn't Elaine on the phone, Gloria. She called me,' Oliver said, as he finished his food and sat back in his chair, waiting for her to explain herself. His tone was sinister. 'What are you up to? Who have you been talking to?'

All Gloria could think of was that Declan knew where Jilly was, but she couldn't trust either man. The Bentleys kept coming into her mind, and all the times she'd seen Roger climbing into one, wearing a pinstriped suit and holding a chestnut cane, grinning at his granddaughter playing on the stone steps and waving him off as he was driven into London for an important meeting. The fine uniform of the driver, which wasn't really a uniform but was bought for him to look the part.

By his mother...

She thought about how many young women had sat beside Roger Wade, believing their futures were about to take off and that they were about to be propelled into stardom.

Linda included.

Then she remembered her promise.

It hit her.

The girl in the doorway. The one who Benton mentioned in his last message. The one who died of an overdose, because she hadn't made it to hospital, had been left in the doorway by a stranger. The driver who took her there and propped her up outside her parents' house so she'd be discovered. But it was too late. She half froze to death, and by the time she was taken to hospital, she'd been beyond help.

The driver pleading with Gloria to save her. Gloria calming him down and promising to ask after the girl and tell him she was okay. But she forgot. It slipped her mind, because there was so much chaos in the office, with the news ramping up over the Manchester drugs scene and the disappearance of young girls.

And her husband's affair with Linda...

It was a busy time. She couldn't remember who she made promises to all the time. She'd thought he'd forgotten about it. Gloria couldn't even remember the girl's name. There were so many of them. And some had got away.

It was Declan's driver who did jobs for Roger, and he'd taken pity on him after the trial and given him a full-time job. He'd relocated him to London and given him a flat, with all expenses paid. *Paid him off*... She'd seen the figures and questioned her father-in-law's sanity. The young driver had been the only familiar face from her Manchester days, but when she'd moved into the lodge with Oliver and Jilly, she hadn't seen him again. And that suited her. She hated the constant reminder of the North-West. Of seeing her husband with the young woman who'd been pregnant when she was viciously murdered by her boyfriend. Or not.

'Gloria—'

She realised Oliver was still talking.

'I have to get out of this flat, Oliver. I can't stay here any more,' she interrupted him.

'Where do you think you can go? Don't be ridiculous, Gloria, the press will cotton on the second you set foot out of here.'

'No, they won't. We used to do it all the time. They won't expect it. They'll be looking for Gloria White. I'll wear something so far removed from her that they'll never spot me. I don't even know if I want to be Gloria White ever again.'

Chapter 58

Gloria opened the service door and stepped out into the fresh air. She'd waited until there was a group of people leaving the gym that was situated underneath the apartment block, and she hid herself among them. She wore a baseball cap, which shaded the top part of her face and covered her hair, and some large sunglasses, found in Jilly's bedroom, with a long lacy shawl, and she carried a large plastic bag of rubbish she'd found in Jilly's utility room. She chatted happily to the group of people, and they were easy to distract with questions about the ongoing problems they'd had with the new windows sticking. She found herself in the middle of the group and they moved en masse to the leisure area at the back of the block, past several journalists and photographers waiting out there.

Once out of sight of the press pack, Gloria dumped the rubbish in one of the recycling bins and looked around. She'd argued with Oliver for a good twenty minutes before finally leaving, and after it all, she couldn't stop him doing the same thing. He'd thought her idea a wonderful diversion, not the ruse to get away from him that she intended, and wanted to come along.

She'd had an idea, but it didn't involve him. For it to work, she must lose him but she didn't know how.

Oliver left via the same back door. He looked comical and was wearing one of Max's oversized T-shirts, with a bandana he'd found in the washing pile. The arrogant arse looked twenty years younger as he swanned past the waiting posse of journos with ease.

Gloria and Oliver walked towards the river and found a bench to sit on. The area was busy with tourists, but they were deliciously anonymous because London hid a thousand other secrets. No one cared who they were.

'Who were you speaking to?' Oliver asked her again.

'Do you know what, Oliver? It's none of your fucking business. Leave it.'

He held up his hands and a couple passing by stared at them.

'Not here,' she said. 'Let's walk. There's a shop around the corner.'

'You don't need any more vodka,' he told her.

'How do you know what I do or do not need?' she asked him, but she didn't expect or want an answer.

'I'm going to the shop, you can follow me if you want.'

She strode away, quite happy to get rid of him and spend some time on her own. She felt like a prisoner and almost laughed at the affinity between her situation and Declan's. Her confinement wasn't anything like the lifer's, but she could feel the restriction on her freedom just by being locked up in Jilly's flat with her ex. She wanted to be near her daughter and wished she could get rid of Oliver. She wanted to fall asleep in her daughter's bed, on her pillow, hugging the soft toys she'd had since she was a girl. She craved something simple and the ability to recreate what they'd had in the beginning. The desire to connect with where she'd come from shocked her. She was much closer to Declan's origins than to those of her family-in-law, or Jilly. All her daughter had ever known was privilege; she'd enjoyed the trappings of her grandfather's empire since the day she was born, and Gloria wanted to strip it all back.

This was her punishment, and whether Declan knew anything or not about who held her – and she suspected he did – it didn't matter. He'd told her in so many words that Jilly's fate was in her own hands, echoing what it said in the letters.

Gloria had to make a choice between herself and her baby. Whatever she did now, it must be about getting Jilly back. She had believed it had always been about that, but Declan had made her realise that she'd been lying to herself the whole time, and if she wanted her daughter back, then all she had to do was tell the truth.

She must make a trade.

What will you choose?

Her life in exchange for the physical well-being of her child.

Declan knew how that felt because he'd once yearned to find his own baby when he'd lost Linda. It didn't matter if Linda's child wasn't biologically Declan's flesh and blood; it was enough that he believed it to be.

Gloria realised that Declan was in a win-win situation and the only people who stood to lose were Oliver and herself. Incarceration had liberated Declan from having to worry about the future, or the past. He existed in a world which was truly in the moment. He knew from experience that the prison service, especially the category A type, was brutal and unforgiving. One must live from day to day or shrivel and die, and Declan wasn't the type of man to give up. His voice demonstrated to her that he'd survived.

She went inside the small corner shop selling junk food, fizzy drinks, cigarettes, alcohol and souvenirs. Everything that was bad for a human under one roof, including the CCTV camera, which, to her, was the worst enemy of all.

She bought a half-bottle of vodka and asked the woman behind the counter to wrap it in a blue plastic bag. She went back out into the sunshine and saw that Oliver had wandered along the river to stand by a railing, gazing into the Thames. She joined him.

'This is the end of the road, Oliver.'

'For Christ's sake, Gloria, why do you always have to pretend the cameras are rolling.'

'I'm not being dramatic, I'm simply telling you what I've suspected all along. Ever since Jilly disappeared. It's our fault. She'd never have been taken if it wasn't for what we did.'

'Don't be ridiculous, Gloria, the fresh air was supposed to relax you, not make you crazier.'

The slur on her character was because she'd hit a nerve. She walked away from him.

Gloria would have laughed at his arrogance if her daughter's life wasn't at stake. But she remembered what Declan had told her about her email spam box. She took out her phone and went to her emails. There was nothing she didn't recognise, so she went to her spam box, and there it was: an email from a private personal address. Tommy Fawcett.

She was floored by Declan's brazen arrogance. He knew she wouldn't inform the police because they were forged from opposite edges of the same sword and neither existed in a world where coppers were welcome. He hated trusting authority because he existed in the shadows of criminality and she lived in the same shadows because she knew the value of protecting privacy, at all costs. It was still a risk for him, though, but then she reminded herself that he was serving a life term and had made peace with his demons.

She clicked on it and saw that it was a link to a video.

She pressed play, looking over her shoulder to make sure Oliver wasn't right behind her.

There was no sound. The first frame was Jilly's front door in Durham, in the snow – so at least six months ago, probably longer. She saw her daughter answer it. Then she greeted the tradesman and asked for some kind of identification. The guy must have had a mounted camera on his chest. He showed his ID and Jilly checked it, nodding. Then she turned and he followed Jilly through the hallway and into the large front reception room, showing him the understairs cupboard. He carried a torch, and it made the invasion more sinister somehow, as if the intruder had thought about how to prove his authenticity to an innocent student who trusted anyone knocking on her door.

She made him a cup of tea and, though the video didn't have sound, she imagined the noises of normality. Jilly laughed with the tradesperson, and Max appeared in the shot.

It was all she needed to know to understand that taking Jilly had been planned for a very long time.

Gloria felt sick.

But she'd made a deal with Declan Lewis.

He was her only hope of ever seeing her daughter again; whoever had her, whether Tommy could lead her there or not, this was another warning that if she involved the police any further, she'd never find her.

The sense of hopelessness was accompanied by a notification on her phone; the kidnapper had sent her another text. It was as if he couldn't leave her alone now. But in a strange way too, it comforted her, because if he was writing his thoughts to her, he wasn't hurting Jilly.

Chapter 59

Dear Gloria,

Death is a part of life. Declan told me that. It's something that we all must process at some point. When Declan paid for my mam to get cancer treatment at the private clinic in Manchester, I thought she'd pull through, because she had big money behind her, but even that couldn't save her. He paid for the finest funeral he could, just for my mam. It was beautiful, and he did that from behind his prison walls.

You have no idea what he was like when Linda disappeared.

You didn't see him give up and hand himself over to the coppers who came to humiliate him. He went with them willingly and they treated him like a savage, but he couldn't see any way out without her. Losing his baby was like losing his will to live, and I'd do anything to save him like he saved me.

You'd never understand loyalty, though, Gloria. He said you never did.

Looking at your daughter in the hole, I can see what she inherited from you and what she inherited from her father, and her grandfather.

I'm sitting on the edge of the hole. I've opened the grate and she thinks I'm going to let her out.

She's begging me.

She's telling me her family has money, that her mother knows people, her mother is famous and can give me anything I want. She's bargaining with me.

Her face is pleading with me and she's starving and thirsty for water, just a little drop to make her cracked lips moist. And she thinks I have mercy because that's what humans have, isn't it? Compassion. We do things to ease the suffering of others. Isn't that what drives us?

But what about when you have nothing left and you don't feel like a person any more? When nothing remains to make you feel anything at all?

She has something in her eyes, something ancient and imploring. It pulls me towards her, and I see them shining in the dark. I can smell the mud that surrounds her, and she looks as though she thinks I'm going to bury her in there. I wonder what that feels like, to be buried alive.

She thinks she can talk her way out. She can pay her way out. She can bribe her way out. But there is no way out.

She doesn't realise that to get out, all she must do is see me, not try to pay me.

Chapter 60

Gloria recalled the night she'd heard Oliver arguing with the new girl late at the office, thinking no one was there.

Oliver had been pacing back and forth, and she'd seen Linda go in there after everybody else had left. The fact that Oliver wasn't even aware she was still at work should have told her everything she needed to know, but she'd been compelled to find out once and for all.

She remembered jumping with fright when she'd heard something smash inside Oliver's office. She guessed it had been a vase or a picture frame. The door was open a crack and Gloria went up close to it, as close as she dared to without being discovered.

'What do you mean, you're pregnant?' Oliver had screamed.

Linda cowered by the door.

Gloria had got even closer then, straining to listen to the conversation.

'I mean, I'm pregnant with your child,' Linda said.

Gloria's heart had smashed into a thousand pieces, but now she knew it to be her ego. Her feelings for Oliver by then had dried up and blown away in the wind, and she knew his character well enough to decide that the marriage had been a mistake. But to have it so blatantly shoved in her face was a slap across it and a blow to her self-confidence.

But was she any better? Carrying on with Declan behind his back?

'I don't want a fucking baby!' Oliver had ranted.

Gloria had believed she'd seen all her husband's flaws in their glorious technicolour over the years, but the way he spoke to Linda that night had made her burn with shame. Yet she still hadn't gone to defend the girl, who was younger than Jilly at the time, and being abused by a man many years older than her, who just also happened to be her boss.

She'd heard Linda begin to cry.

'I want you to get rid of it,' Oliver had said. His voice had come down an octave and he was calmer, but his tone was more threatening.

'I don't want to,' Linda replied. Gloria's stomach had sunk to her toes because she knew what Oliver was like when he was disobeyed.

'You don't have a choice,' he spat.

But then he changed mood.

'Listen to me. I'm married to Gloria, and this would destroy everything for me.'

'That's your fault,' Linda shouted at him.

The girl was asking for trouble, and Gloria had wanted to hear no more of it, but she knew now that doing nothing had been a cowardly act and the girl had needed somebody – an adult, or at least somebody older than she was – to stick up for her in that moment.

'I'll take care of it – you have no choice,' she'd heard Oliver say.

Gloria remembered thinking back then that Oliver had sounded like a man who made problems disappear. Just like his father.

'We don't have to go public,' she'd pleaded. 'No one needs to know.'

She was begging him, and the tragedy of her predicament made Gloria fear for the safety of the girl, and she willed her to leave and comply with Oliver's wishes.

Do as you're told…

Give into the bully…

'I'm keeping it,' Linda said defiantly.

'No, you're not,' she heard Oliver warn her.

Gloria hated bullies, but she'd also interviewed countless people who were victims of tyrants who said they didn't see it happening as clearly as they thought they would, and by the time they were in danger, it was too late. But Gloria hadn't thought about those things at the time.

'Get rid of it – I'll take care of it. If you don't, your career is over – not that it ever began.'

'I'll tell Gloria and see what she thinks.'

Gloria froze. She had willed the girl to take it back, to appease him and to promise she wouldn't, but she detested the memory of those wishes. She championed women standing up for themselves all the time, and yet she had left Linda alone in that office with a man who was willing to do anything to silence her.

'You're sacked. And try to prove the brat is mine, and I'll tell Declan Lewis everything you've done for us.'

That was when Linda had opened the door to leave, and Gloria had hidden behind the water dispenser and watched her run from the office in tears. Gloria had stayed there for around an hour until she saw Oliver leave and turn out the lights. Only then had she come out and breathed normally, but she'd never told anyone what she'd heard.

Three weeks later, Linda disappeared.

Gloria watched him now, staring at the Thames, and she wondered if he was gawping at the river thinking the same as she was: that his past miscalculations were coming back to haunt him and he'd never see his daughter again because he didn't deserve to. She wondered if he was ashamed to think that Jilly might discover who he really was. She questioned if somebody like Oliver even felt shame and regret.

He received a call and she watched him answer it.

Gloria glanced up into the sunshine and allowed it to warm her face. She craved liberation from the nightmare they were in.

Oliver walked towards her, still on the call, and sat down next to her on the bench and mouthed that it was Pete on the phone. He looked buoyant, as if he'd heard some good news. She listened to their conversation, unable to work out what they were discussing, and waited until Oliver ended the call.

'Max remembered Jilly telling him about somewhere Declan Lewis mentioned in their session together. Some beach where he has a property.'

'Jesus, we need to tell Lucy and Eddie.'

Gloria jumped up, ready to deliver the news.

'Wait.' Oliver pulled her sweater.

'What? Oliver, she might be there. Come on! What are you doing?'

'Just hear me out – it'll only take a second,' he said.

She sat down next to him and crossed her legs, swinging one over the other in frustration.

'I think we should let Pete investigate. Think carefully about it. If we lead them to this address and it's a trap, it could expose everything. Let Pete check it out first. The whole point behind contacting you with those letters was to draw you in and make you reveal everything. That's exactly what he wants. Let's not rush in and give in to him. We're in charge, not him.'

She stared at him, with her mouth agape.

'You're playing with our daughter's life, Oliver,' she breathed helplessly.

She was reminded of the moment she'd stood outside his door listening to Linda's misery when he told her that he didn't want her baby, and she knew this was one of those opportunities. She'd hated herself for twenty years for not stepping in and now he was forcing her to do the same again, to save him, and to put Jilly second, like all the women in his life.

But, on the other hand, what he was saying made sense, and she hadn't forgotten how she was implicated in everything Oliver had done. She wasn't innocent herself. She'd sat back and allowed him to run the office like a tyrant. She'd told herself that hard work was tough and those who wanted to make it should step up and take the abuse, like men.

'Man up,' she'd heard a thousand times…

'Just give Pete a couple of hours to drive there.'

'Where?'

'Some beach in Norfolk.'

'Norfolk? Where is he? How long will it take?'

'He's on his way there now. He'll be there in two hours.'

'I thought he was in Stevenage?'

'No, he left there already, after Max was discharged,' Oliver said, and she suspected he wasn't telling her the whole truth, but she let it go.

'If I'm exposed along with my father, then the Wade Group will vanish into oblivion, and you'll lose everything you've built over twenty years.'

She stared at him.

She wished she could conjure up some of her trademark confidence like she did when she was on her orange couch in the studio, contemplating other people's problems and dishing out advice as if it were confetti, but she couldn't put her finger on it. She couldn't locate it when she needed it most.

She nodded.

'This is our best hope of getting Jilly back,' he told her, smug with his own cleverness. He acted like a hero sleuth who'd just cracked the case on his own. If he could pat his own back, she reckoned he would. But she felt dead inside.

'Fancy some waffles to take back?' he asked.

'Okay,' she said. 'Get some and take them back to the flat, I'll join you there.'

He smiled, satisfied with himself.

She watched him walk across to the waffle van, and then looked up and down the river. Southbank was busy, and if she threw off the scarf and clipped her hair up on top of her head, and walked very quickly, with her head down, she could be at

Waterloo station in ten minutes, where she could get the tube to King's Cross.

She shot off north along the river before she could change her mind.

Movement was the only thing that was going to relieve her.

And Oliver was lying, she could tell.

The place in Norfolk was exactly where they should be looking, but Oliver putting her off going there was a massive red flag to Gloria. He was going to use their daughter to make sure nothing came out about Linda, and Pete was in on it.

If she knew her husband, then he could have planned this all along. And it wouldn't surprise her if Pete's aim was to take out Benton before the police even knew where he was, and silence him forever.

Not if she got there first. Max might have recalled a random reference to a house that Jilly mentioned but Gloria knew the exact location, and it wasn't easy to find.

She had no time to lose.

Chapter 61

Gloria glanced back once and couldn't see Oliver, who'd been lost in the crowd that had formed outside the waffle truck, so she kept her head down and broke into a gentle jog, but after five minutes, she had to stop. She just wasn't that fit any more. Her throat was parched and her head thumped.

Besides, it was probably less conspicuous to walk. A middle-aged woman running in plain clothes anywhere in London would raise suspicion.

She passed the National Theatre.

When she'd walked a short way and the promenade began to get busier, Gloria took out her mobile and rang the number Declan had given her.

It didn't take long for him to answer.

'Gloria, you've just brightened my day,' he told her. 'That was quick, you couldn't wait to speak to me.'

'What does he want?' she asked him.

'Who?'

'You know exactly who I'm talking about. Benton Cooke.'

'You figured it out? It took me some time.'

'Bullshit, you've known all along.'

'I haven't, actually. But I'm not surprised you don't believe me – your moral compass has always been a little suspect.'

'Declan, I'm sorry about Linda. I didn't know—'

'You did. You let her down, Gloria.'

'Me? What about you? You knew she was carrying on with Oliver – I told you! Yet you allowed her to continue to walk into that trap. You knew what he was capable of, what his father was capable of, and yet you still allowed her to spy for you, knowing the risks. Don't pin this all on me.'

He didn't reply and she kicked herself for jumping in too soon; she worried she'd lost the connection.

'Declan?'

'I'm here, Gloria. I've got nothing in my busy schedule for the next few years. I'm all ears. You were on the bit where you were telling me this is all my doing. Forgive me if I reserve a little bit of smugness for myself at the irony.'

'You got clever.'

'I was always clever.'

'You were rough around the edges. You've been reading.'

'Funnily enough, people like me can read. There is salvation in education.'

Gloria stopped walking. Benton had written that exact phrase in one of his letters. She swallowed hard and reached into her bag for a swig of vodka. It took the edge off and she wiped her brow of sweat.

'You're breathing hard, Gloria. Are you in a rush?'

'I have somewhere to be, thanks to you. I remember. You know exactly where she is.'

'It was a guess – I can't promise.'

'Bullshit. Tell me about your house in Norfolk, is it still the same?'

'Clever girl – Jilly remembered.'

'What?'

'I mentioned it in my session with her.'

'It was on purpose?'

'I had a hunch.'

'So, you do think she's there?'

'It depends on how you handle the police.'

'This isn't a game.'

'No, you're right about that, Gloria, but you're the one making it gameful. Buying time, cheating, double-crossing. All I want is for you to trade one body for another.'

Gloria closed her eyes. 'Please don't say that, Declan.'

'I want you to tell the police that your stalker is offering the location of a body in return for the location of Jilly.'

'My stalker? How do you know? You knew? You knew all along. Wait, you planned this whole thing? Hold on, the location of whose body?'

The question was met with silence.

Gloria finally understood.

'You know where Linda is?'

'I have a hunch.'

'This was engineered to get you to this point of leverage, to arrange the quashing of your sentence.'

'You give me far too much credit. You'd like to think that, wouldn't you? That I've been plotting revenge all these years. But I do know the person you might be looking for and where he might be. Loyalty is a powerful attribute and the person you're looking for has it in abundance. I can't monitor everything from behind bars – there is such a thing as free will. But it's about time you started bargaining with what you have, because you won't have it for long. It's time to make your choice, Gloria.'

'Declan, wait, don't hang up.'

She spotted a young couple holding hands, strolling under the trees which were covered in sparkling fairy lights by night and swayed under the clouds by day. Children screamed in the distance and the London Eye looked like it always did – unmoving. She admired the couple's easy nature with each other. She'd stayed with Oliver for eleven more long years after leaving Manchester, even after learning of Linda's disappearance and choosing to believe Oliver about who was behind it. And after giving birth to her own daughter, keeping her affair with Declan Lewis a secret throughout.

'I'm still here,' he said.

Oliver never suspected. And he still didn't.

'Declan, Jilly is your daughter.'

Chapter 62

Oliver had driven her car that night, with her keys jangling off the Little Miss Sunshine key fob. The key ring she'd lost years ago.

Disappeared, like all problems facing the Wades.

The night Linda thought she was going back to Roger's suite with him – number 724 – she trusted him. After all, he was the man who was going to make her rich and famous.

Roger Wade commanded air like God.

Linda wasn't the first to try to bend his will and lose.

She must have been puzzled at first when they'd arrived at a different destination: her own flat. Did Roger plant evidence to frame Declan that night? After he killed her. That's what she now believed to be true. Enabling him to depict Declan as a heartless boyfriend who exploited her, then killed her when he found out she'd double-crossed him, then hid her body. Gloria recalled the jury all those years ago, entertained by the most expensive QC in London, lapping it up, wooed by the story and then hooked. They believed the prosecution's argument that lack of forensic evidence was down to Declan being a clever killer and doing an excellent cleaning job. Everybody in that courtroom who knew anything about the behaviour of organic matter knew that such an outcome was scientifically impossible. But the jury bought it.

Gloria hadn't told the police any of that at the time because she was never interviewed, and she was so relieved to be left out of such a high-profile case that she'd crawled back to London, with her own unborn child inside her, thankful to leave it all behind.

Gloria had convinced herself that she didn't tell the police about any of it because she wasn't asked. She didn't tell them about the women who were taken to his flat. She didn't tell them that Oliver was the father of Linda's unborn baby. Just like she told no one that Declan was the father of her own. She never testified to anyone that Declan wouldn't have hurt Linda. She never attested to his good character. It had been easier to go along with the prosecution's story that Declan was a gangland killer and murdering his girlfriend was no different to punishing his enemies on the street. She was a coward and behaved like one, thinking it was better off for her child to be a Wade than the daughter of a convicted killer. She chose a baby with a powerful name over the truth.

She considered her choice and believed it to be the most irresponsible decision of her life. One man went to prison rather than dragging her into court, which he could easily have done, knowing what a strong witness she would have made. The other man scurried around his father to protect his inheritance.

Declan knew.

He had to have known, or at least suspected. That's why he'd wanted to see Jilly in the flesh. To see if he saw a resemblance. It's why he paid Professor Love to arrange it. It's why she knew he'd never hurt her. To have defended himself would have caused Jilly's paternity to be revealed.

Oliver delivered Linda to his father because he was more scared of him than he was of what might happen to an innocent woman.

And Gloria had been too much of a coward to face the truth.

She'd thought it had been her choice to protect Jilly, but it hadn't, it had been Declan's all along. If she'd gone on the stand, then it would all have come out. And by waiting twenty years, he also knew that for it to come out now would cause much more damage to her.

Vengeance served immediately would have been less satisfying.

And of course, he couldn't do it himself, not just because he was incarcerated, but because he wouldn't have been able to inflict pain on Jilly himself.

Her terrible secret all these years hadn't been a deception at all.

She'd only fooled herself.

And protected Roger.

Chapter 63

Gloria's train sped north through the countryside from King's Cross to King's Lynn. She'd ordered an Uber for when she arrived and the house was ten minutes by car from the station. She was working on the assumption that it would take Pete hours to find the place. All he had to go on was Max's fuzzy memory of a snippet of information randomly passed on by Jilly.

Her guts turned over and over as the train rocked from side to side.

She recalled the last time she'd been there.

It was a party.

Thrown in her honour.

And only two people were invited.

He'd had food flown in from London by helicopter. They'd eaten his favourite Attilus Royal Siberian caviar, as well as divine foams over morsels served in terrines carried into the kitchen by three of the restaurant's staff.

Gloria had hidden from them in the lounge, even then terrified of exposing herself.

It was the last time she'd seen Declan a free man. She'd toyed with telling him then, about her pregnancy, so swept away was she by the romance and danger of what she'd got herself into, and the anger and betrayal of her husband.

But more pressing matters got in the way.

She remembered the remoteness, the helipad, the luxury and the long drive up to the house. As well as the feeling inside her abdomen and going over the dates two or three times to be sure...

Now, Gloria figured she could get there with a Google map. She'd already looked at the area and reckoned she knew where to start. Twenty years might have changed the landscape but she was sure she'd know the house.

The afternoon sun in Norfolk was turning orange, and tourists and locals who'd no doubt flocked to the beaches in the heatwave would be starting BBQs or going to the local pub for Cromer crab and chips.

Gloria stared out of the window.

She'd missed dozens of calls from Oliver and Lucy Holt.

Thinking about her phone jolted her, and she remembered something from the footage of the tradesman visiting Jilly's flat. She took out her phone and replayed it on silent, and rewound it, again and again.

There.

She'd thought it odd and distracting the first time she'd watched it, but now it made complete sense. During the visit to her house, the man had spoken to Max as he waited for Jilly to tidy the understairs cupboard so he could get in and pretend to read the meter, but as he was doing so, he filmed himself picking up a hairbrush, which was on the floor.

Declan did nothing by accident.

Then the brush was gone, and Max could be seen in the background turning away...

There was only one reason anybody would steal a hairbrush from a house full of expensive jewellery and other items.

To get DNA.

Declan always said Tommy had predicted how valuable DNA would become to the police in years to come.

When Declan met Jilly at the prison, he'd already known she was his, because he would have had Jilly's hair tested at a private lab – or rather, Tommy would have.

Gloria had kept her secret, never quite daring to believe the paternity herself. But when her baby was born, Gloria had known instantly. Oliver had been oblivious and focused on what he imagined was her strong resemblance to the Wade ancestry, but Oliver was simply smelling the power. Gloria was looking at her nose, the arch of her forehead and the colour of her hair. Jilly was Declan's and she'd got away with it.

On the train, Gloria contacted the two newspapers which had published the stories about Roger this week and asked for the details of their lawyers. She'd made the choice to take a posthumous stand against her father-in-law, by tipping off the police about the possible whereabouts of Linda's body. Just like Declan knew she would. It was a hunch, nothing more. It was the only place she could think of that a narcissist like Roger would feel safe.

And the place she'd seen the two men who intimidated and assaulted Linda in the Bare Bunny, the two men who even Tommy Fawcett had never been able to identify. The same two men he'd no doubt spent the last two decades trying to trace from the CCTV footage he kept from the police, at Declan's request, so he could punish them his way...

The same two men Roger used for his own dirty work. The men she'd seen coming in and out of the Wade estate barn on one particularly sunny Sunday, having done odd jobs for Roger. They'd been draining the pond adjacent to Roger's memorial tomb and had cleaned the marble structure.

They'd whistled as they worked.

The new information could reopen Linda's case and potentially exonerate Declan Lewis.

Gloria knew her decision was career-ending. So much damage had been done to the Wade name that public knowledge she'd covered for Oliver would damn her to hell, because even though that wouldn't come out, her discerning fans would set about reaching that conclusion from behind their TV screens. The keyboard warriors would close in on her. The betrayer of women. But she'd made her peace and it was long overdue. Watching Jilly grow had been agony in so many ways. Lying to her about her paternity was only one reason. Gloria's involvement in a woman's death – albeit as an innocent bystander who did nothing – was another.

The Uber was waiting for her at King's Lynn station and they sped away into the countryside. Gloria prayed she wasn't mistaken. She'd settled on one particular estate that sat nestled behind one of the quieter beaches, near Sheringham, and she remembered it had a high wall built around it, with tall wooden gates.

When they arrived, she knew it was the right place, but it was getting dark.

She was shocked to see no police cars outside the property.

Nobody had worked it out yet.

Gloria felt clever, but her mood soon turned serious again. The Uber dropped her at the huge gates, and now she had to work out how to get in, but as she approached them, they opened and she walked straight through.

The walk up the long drive seemed endless, and Gloria realised she was ravenous and dehydrated. All she'd consumed was the bottle of vodka, and a bowl of Special K in the morning, and a whole sheet of pills, over the three hours it had taken to get here. Her gait was slightly off and she tried to concentrate on the house that came into view up ahead.

The property looked deserted, but Gloria knew where she was going. And she knew that someone was expecting her.

The ground, the sea, and the sky all looked the same as she began to speed up, and soon she was jogging, right past the house, round the side of it, towards the sea. She ran across the huge lawn and then she stopped and squinted.

She saw something on the ground. Something white.

She jogged carefully now, trying to make out the shape. Then as she got closer, she realised what it was.

It was the shape of a body, lying on its side.

And it wasn't moving.

'No, no, no, no...'

She sprinted to the figure and fell to her knees, gently picking up the limp frame of her daughter, Jilly.

Then she heard a noise and turned to see a man standing behind her with a bottle of water.

'Benton?' she asked.

Chapter 64

'She's unharmed,' he said.

Benton Cooke looked like a grimy ghost from her past and she shuddered to think of him hurting her daughter.

Gloria glared at him and rocked Jilly's body back and forth.

'Stay away from me,' she hissed. 'Of course she's harmed, you idiot – look at her!'

He wasn't how she remembered him. He looked old, and she shuddered to think he'd held her daughter here, in the middle of nowhere. She recalled him now, sat in his suit, behind the wheel of a car, waiting for her outside the Bare Bunny. Driving Linda anywhere she wanted to go. Anywhere the men in her life wanted her to go.

'I can't believe you're here,' he said, speaking like an ardent fan and grinning like he was about to ask for her autograph. It sickened her.

'She needs water,' Benton continued. 'She tried to climb up and fell.'

His voice was panicked, and she realised that he'd failed his brief. He was supposed to keep her alive.

Just then, a mobile phone rang and Benton reached into his pocket to retrieve it, at the same time putting a bottle of water beside her. Gloria took it and opened it, before dribbling some water across her daughter's mouth.

'Jilly,' she said. 'Jilly, please wake up.'

She held her baby and felt her body was ice-cold. Gloria took the flimsy shawl she'd carried all the way from London and wrapped it around Jilly, and cradled her against her own warm body. After a while, she pulled away, just a tiny space, and Jilly looked up to her and opened her eyes.

'Mum?'

'Oh, thank God, Jilly! My baby, you're alive! I love you.'

'Was I dead?' Jilly asked.

Gloria laughed through her tears and cuddled Jilly's body close to hers.

'Are you hurt?' she asked her.

'No. I'm just really weak. Are the police here?' she asked.

'No, not yet, they're on their way.'

Gloria couldn't help herself. Perhaps she was a pathological liar, but she couldn't bear to tell Jilly she'd come alone. But one thing was for sure, she wasn't afraid of Benton Cooke.

Jilly peered behind her mother and screamed. 'Oh my God! He's here!'

'It's all right, Jilly. Calm down, he's not going to hurt you. Please, believe me, you're safe.'

'What?' Jilly was exhausted but still had fight in her, although Gloria could tell she was petrified. Gloria watched as Jilly drifted in and out of consciousness.

'Jilly, stay with me!'

Gloria saw the hole in the ground next to them and the grate that had once been locked above it. This must have been where Jilly had been kept and the very thought of it made Gloria's body rigid with rage and disgust.

Then she saw Pete, the private investigator. Gloria's insides turned to lead. He sauntered over to where they were and smiled at her.

He held his hands up. 'I come in peace. That was quite a show.' He turned around. 'Benton, go back up to the house. Get your things and disappear.'

'Benton!' Gloria shrieked. 'You were there the night Linda disappeared. You drove her there – you're just as much to blame as we all are for not protecting her. Does your boss know that?'

Gloria was growling and the sound betrayed an aggression she didn't recognise.

Jilly looked up at her, puzzled.

'Mum, what are you talking about? You know about Linda Wilson's murder? It wasn't Declan Lewis who killed her?'

Pete spread his hands. 'You might as well come clean now, Gloria. This is why you're here after all.'

'Mum?' Jilly asked.

'You bastard, Pete. Were you always playing both sides?'

'I follow the money, Gloria. Declan always paid better than Roger, who, I might add, was a tight-fisted bastard.'

Jilly pulled away further. Gloria realised that her daughter was surrounded by people who had either incarcerated her, lied to her or betrayed her.

'Mum, what's going on? Where's Max?'

'Jilly.' She turned to her daughter. 'I've got a lot to tell you – let's get you safe first.'

'What about the police? They're not coming, are they? You did this to me?'

'No, I didn't.'

'No, she didn't.' Pete at least backed her up. 'But you need to let her explain. The boss will be on the phone when you've finished,' Pete said, turning to Gloria. 'Max won't be around for a while,' he added.

'Why? Who's the boss?' Jilly asked.

'Declan Lewis.'

Chapter 65

Oliver had given up searching for Gloria hours ago.

He'd had a feeling it might end like this. The world – his world – caved in on him slowly and he saw no way out.

The letters Gloria had shown him were similar to the ones he'd received. Not the same, but alike. They came from the same hand. It hadn't even crossed his mind that Gloria had been a victim too, but what man reports harassment? Not a real man like a Wade.

He bowed to no one, especially a down-and-out like Benton Cooke. He had Gloria to thank for the ID, but once she'd figured it out, it had made sense.

Oliver had no recollection of the man until Gloria reminded him, and only then had he recalled him driving Linda away from the Bare Bunny.

It was the last time he saw her.

She'd gone from begging him to raise their child to swearing her revenge in the space of a day. So he'd allowed his father to have her.

Linda had believed she could play both of them but she hadn't factored in the determination of Roger Wade. Oliver had kept his father from her by telling him she was off limits, because she was his. Roger Wade had raised his big, bushy eyebrows and shrugged.

'Good choice, son, but it's a pity, she's a fine specimen.'

His father always spoke like that about women. They were either pedigree animals or mongrels. To Roger Wade, Gloria had been a prized racehorse, raking in money faster than he could spend it. But Linda had been a rough cross between a well-run greyhound and a mutt from the slum. Just as useful but one was more dispensable than the other.

But when Oliver finally gave him the green light, his old eyes had lit up as if Linda was a thoroughbred.

Roger Wade made problems go away. That night, he proved it literally. Oliver could protest all he liked that he'd had no idea what his father's intentions were, but deep down, he knew exactly what her fate would be. Oliver had left her to the two men and Gloria had worked it out. He'd driven her car, with the Little Miss Sunshine key fob. He'd been nervous as hell. And when Gloria told him the letters contained a reference to Little Miss Sunshine, he'd known immediately what they were facing.

He looked around Jilly's flat, knowing Gloria wasn't coming back, and picked up framed photos of his daughter, with Max, with her professor on graduation day, with Gloria and with her grandfather. With him. His heart ached with love but also with regret.

Linda had looked just like her.

Full of hope, passion and trust.

An open face with blonde hair and blue eyes. Suddenly, it made him want to heave as he imagined Linda with his father.

He'd delivered her like an exquisite meal at a Michelin tasting.

He sat down in front of the balcony and stared out over the city.

Apart from him and his father, there were only three people who knew where Linda was buried.

And two of them had been taken care of years ago.

The other wasn't answering his phone.

Pete Young had gone off-grid and Oliver felt the distinctly oily sensation of betrayal seep out of his pores. His clothes seemed suddenly tight and the flat airless.

He'd run out of people to separate his past from his future.

Even Gloria had abandoned him.

The doorbell made him jump and he got up to peer through the spyhole.

It was the two detectives. Dumb and Dumber.

He opened the door and forced a smile but it fell from his face as the gravity on Lucy's and Eddie's faces became clear.

'Have you found her?' he asked.

'Yes, we have,' Lucy said. 'Or, rather your ex-wife did. Jilly is safe.'

'Oh my God,' Oliver gasped. His knees almost gave way and he wanted to hug the female detective, but he got the impression she wouldn't let him. He found women so uptight nowadays.

'May we come in?' Eddie asked.

'Of course,' Oliver said, opening the door. 'When can I see her? Where is she?'

'Recovering at a hospital in Norwich. We need to talk about another matter.'

'I don't have time, I need to go to Jilly, right away,' Oliver said.

'Not right now. We've had a tip off. And we have a warrant to excavate a site on your father's estate. We've also traced a VW Beetle car, which is being processed at a secure forensic facility. It was once registered to yourself and is suspected of being involved in a crime. We've been provided CCTV footage – old tape, as it happens – that makes you a person of interest in a historic case we're thinking of reopening, depending on what we find at your father's Buckinghamshire estate.'

Oliver's face went cold, and tiny prickles of heat made his scalp feel as though it was on fire.

'Can I see my daughter?'

'I'm afraid not yet, Mr Wade,' Eddie told him. 'You need to come with us.'

Chapter 66

On a fine Sunday near the end of September, human remains were discovered buried underneath a plinth of marble that edged a colossal tomb in the middle of a pond on the estate of the late Roger Wade. The skeleton looked like any other, but the clothes, shoes and handbag suggested she was female and she'd been dressed up for a party.

Lucy Holt and Eddie Tate were both in attendance.

Oliver Wade had been arrested in connection with the 2005 murder of Linda Wilson. It threw Declan Lewis's conviction into chaos and an army of lawyers had pushed through a motion to quash it on the grounds of a miscarriage of justice. Hotshot barristers in the city had told him he could claim upwards of five million quid in damages.

He didn't want, or need, any of it.

What he really wanted was for his daughter to write a book about him.

He'd been approached by no less than seventeen publishers, but he'd rejected them all. Jilly Wade was his first choice for his official biography. And she'd finally said yes.

She sat in the visitors' reception inside Frankland Prison and watched the door pensively. They were allowed to see each other every week, but it seemed an endless process waiting for the paperwork to be processed and finalised before a decision was made on his release. Campaigners warned that if he came to any harm during the time he'd been forced to wait for the judges to sign off his release, they'd sue the government for millions. It had fallen on deaf ears. The British penal system was like lightning when it came to locking people up; release was a whole other ballgame.

But here he was.

Almost free.

Jilly knew that her pursuit of the truth had paid off in more ways than anybody could ever imagine. It had been painful beyond words finding out that her 'father', Oliver Wade, had betrayed them all, and had brought her up believing a lie. The same could be said of her grandfather.

Wade Media Group's stock plummeted and was worth pennies by the time the dust settled, allowing the vultures to swoop and fight over it. Her mother had walked away from fame with no pension, a reputation in tatters and no future. But Jilly secretly suspected that she didn't mind at all.

Declan sat down in front of her. He wasn't cuffed.

He rubbed his wrists as if he missed them and she gave him a hug.

She hadn't been able to call him 'dad' just yet, but it was early days. She'd been getting to know him. And he was honest with her. He'd promised to tell her everything and it had taken seven visits so far. It kept him busy and made the time he had left go quicker. Each time she visited, she gave him news from his legal team and he dared hope a little bit more that soon he'd be a free man. His legal team wanted to manage his release perfectly, to make sure he got the maximum publicity...

He wanted none of it. All he wanted was to sleep in a proper bed and eat some takeaway food in an average fast-food place in Manchester with his daughter.

He'd explained to her that Benton had been a disturbed soul as a kid, that's why he'd taken him on, to get him off the streets. It had been his obsession with Linda that had made Benton abandon her to a man like Roger Wade. He'd been so eager to spend time with her that he'd missed the danger she was in.

So far, Benton Cooke hadn't been found.

He'd walked off the estate in Norfolk as if disappearing into thin air and had vanished just as surely as Pete Young had. The police explained to her that her mother had been blackmailed by a man called Andy Knight, who'd been paid by Pete, to extort as much money as possible.

Their plan hadn't worked, and it was only her mother's quick thinking, once she'd been tipped off by Max about the Norfolk property, that saved her.

Her mother was a hero.

Jilly didn't quite see it that way, but she kept her mouth shut for Declan's sake.

What hurt the most, more than anything else, even more than Oliver Wade's betrayal, was Max's, and she shivered each time she replayed the last three years together, and all the time him pretending to be her best friend. He was still on the run, AWOL. The police weren't even sure that Max was his real name.

There was only one other question that kept popping up and bothering her each time she saw her father. She'd asked him several times. But it was getting less frequent.

He reassured her a little bit more each time that Benton had been aided by Max, who, for a price, had taken care of the logistics. She seemed to be surrounded by people who were willing to betray her and she finally understood how her mother felt.

'You didn't have anything to do with Benton taking me?' she asked again.

'Jilly, I promise,' he said, 'I'd never do that to you. You're my daughter and I love you.'

Chapter 67

Gloria felt the soft sand between her toes.

She wore a floppy hat and dark glasses and took her time walking along the sandy bay, just a mile away from her house, from which she could see and hear the Pacific Ocean every day and every night. Before she went to sleep and when she awoke, it was there, caressing her and encouraging her to breathe deeply.

A man walked past her and smiled, but she looked away. He could be paparazzi, or a local fisherman, but she didn't care. Her interest in men had been incinerated. He reminded her of Max, Jilly's old friend who'd disappeared after leaving hospital. He hadn't been recovering with his parents after all, and no one knew where he was.

Gloria reckoned that he was either paid off or dead, but she didn't tell her daughter that.

The man walked past her and got the message she wasn't interested.

Gloria concentrated on what made her happy, like Jilly getting to know her real father. And she was satisfied that Linda would finally have a chance to be laid to rest. She had no doubt that the remains found on the Wade estate were hers, and she wouldn't be surprised if the police found more besides. Roger had always preyed on the misfits and the unmissable.

Until Linda.

Gloria wasn't happy that Oliver was locked up and facing trial for murder, or at least as an accessory to murder, but it was the safest place for him.

For all their sakes.

It was hard on Jilly, but she finally had her truth, as she saw it.

She kept in touch. They had Zoom calls and Gloria was, of course, summoned to give evidence to the police as they pieced together their case against Oliver Wade.

One thing that they'd found alongside Linda's body was Gloria's old Little Miss Sunshine key fob and Lucy Holt had told her that it had blood on it, and there was a chance that it contained usable DNA.

Gloria enjoyed allowing things to develop off her watch. She'd stepped back from life and no one recognised her here at the beach.

She didn't watch TV.

In fact, she didn't even possess one.

She'd heard second- or third-hand that the new face of daytime TV was a woman half her age.

Good luck, she thought.

She was happier to let things go and not have to be forever picking up pieces and fitting them together.

She found herself not wanting to drink, here in her new home, and she was off the pills. It had been a curious journey for her to realise that as soon as she hit a dead end and had nowhere else to go, once the wheels came off her life and she was exposed, she no longer wanted to self-destruct. It took living her reality to want to keep it.

It had been ugly in the beginning, but it was true.

Her phone buzzed, and it reminded her that she was still attached to the UK and she always would be. It's how Jilly kept in touch.

She looked at it and stopped walking. Suddenly, the sun felt too hot on her skin and the hairs on the back of her neck stood up.

It was a text.

> Hello, Gloria.

Acknowledgements

I'd like to thank my agent, Peter Buckman, for his support for each and every random idea I put to him. I'm lucky to have somebody in the industry who is patient, honest and wise.

The Famous started out as a commentary about cancel culture and turned into a thriller I'm extremely proud of. I had so much fun inventing personalities who live in the telly-world.

This is my sixteenth published novel with Canelo and I'm fortunate to work with a publisher that always relishes new ideas. Louise Cullen has been my editor since the very beginning and I love working with her and Alicia, who have watched my books grow since 2016.

I'm eternally grateful to people who buy my books from all over the world, and the ones who send me notes on social media, asking questions, sharing thoughts and generally communicating their love of crime fiction. It's an honour to be anchored in such a community.

I couldn't focus on my work if my family weren't behind me supporting me and shouting about me at every opportunity. Thank you to Mike, Tilly, Freddie and Poppy for being my biggest fans. I love you.

And finally, my writing chums who keep me sane when all I want to do is throw away my work. Your wit and down-to-earth companionship see me through the darkest days of a challenging job. One minute we're up and the next we're down, but you're always there, to Marion Todd, Sheila Buglar, Jeanette Hewitt and Sarah Ward. Big love.